THE
SECRET
SCROLL

To Rita,

Enjoy!

Ronald
Cutler

3-11-08

THE
SECRET
SCROLL

A NOVEL BY

RONALD CUTLER

BEAUFORT BOOKS
NEW YORK

www.thesecretscroll.com

Library of Congress Cataloging-in-Publication Data

Cutler, Ronald.
  The secret scroll : a novel / Ronald Cutler.
     p. cm.
  ISBN 978-0-8253-0515-3 (alk. paper)
   1. Archaeology teachers--Fiction. 2. Americans--Jerusalem--Fiction. 3. Scrolls--Fiction. 4. Christian antiquities--Fiction. 5. Christian sects--Fiction. 6. Jerusalem--Fiction. I. Title.

  PS3603.U86S43 2008
  813'.6--dc22

                                                        2007043678

Published in the United States by Beaufort Books, New York
www.beaufortbooks.com
Distributed by Midpoint Trade Books, New York
www.midpointtradebooks.com

First Edition

Printed in the United States of America

DEDICATION

To my family and friends
To my ancestors
To all the people I loved who are no longer with me
and
To you, my readers

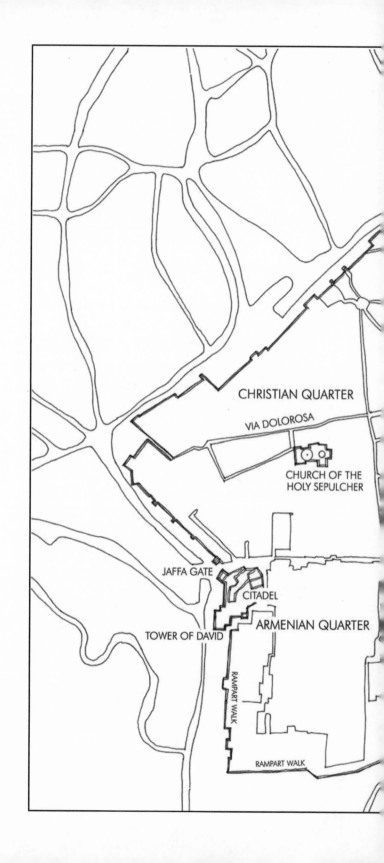

ROCKEFELLER MUSEUM

VIA DOLOROSA

LION'S GATE

TEMPLE MOUNT

MOUNT OF OLIVES

DOME OF THE ROCK

TEMPLE MOUNT

WALL

R

RAMPART WALK

DUNG GATE

JERUSALEM

THE
SECRET
SCROLL

Chapter 1

JOSH COHAN WAS FEELING SPIRITUALLY HEIGHTENED. He had visited countless sites in more than thirty countries, but Masada was like no other. It sat like an island in the sky, a fortress atop a desert mountain plateau keeping eternal watch over the Dead Sea some thirteen hundred feet below. Josh moved away from the crowds to an ancient stone ledge and, from there, stared at the deep, blue, cloudless sky above. He cast his eyes downward to the Dead Sea and realized that he was taking in the same view that the Jewish fighters had nearly two thousand years before, when they faced the might of Rome. The landscape hadn't changed.

He closed his eyes and listened to the rustling of the wind. He allowed himself to sink into the moment, but instead of lulling him, the sound grew louder and louder, first becoming the ominous hiss of a serpent and then swelling to a crescendo of voices. Like a Greek chorus, the thousand voices chanted...

From the beginning to the end: freedom, compassion, tolerance, sacrifice....

In his mind's eye, Josh saw a lamb being washed away in a river of blood. Flames rose from the earth, suffusing the clouds with a deep, bright red.

The disembodied voices reverberated in Josh's ears. When he opened his eyes, he saw the shadows of countless people on the ground.

One...one...one...one...they chanted.

But when he looked upward to see who cast the shadows, there was nothing but sky and the fluttering sound of invisible wings.

Josh had visited Masada three times before, and three times the voices had whispered to him. But he had never experienced anything like this before. He was a man of science, and although he loved the stories this desert held, he was trained to find the truth in artifacts and bones. The historical power of the place had simply caused his imagination to play tricks on him. The voices, of course, weren't real.

But what if they were? Even if they were purely the product of his imagination, might they carry some meaning beyond the safe perimeter of the ancient past?

Josh drove north toward Jerusalem on Route 90, an Israeli-protected road. To his right was the deep blue of the Dead Sea, and beyond, illuminated by the late afternoon sunlight, the Jordanian mountains. To his left, the Judean desert stretched outward in an expanse of hills and caves so vast that it had concealed the Dead Sea Scrolls for nearly two thousand years. Josh wondered what secrets were still buried there today.

But he was taking a leave from active duty as an archeologist. This sabbatical was precisely what he needed: a restorative break from the departmental politics back at the university museum. Israel beckoned to him not only as a scholar, but also as a man—a cultural Jew if not a practicing one—and it was time to heed the call. He had felt transformed the moment he landed at the airport in Tel Aviv. Gazing at the azure sky, smelling the air, Josh sensed that he had touched sacred ground. He belonged in this place. Something bonded him to the land itself.

His thoughts returned to the solemn majesty of Masada

and he felt himself walking amongst its ancient citizens. The energy of the place was undeniable, even all these miles away.

In his reverie, the image of the cave ahead barely registered. It was enough, though, to unleash a torrent of remembered dreams—years' worth of visions Josh had no ability to explain.

He is reeling through the desert, the menacing hiss growing louder as the flying serpent spits and lunges closer and closer behind. And then the sand around him ignites into an other-worldly fire, the flames stretching out ahead of him on either side as if in protection, lighting his way through the dazzling white-ness of midday. He follows this path toward the hills, but the Earth seems to have been upended, with the sky below and the solid rock somehow hovering above. And directly in front of him, suspended from the ropes of flame, is the opening of a cool, dark cave, its lip curving dramatically downward to the heavens.

His head spinning and the blood thumping in his eardrums, Josh jammed on the brakes and the Land Rover fishtailed off the side of the road. Fortunately, there were no other cars nearby and he came to a skidding stop with nothing more than the sound of gravel crunching beneath his tires. Josh took a deep breath and tried to steady his hands against the steering wheel. But still dizzy after another minute, he opened the door and stumbled out to find some grounding.

The hot sun felt heavy, as if it were weighing down against his skull, and he bent over at the waist, head hanging and elbows braced against his knees. Josh was afraid he was going to throw up, but instead the spinning sensation passed as suddenly as it had begun. Breathing more easily now, he opened his eyes and stared between his knees at the expanse of desert beyond.

It was exactly as he had seen it all of those nights—the sky below, the hills above...and the unusual shape of the opening itself. He had seen nothing else like it in Israel, nothing like it anywhere in the world.

Slowly, with mounting trepidation, Josh got his backpack from the car and began to climb toward the cave. Within minutes the dirt and sweat had mingled in muddy streaks down the back of his neck. He'd been this close before in his dreams. He'd been to the edge of the cave—but never inside. As he approached the curving mouth, he wondered if it was actually possible to enter. He'd always awakened before he could take that step. What would happen now?

Josh's nerve endings bristled as he stepped across the threshold. Something was waiting here for him; he knew this with certainty, just as he'd known it in every interrupted dream. He turned on his flashlight and aimed it ahead of him, moving deeper into the unknown. As he walked, his nervousness dissipated, replaced by a sense of tranquility he'd rarely experienced before. Even as his curiosity remained on high alert, his body felt incredibly relaxed.

Moving deeper, he saw rock projections jutting out from every side, ready to trip unwary trespassers. Josh wouldn't stumble here, though. He beamed his light onto the wall across from him, revealing a series of faint drawings. He moved closer and observed letters that he recognized as Aramaic and, under them, a broken line. He held his flashlight two to three inches from the inscription, but realized that it would be impossible to translate. Parts of letters were totally missing, while other characters had faded away through age and decay. Josh looked instead to the broken line. It appeared to point downward.

It's telling me to dig.

It wasn't a thought; it was a conviction.

Josh dropped to his knees and felt the ground at the bottom of the wall directly under the markings. It was nearly as solid as the rock—much too hard to dig—but he knew he had to try. He retrieved a small spade from his backpack and began to probe the resistant topsoil. After long minutes, he'd made it ten inches below the surface. There, he noticed the top of a buried object. Josh reached down and touched what felt like clay. When he examined it more closely, he immediately recognized it as an artifact from a distant age.

In every version of the dream he had known that there was something waiting for him in the cave, though he never got to enter. Josh was certain now that he was supposed to find this object.

He worked feverishly, losing all concept of time. As he dug, he couldn't help but remember the last dig he'd been on—the one that drove him toward this sabbatical. It hadn't been his project; in fact, it wasn't even his area of expertise, but when a senior colleague makes a special request for your assistance, you can't politely decline. Josh knew that much about departmental politics, even before he left for Mexico.

For more than a month he had labored under the merciless Yucatan sun, filtering the dirt, searching for some relic or artifact. This was a standard part of any archaeologist's work—many hours and few discoveries. The excitement and the mystery of the exploration made the search rewarding even if it netted nothing.

Josh had the reputation of being meticulous in his execution of even the smallest tasks, so it was often the smallest tasks that he was assigned. But one day, unexpectedly, he unearthed the tip of a stone unlike the others. Digging with even greater care, he uncovered a statue of an unknown Mayan god. His heart thrilled as it emerged from the earth; this was what he lived for. Josh delicately wrapped the six-inch artifact and went to Coughlin, the gruff yet tenured head of the dig.

"Cough," he said, unable to conceal his excitement, "I've just discovered something you should look at."

His supervisor studied the artifact. "It appears authentic," Coughlin said as he stroked his beard thoughtfully. "But I wouldn't get too excited until we get back to the university and do extensive testing."

Six weeks later, in a meeting at the University of Pennsylvania's world-renowned museum, Coughlin announced the discovery to a packed room of faculty, reporters, and students.

"Gentlemen and women," he said, stoking the drama of the moment, "I've made a major archaeological discovery— the statue of an unknown Mayan god. The artifact is in excellent condition and may give us clues to the Mayans' demise, as it dates from the time period just before their civilization's disappearance."

Josh was stunned. Coughlin had failed to acknowledge that Josh had been the one to make the discovery. At that moment, he realized that his department was as much—if not more—about positioning and power than it was about pure science. The notion made him sick.

The next day Josh went to Coughlin's office.

"I tried to talk to you yesterday after you announced our discovery," he said, "but you left so quickly."

Coughlin picked at his right ear. "What's up? You look upset."

"Yesterday you never acknowledged that I discovered the artifact."

"Josh," he said condescendingly, "you're part of a team, that's all. I'm the team's leader."

Josh felt his blood run cold. "A discovery of this scale doesn't come along very often. This was a huge thing for me."

"Welcome to the real world, Cohan. When you get to my level maybe you'll understand."

"I'm not just going to sit back and take this," Josh said, seething. "I'll go to the media. I'll…"

Coughlin put a hand up to stop him. "I don't think you get the point. I have decades of experience. With that experience comes plenty of influence. If you do anything to undermine me, I can arrange it so you'll never go on another meaningful dig for the rest of your career."

Josh was so furious he couldn't speak. His intuition told him not to proceed, but he did anyway, challenging Coughlin's false claims. It did him no good. Cough was too well protected by his cronies. Josh knew that he had upset the status quo and that at least a few people saw Coughlin for what he really was; but after all was said and done, that didn't improve Josh's situation.

At least he managed to escape the career-ending consequences that Cough had threatened. The only action taken was that Josh was prohibited from working with Coughlin again, and he considered that more of a reward than anything. He assumed that, while they wouldn't validate his charges against the more senior archaeologist, the university didn't want to punish him in the face of his obvious accomplishments, either.

Still, the whole experience had left Josh more than a little disillusioned. Maybe he should have listened to his intuition and simply walked away from the entire mess. His instincts had rarely failed him, and he should have known better than to let his ego do the talking. As it was, conditions at the university were too difficult to bear. He applied for a sabbatical in a place where he felt an emotional connection and left for Israel.

It was interesting, Josh thought, that the very mess he had thought might ruin him had helped to bring him here. If it hadn't been for Coughlin, he may never have been driving down that particular road or made the connection to his dream.

At last, his work paid off. Josh put on a pair of surgical gloves and carefully raised the cylindrical jar from the ground. Although considerably smaller, it was similar to the storage jars that had contained the Dead Sea scrolls, found not more than ten miles north of this cave.

Josh took off his T-shirt, delicately wrapped the jar, and placed it carefully in his backpack. He would be able to do a much better inspection of the artifact back at his hotel than here in the dimly lit cave.

It was almost dark as Josh moved carefully down the hill back toward the highway. As he neared the road, he saw a beige military jeep parked next to his Land Rover. Beside it were two Israeli soldiers, tall, well-built, and serious. And both with their guns pointed directly at him.

"Take the backpack off and put it on the ground," they ordered, "then put your hands on your head."

Josh complied. "I'm an American archaeologist vacationing in Israel," he told them, his voice shaky.

The fairer of the two soldiers walked toward him, lowering his gun. "What's your name?"

"Josh Cohan. I'm a professor at the University of Pennsylvania."

"Where is your identification?" the man demanded, heavily armed and now only a foot away.

Josh's heart pounded and his mind began to race. If they opened his backpack and found the jar, it would be confiscated on the spot. He couldn't lose another find, especially not to a couple of overzealous kids who'd probably destroy the artifact just trying to figure out what it was. He would have to talk his way out of this, but how?

The other soldier's rifle still aimed at his heart, Josh weighed his options and decided to go with the friendly foreigner approach.

"So how about that desert?" he joked, trying to lighten the tension in the air.

But neither soldier answered. Instead, the blond one swung his own weapon around onto his back and took one more step forward. Josh could feel the man's hot breath on the side of his neck.

"Documentation," he demanded again, sweat glistening in the furrows of his stern set brow.

"I'm afraid it's inside the car," Josh said, hoping the lie wasn't evident on his face.

He heard the safety disengage from the other soldier's rifle as he was pushed toward the front of the Land Rover, legs spread and arms out against the hood. Not wanting to draw attention to his backpack, Josh waited until the soldier was kneeling down, frisking his calves and ankles, to steal a glance in the direction where it lay, all but forgotten for now.

Suddenly there was a hand in his back pocket, and then without explanation the soldier walked away. Josh heard the crinkling of paper and then the static of a walkie-talkie as the soldier radioed in to his command center. He had found Josh's driver's license and the photocopy of his passport he always carried when he was on the road. Josh was stunned. He was certain that they had been in the backpack. He was nothing if not methodical....

After a long, uncomfortable silence, the walkie-talkie crackled again and someone on the other end reported back, "He's okay."

The Sephardic-looking soldier lowered his weapon at last.

"Can I pick up my backpack?" Josh asked, as casually as he could manage.

"What's inside?"

"Only personal items and a few souvenirs. Would you like to inspect it?"

It was a gamble, but one Josh was hoping would pay off. He'd already been cleared by the higher-ups, and he was betting that the two kids were as eager as he was to get out of the heat and back on the road.

The blond soldier looked at the backpack for several seconds, then finally raised his eyes back to Josh. "That won't be necessary."

Josh grabbed the pack and flung it over his shoulders.

Another military jeep pulled up, carrying two more armed Israeli soldiers. "Is everything okay?"

"Yeah," said the soldier with the dark hair. He nodded to Josh. "You can go."

Josh hoped that his relief wasn't obvious as he returned to his car. What would have happened if they'd discovered the jar in his backpack? He never could have convinced them to let him hold on to it. That business with Coughlin would have been nothing compared to losing this artifact. Josh wasn't too big on messages from the beyond, but something in that jar had been calling to him for many years.

The full moon shone brightly on the desert as Josh drove toward Jerusalem. In less than an hour, he'd be back at the Jerusalem Pearl Hotel. There, at last, he could inspect his discovery.

As he drove past the oasis of Ein Gedi, the import of the last few hours settled on Josh. His recurring dream was no longer just a dream. It had led him to the jar...where would it lead him next?

Chapter 2

THE WINDOW IN JOSH'S HOTEL ROOM FACED THE ancient wall of the Old City. He loved the location, close to the spiritual center of three great faiths. Josh had taken numerous trips to the Old City over the years, and every time he returned he felt he was home. This was the place of his ancestry and he just seemed to resonate differently here. Though he could barely wait to open the jar, he still took a moment to gaze out on the city before beginning. There was so much magnificence here. And sadly, so much danger. There had never been more perilous times in the Middle East, and this city stood at the center of the conflict. It was a tragedy within a tragedy.

He picked up his pack and carefully unraveled the t-shirt-covered cylinder. An electric thrill raced through his body. There was a reason why he found this jar. Now he would take the first step to discovering what that reason was.

Under Israeli Law, all archaeological findings belonged to the state and were under the control of the Israel Antiquities Authority. Josh knew that he would have to turn the jar over to the IAA, and that once he did they could exclude him from taking part in his own discovery. He couldn't recall anything in the law that said when he had to give it up, though. In his estimate, the jar had already lay buried for millennia. The IAA could live without it for a few more days.

He once again slipped on surgical gloves and began the

first part of what he was certain would be a long and delicate process. The top of the jar had been closed tightly with sealing wax. Opening it would require the utmost care, as breaking the jar or damaging its contents even slightly would be an unforgivable sin. He pulled a small knife from his backpack and worked very slowly, dislodging the lid after several minutes.

Inside Josh found a cylinder of wound linen cloth. He hesitated for a moment, and then carefully removed it from the jar. The linen was in such good condition that he began to question its authenticity. When archeologists discovered the Dead Sea scrolls, they found hundreds of fragments representing approximately 850 scrolls. In only ten cases had more than 50 percent of the original scroll survived. Only one, the Isaiah scroll, was complete. If this jar was more than two thousand years old, how, then, were the contents so perfectly preserved?

Gingerly, Josh unwound the linen wrapping to reveal a scroll. The scientist in him was both dubious and thrilled at the possibilities...but once again, that feeling of tranquility overwhelmed him. How could he feel tranquil at a moment like this? When he discovered something in the field, his system burned with adrenaline. Now, though, he felt inexplicably peaceful.

He unrolled the first section of the scroll and examined it closely. The words on the sheet were Aramaic, a mostly forgotten language once spoken in this region. Josh learned it while pursuing his doctorate in Biblical Archaeology. Tiny specks surrounded many of the letters on the sheet. They were the document's only obvious signs of aging.

He turned on every light in the room, took out his magnifying glass, and began the slow, arduous task of translating. Though it would take him until morning to complete the first paragraphs, he took no notice of the time. The words he read held him so completely in thrall that he was certain he could have gone days without stopping.

I am Yehoshua ben Yosef. In the next two weeks, I will meet my fate. I write this scroll so you will know the truth of who I am and what I preach and believe. I am a prophet with visions of the future and I write this scroll to prevent my worst fear— that my teachings will be forgotten or, worse, that I will be mis- interpreted and my message subverted by the teller of lies.

I taught in parables, but even my closest companions had trouble understanding their true meaning. I write now in a way that the simplest of men and women may understand, yet will touch the hearts of even the brightest minds.

I was born in Nazareth in Galilee during the last year of the reign of Herod the Great. My parents, Miriam and Joseph, were religious Jews who kept the Laws of Moses and the sancti- ty of the Torah. I grew up studying every word of that sacred document. As a child, I had dreams and visions that made me feel my life had a special purpose. I prayed every day, studied the Torah, meditated, and learned healing. My mission was to seek the path of helping others, particularly the poor, the hopeless, and the spiritually starved. My plan was to free my people from Roman occupation and to establish a heaven here on earth.

Josh leaned back from the scroll and rubbed his eyes. When he looked out the window, he noticed sunlight streaming through. He stared back at the scroll. There was so much more to translate. So much more to discover. What he found already, however, was breathtaking.

If he could believe what he read so far, the author was the man known today as Jesus Christ.

Josh paced the small hotel room, barely able to com- prehend what he'd just read. The document had to be a fraud. How else could you explain the condition of the scroll? If it wasn't a hoax, however, it was the most monumental archaeological find in history.

Josh ran his hands through his hair, trying to collect his thoughts. Should he call the IAA? They had the tools and research resources necessary to determine the scroll's authenticity. How much would he lose if he called them, though? Would they let him be part of the research team? Would he get credit for the discovery?

Josh decided not to take chances. He would make a copy of the entire scroll and then turn it over to the IAA, under the condition that they involve him completely. He cleared the floor and carefully unrolled the scroll until it extended the length of the hotel room. Then he took out his digital camera and snapped furiously away. When he was done, he carefully rolled the scroll back into place and took pictures of the linen cover. He neatly placed the scroll back into its jar and fixed the lid tightly on top of it.

He grabbed his laptop, connected it to his camera, and transferred the photos of the scroll's contents onto the computer's hard drive. Even if the IAA kept him from the scroll itself, he now had his own digital copy to work from. It wasn't much, but it was the best he could do under the circumstances.

Now that the text, at least, was somewhat safer, Josh noticed the rumbling of his stomach and realized that he hadn't eaten in nearly 24 hours. Still, he was more exhausted than hungry. With visions of an extraordinary day flashing through his mind, he lay on his bed and fell quickly into a troubled sleep.

Chapter 3

JOSH IS FACING ROWS UPON ROWS OF CROSSES. HE CAN see hundreds of men in agony, their wrists tied with ropes, nails driven into their heels, their bodies left to rot under the deadly desert sun.

A group of centurions laugh scornfully, light gleaming off their helmets and the sharp tips of their spears, as their victims suffer painful, humiliating deaths. "This is what you Jewish dogs get when you defy the power of Rome," one of the soldiers taunts and the others join in with cynical glee.

Josh awoke, soaked with sweat. The nightmare had felt all too real. Now that he'd discovered the jar, every dream took on a new dimension. What did this one mean? Were all of his dreams fated to come true in some way?

He couldn't worry about this now. There was too much to do. Too much to learn about the scroll.

He showered, shaved, and headed down to the hotel's spacious lobby. It was only a little after 9:00 a.m. He hadn't been sleeping long. He bought a cup of Turkish coffee and a piece of rugulach from a kiosk and headed to a pay phone in a quiet corner of the room. He got great cell phone reception here, but wanted to avoid being traced. Josh wanted the people he called to know as little about his identity as possible until he deemed it was okay.

"Shalom, Israel Antiquities Authority," a woman answered. "How may I assist you?"

"Shalom. I'd like to speak with the person in charge of archaeological research."

"Can I have your name please and the purpose of your call?"

"I think I may have discovered something that would be of great interest to your research department."

"One moment."

Josh looked around the bustling hotel lobby. People moved about, starting their day as either tourists or workers. What would it be like to work here every day, to try to do a normal job and live a normal life when danger could strike at any moment? The city of Jerusalem was peaceful most of the time. Yet, there was an uneasy feeling when people boarded a bus or went to a shopping center, café, or nightclub.

At this point, people who lived or worked in any major city around the globe held at least some unconscious fear of random violence, but here the odds were so much greater that it would actually happen. There was a part of these people's lives that he, as an American, could never understand. The bravery it must require to go about daily life under such circumstances touched Josh deeply.

After a few moments, a thickly accented Israeli voice came on the line. "Hello, this is Moshe Ben Daniel. To whom am I speaking?"

"I'm an American archaeology professor. My specialty is Biblical archaeology."

"What can I do for you?"

"Would you mind telling me your position at the IAA?"

"I'm an archaeologist," the man said a bit stiffly. "I head many of our research projects."

"I'd like to meet with you," Josh said.

"What about?"

"I might have discovered an artifact that will be of great interest to you."

The voice on the other end of the phone chuckled. "You American archaeologists think you know everything. You destroy more artifacts than you discover."

Josh felt his ire rise. He hated being stereotyped and had always taken extraordinary care at every site he visited. "If you're not interested," he said brusquely, "I'll take my discovery back to the States."

"That's against Israeli law."

"Only if the artifact is authentic and, as you're not interested, you'll never know."

Moshe sighed loudly. "Fine, tell me about it."

Josh cupped the receiver with his hands so no one around him could hear him clearly. "I found a jar in a cave near the Dead Sea and it looks like it's from the Second Temple period. If you determine it's authentic it could be a major discovery."

There was a moment of silence on the other end, and then Moshe said, "Where is the artifact now?"

"It is safely in my possession."

"And where are you?"

"I'd rather not say until we meet. I'd appreciate it if we could do so at your earliest convenience."

The next silence stretched longer than the first. Why was this guy hesitating? If Josh got a call such as this one, he'd have the caller in his office instantly.

"I can meet with you at noon."

Three hours? It would feel like an eternity. "Where? You have offices all over Jerusalem."

"Our headquarters at the Rockefeller Archeological Museum, Sultan Suleiman Street, East Jerusalem. But you will not be cleared by security unless you tell me your name."

Josh knew he was telling the truth, but hesitated for a moment. He would have to trust this man, sight unseen. "It's Josh Cohan," he said. "I'll see you there."

Josh hung up the pay phone and looked around the lobby. There were more people out now than when he placed the call. He searched for any faces paying undue attention to him, and then realized he was being overly paranoid. No one knew what he had in his possession or what it could mean to the world.

Why, then, did he feel so uneasy?

He had things to do before his meeting. The first was to find an Internet café where he could upload the manuscript photos to his secure server at the University. The file would be much safer there than it was on his laptop. The department had multiple security systems to prevent hacking, and Josh gave the file a special encryption for additional protection.

Then, with both the jar and its precious contents in his backpack, Josh walked across town to meet up with his old high school friend, Avner Katz. Avner was a six-footer with a wide body and a wider smile. After high school, Avner had fulfilled his lifelong dream of moving to Israel and studying at a Yeshiva. He had lived in Israel for fifteen years now, the proprietor of a souvenir and antique store in the Old City's Jewish Quarter.

"Josh," Avner said when he walked through the door of the shop, "I don't see you for years, and now I've seen you twice in a couple of weeks. To what do I owe the honor?"

"I just can't get enough of that gorgeous face," Josh said, grinning. "In fact, now that I've seen you again, I'm thinking about moving here permanently just so I can look at you all the time."

Avner guffawed. "Spoken like someone who needs to borrow a few dollars."

The smile left Josh's face and Avner's expression darkened, as well. Josh leaned toward his friend, glanced around the shop at the two patrons, and whispered, "I actually do need a favor."

Most of Avner's smile returned. "And I thought they paid you well at the university. Of course. How much do you need?"

Josh shook his head briskly. "I don't need money. I need for you to put something in a very safe place for me."

Avner said nothing, but his face spoke loudly.

Josh looked around again. Someone new had come into the store. Had Josh seen the man before? Again, he pushed away the paranoia. "I discovered something on a dig. It might be a hoax, but if it's real, it's monumental. I can't keep it in my room and I'm not going to give it to the IAA yet."

"Do I get to know what it is?"

"I'll explain the whole thing over drinks in the near future. For now, if you could just do this for me without asking any questions, I'd appreciate it."

Avner patted him on the shoulder. "For you, anything. You will, of course, be *buying* the drinks when you tell me this story, right?"

"As many drinks as it takes."

"Don't make promises you can't keep, my friend. Come—I'll take you down to my safe. It's built like a fortress. I have quite a few valuable things myself."

Josh scanned the room a final time. The man who'd entered minutes before was gone. Why did he seem so familiar? Josh could not place the face.

He turned and followed Avner to the back of the store.

Chapter 4

JOSH TOOK A TAXI INTO EAST JERUSALEM. THE AREA lay north of the Old City and ran from Damascus Gate to Herod's Gate and downhill along Sultan Suleiman Street to his destination, the Rockefeller Archaeological Museum. Built with two million dollars donated by John D. Rockefeller in 1927, the museum contains one of the most important archaeological collections in Israel.

They drove through portions of East Jerusalem that made Josh apprehensive. He knew that mingled among the vast majority of peaceful and quiet people were a few with the potential for great violence. This was the home of Jerusalem's Palestinian Arabs, and the part of the city they claimed as the capital of a future Palestinian state. It was a place with a violent past and an almost certain violent future.

The Museum itself was near the walls of the Old City in one of the better districts in the area, close to the affluent Arab neighborhood on Nablus Road. It was a 1930s Jerusalem landmark, elegantly constructed of pink and white limestone with a distinctive, dramatic octagonal tower. The building beautifully combined the architecture of Byzantine, Islamic, and Art Deco, and was the home of the Israel Antiquities Authority.

The Department of Antiquities was created in 1948, with the founding of the State of Israel. In 1967, the offices of the Department of Antiquities had moved from the Israel Museum to the Rockefeller Museum building. With the passage of a new law in 1990, their name changed to Israel Antiquities Authority.

Josh knew that the IAA was in charge of the country's antiquities and antiquity sites—their excavation, preservation, conservation—as well as the country's antiquity treasures. The authority was also responsible for inspecting commerce of antiquities and combating robbery and theft. They even had their own security force with the same authority as regular police. Known as inspectors, most of these security people were former members of the Israeli Defense Forces.

Although headed by the Director General, the IAA was run by an Authority council of sixteen members composed of government ministers and archaeologists from some of Israel's major universities.

At the Rockefeller museum's entrance, Josh was met by two guards who asked for his identification and the purpose of his visit. They were more polite than the soldiers on the side of the road yesterday, but no less serious. After a battery of questions, obviously designed to ascertain if he was a risk, they sent him through. He'd grown accustomed to such security upon entering a building here, but today, with his own threat system already on high alert, the precautions made him especially uneasy.

Josh waited fifteen minutes in the reception area before a balding, middle-aged man walked distractedly into the waiting room.

"Josh Cohan?"

"Yes, I am." Josh rose and shook the man's hand.

"Shalom. I'm Moshe Ben Daniel. Welcome to the IAA."

"Thank you for meeting with me."

Moshe walked Josh back to his office, a small, windowless room that looked as if its contents had literally been thrown together.

"Please excuse the mess. I've been especially busy lately. Did you bring the artifact?"

"No, I didn't."

Moshe stared up at him irritated. "Why not? I assumed that was the purpose of our meeting."

"I wanted to have a conversation with you first and then arrange to leave it with you safely."

The man grumbled and sat behind his desk. "You know, under Israeli Law, if the artifact is authentic it belongs to the state."

"I know that."

"I assume you also know that you must have a permit from us to dig, which you did not."

"Yes, but I didn't plan on doing an excavation. I accidentally discovered the artifact."

Moshe glared at Josh. "I find that hard to believe."

Josh rose from his chair and stared directly into Moshe's eyes. "That's what happened. If I didn't want to do the right thing, I wouldn't be here. I came to you even though this is by far the most significant discovery I've ever made."

Josh could tell that Moshe didn't know what to make of him.

"You don't even know if the artifact is authentic," the older man reminded him.

"Yes, but I sense that it is. Strongly...very strongly. That's why it's critical to me that I be on the research team that determines its authenticity."

Moshe looked at him as though Josh had been speaking in tongues. "That's a lot to ask. We rarely have outsiders involved in research. I don't recall any of them working in our laboratories."

"I'm afraid I really must insist. I'll also be an asset to

your team. I've done radiocarbon dating and I've used all the main dating techniques including pottery typology. For the last ten years I've been a professor of archaeology at the University of Pennsylvania."

"Well that is something, at least. Do you have a CV?"

Josh nodded. "I brought a copy with me. I had a feeling you might ask."

Moshe took the sheet from Josh, scanned it briefly, and then cleared a stack of papers from a chair and motioned Josh to sit. "Now tell me about the discovery."

Josh relayed the story about finding the cave, tactfully leaving out the part about his dreams, and told Moshe how he came upon the jar.

"Do you remember where the cave was?"

"Between Masada and Ein Gedi, about a quarter mile off the road. I'm sure I can find it again."

"If the jar and its contents are authentic, we will excavate the cave. Where is the artifact now?"

"It's in a safe location."

"You *will* have to turn it over."

"I know. I'll do so as soon as you let me know if I can be on the research team."

"Yes, that again." Moshe was silent for a long moment and Josh wondered what he was thinking. He knew he didn't have much leverage here and he was certain that Moshe knew it as well. Still, he would fight this one to the end.

A knock on the door broke the silence. "Dad, I...oh, sorry, I didn't realize someone was in here."

Josh turned toward the head peeking into Moshe's doorway. The vision was shocking. This was the man's daughter? The most generous thing you could say about Moshe's physical appearance was that he was average looking. The woman who just called him "Dad," however, was more than merely attractive. She had big, shining blue eyes, raven hair, olive skin, and shapely lips. She wasn't classically gorgeous; she had what he'd often heard referred to as an "interesting face." But she was something to look at. She seemed natural, exotic. The notion of Cleopatra came to mind, but Josh figured that was probably because he'd been so focused on the Biblical era since he discovered the scroll.

"It's fine, Danielle," Moshe said. "In fact, I'm glad you stopped by."

Danielle entered the room and turned toward Josh. He didn't often take much notice of women, but this was one extremely noticeable woman. More than anything, Josh had the strangest feeling that they had met before, although he most certainly would have remembered such a meeting.

"Danielle, this is Josh Cohan. He's an American archaeology professor. Josh, this is my daughter, Danielle."

She reached a hand out to him and he took it. Her grip was both soft and solid at the same time.

"Nice to meet you, Josh," Danielle said. "I love America."

Josh smiled. "I'll be sure to send my regards," he said, instantly regretting blurting something so inane. Danielle smiled back politely, though he was sure she must have thought him socially inept, at best.

"Danielle is also an archaeologist," Moshe said. "We work together on occasion."

Danielle turned toward her father. "That's why I stopped by, actually. I have an update from the excavation at the Temple Mount rubble. I'll come back when you aren't busy."

"No, stay. I'd be interested in your thoughts about what Josh has discovered. It's a jar that he thinks comes from the Second Temple period."

Danielle's eyes grew wider, though Josh would have sworn a second ago that such a thing was impossible. "Really? Do you think it's authentic?"

"I don't know for sure," he told her, "but my gut tells me it's something special."

Again, Josh related the story about his dig in the cave and the remarkable results. Danielle listened attentively and then asked, "What made you go into the cave?"

Josh hesitated. "It was luck."

"Pure luck?" Danielle asked with a look of disbelief. She gazed into Josh's eyes. "I don't believe you."

She was hard to look away from, but he felt accosted by her confrontation. "You don't have to believe me. I found the jar. How I found it isn't relevant. If you're not interested, I'll just take it home with me."

Danielle watched him carefully for several additional seconds. He thought he detected the beginnings of a smile at her lips. *She's fascinating—and I think I'll stay very far away from her.*

Abruptly, she broke eye contact and turned to her father. "Have you seen the jar?"

Moshe's brows narrowed. "Josh has some issues he feels need to be addressed before he's willing to show it."

Danielle angled a sideways glance at Josh. Somehow, her recrimination was so much harder to endure than Moshe's was. Josh put his hands up to protect himself. "I believe this is the most important discovery of my life. I need some assurances that I'm not going to be eliminated from the process."

Danielle leaned toward Josh as though she was going to remove a piece of lint from his collar—or slap him in the face. Then she put both hands on her legs, looked toward her father, and rose. "The two of you need to work this out. We have to find out if this jar is real."

She turned and departed. How could she leave so suddenly? Weren't they in the middle of a conversation?

"Danielle has no patience for dickering," Moshe said.

"This profession must drive her crazy. Dickering seems to come with the territory."

Moshe offered a subtle smile. "Don't get me started on that." He shook his head and seemed briefly lost in memory. The gesture was surprisingly disarming. Then he recovered and made hard eye contact with Josh. "It would be hard for me to go to my research team and argue for you to be an observer without me first examining the jar myself."

Josh regarded Moshe warily. "I can take you to the jar, but first I need your word that once you've seen it you will speak on my behalf to your associates."

"If the jar seems as authentic to me as it does to you, I will do that."

"I also need your promise that you will not tell anyone—and I mean anyone—that you're meeting with me or that you know the jar's location."

After a moment, Moshe shrugged. "I will try."

"Trying isn't good enough."

Josh started to get up to leave when Moshe said, "Okay, I won't tell anyone and, if the jar's examination meets my approval, I will do my best to convince my research team to allow you to be part of the project."

Josh searched Moshe's face for signs of deception. "Meet me in front of my hotel tomorrow at nine."

"The Jerusalem Pearl?"

Josh hadn't said where he was staying. How did Moshe know?

"It was a logical assumption," Moshe said, answering the unasked question.

Chapter 5

Moshe arrived promptly at 9:00 a.m. to find Josh waiting for him outside the hotel's entrance. Josh climbed into the car and they proceeded to the Old City, where he directed Moshe to park near the massive stone Zion Gate. Built in 1540, it marked the dividing line between the Jewish and Armenian Quarters.

They headed to the Jewish Quarter. Walking down the narrow stone streets, Josh couldn't shake the feeling they were being followed. He always followed his instincts, but he wondered how reliable they were right now. Since discovering the jar, he'd been hypersensitive to everything around him, seeing everything as either prophetic or potentially threatening. He didn't like this feeling, yet was powerless to prevent it. He stopped and looked behind him but didn't find anything suspicious in the faces and actions of the people nearby.

They proceeded to a street full of small tourist shops and stalls. Josh's sense of apprehension grew. He grabbed Moshe's arm and ducked into a small souvenir shop.

"What are we doing here?" Moshe asked, more perturbed than anxious.

"I think someone is following us."

"I didn't see anyone."

Josh peered out the store's window. Only a few people were outside—two tall priests and a few female tourists.

"Moshe, are Catholic priests usually found in the Jewish Quarter?"

"The Old City is the religious center of the universe. Holy men are everywhere. I wouldn't worry about a couple of priests if I were you."

Moshe's words did nothing to reassure Josh. His intuition spiked. *What if Moshe leaked information of my discovery to the wrong people?* Could he trust this man? Should he? Josh only knew that if he was going to move things forward, he had to show Moshe the jar. He wasn't getting anywhere pretending to be a master spy.

Josh led Moshe out to the street and then to Avner's store, only some fifty yards away.

Avner greeted Josh warmly when he saw him. "It's like we're back in school," Avner said, leaning closer to his friend. "I hope you aren't coming to take me drinking now. It's a little early."

Josh laughed. "We'll drink later. For now, I want to introduce you to Moshe Ben Daniel."

Avner shook Moshe's hand and welcomed him to the store.

"Is there anyone else here?" Josh asked, looking around.

Avner made an elaborate, over-the-top scan of the room, then grinned at Josh. "Not unless they're hiding behind one of the counters."

"I want to show Moshe the jar, but before I do, I need to be sure we weren't followed."

Josh walked toward the window and glanced outside. The two tall priests were still milling about, but they weren't paying attention to Josh or the store. His senses tingled, but they truly seemed preoccupied with something on the opposite side of the street. He turned back to face Moshe and Avner.

"Avner, Moshe and I need to go to your back room.

Can you please stay here and watch for any suspicious people?"

"You *are* paranoid," Avner said, laughing. He punched Josh's shoulder playfully.

"No," Josh said portentously, "just careful."

Avner shook his head reproachfully. It was obvious that he found his friend's cloak-and-dagger theatrics entertaining, and it irritated Josh a little. Maybe if Avner knew what was at stake he wouldn't be so lighthearted. Of course, that would require telling Avner what was at stake.

"Wait here," Avner told them, walking toward the back of the store. "When I get the artifact out of the safe, I'll call you to come in."

Less than a minute later, Avner summoned them. They stepped into the crowded stockroom that doubled as Avner's office. Moshe walked briskly to the desk, pulled a magnifying glass from his coat pocket, and began to scrutinize the surface of the jar.

Moshe's examination was thorough, reviewing a number of features several times. "It definitely resembles some of the jars from the Second Temple period," he said, lifting the top from the jar. He noted the presence of the linen-covered scroll, and then re-sealed it.

"Aren't you going to look at the scroll?"

"It would be better at this point if I didn't take it out. I've seen enough to be interested in having my team examine this artifact to determine its authenticity. I will assemble the group this afternoon for a meeting."

"At which point you'll convince them to let me join you?"

Moshe paused. "I reviewed your CV and did a little Internet research on my own. It turns out that I even knew one of your works, though I didn't recognize it from your name. I'll do everything I can to get you on the team."

Josh nodded and then called for Avner. "Thank you, Avner. Could you please put the jar back in the safe?"

"In the safe?" Moshe said surprised. "I thought we could bring it with us."

"For the moment it stays here. When you confirm that I can participate in the authentication, I will deliver it to you at the IAA. But remember, you are to tell no one about the scroll's current location."

Moshe seemed about to argue, but then his shoulders sagged. "I can see it is going to be a challenge working with you."

Josh thanked his friend and he and Moshe exited the store. As they turned up the street, the two priests were still lingering outside a nearby textile stall. One of them leaned over to touch a bolt of linen and his crucifix slipped loose, catching the light from the late morning sun overhead. The priest smiled placidly at Josh as they passed, but as he furtively tucked the necklace back under his collar, Josh noticed that it wasn't like any cross he'd ever seen, but some other icon entirely.

Chapter 6

SEATED AROUND THE CONFERENCE TABLE AT IAA headquarters were five of the top minds in Israel. They were an eclectic bunch, comprised of Christians, Jews, and agnostics from three continents, some with decades of fieldwork under their belts, others still basking in the glory of graduating top of their class from Hebrew University. Two things they all had in common: each was a world-class specialist in Biblical archaeology, and each had been hand picked for this team by Moshe.

Even before the intrigue had begun, Moshe knew that this would be a sensitive project. That meant that everyone involved needed to be not just brilliant, but also highly diplomatic. Israel as a whole was an archaeological mother lode, but the area around Jerusalem was particularly rich, and particularly complex. Home to some of the holiest sites in Judaism, Christianity, and Islam, it was rich with history and rife with conflict. This meant that any new discovery could potentially affect the spiritual lives of much of the world's population. Of course, most digs proceeded according to routine, attracting plenty of tourists but arousing the passions of only academics and the most avid lay enthusiasts. Still, there was always the chance that someone would stumble upon the next House of David Inscription or Dead Sea Scrolls.

Given the unusual circumstances of this find and the strange events of the past couple of days, Moshe was glad to be working with such a solid—and strategically diverse—team. Between them was enough expertise for any eventuality related to the work itself, and enough influence within the various faith communities to ease any political tensions. Most importantly, he'd worked with several of them for years and felt he knew all of them intimately. When any group had worked as closely as these men had, there was little to hide.

"Thank you for assembling on such short notice," Moshe said, calling the meeting to order. "I have brought you here because an ancient jar has been found near route 90, about two miles south of Ein Gedi. The jar was discovered by an American archaeology professor named Josh Cohan."

"Why this meeting?" interrupted Reverend Barnaby Smith, a fifty-year-old American Protestant with a full beard and ill-fitting wire glasses. "Why are we not following the usual procedures?"

"The artifact was not found on the black market or the usual places for fakes and forgeries," Moshe told them. "Nor was it found on an archaeological dig. Cohan found the jar accidentally, buried in a cave. What's more, it contains a manuscript, the contents of which he claims are in better shape than any of the Dead Sea scrolls."

Father Andre Billet, a Catholic priest with a reputation as prominent as his bald spot, raised a pudgy hand. "Are we in possession of the jar?" he asked in a thick, French accent.

"We are not. That's why we're here. Cohan won't release it until we allow him to be part of our research team."

"We've never let an outsider participate in our research," Alon Paul, a young Israeli, protested. The son of one of the museum's major benefactors, he could be defensive about anyone receiving preferential treatment and worked hard to earn the respect of his colleagues. He expected others to do the same.

Michael Berg, another Israeli prodigy, agreed. "It would be a terrible mistake," he said sharply, never one to be shy about venting his opinions.

As Moshe scanned the room, Father Billet and Reverend Smith nodded in agreement with Michael.

"He has to turn it over to us," said a man with a huge walrus mustache and flaming red hair, by appearances more beach bum than brilliant archaeologist. Jonathan Levi was the fourth Israeli in the room. "It's the law. We should just send some of our security people over to take it from him."

Moshe shook his head. "I don't think that is the right thing to do in this instance. I've met with Professor Cohan on two occasions already. He won't give up the artifact easily."

Berg slammed his hand on the table. "He has no choice."

"That may be true, Michael, but I actually think Cohan might be an asset. He's written several important papers in our field. He was also a key contributor to *Making the Impossible Possible*."

"I've read that book," said Reverend Smith.

"We all read that book based on your recommendation, Barnaby," said Father Andre. Others around the room nodded.

Michael leaned forward. "Why are you lobbying for him to join us? Even if he's highly credentialed, what can he offer us that we don't already have?"

"Michael, you know as well as any of us how important passion is in our work. Trust me when I say that Josh Cohan has an abundance of passion."

Alon shook his head briskly. "I don't like the idea of adding someone new to our team. What else do you know about him?"

"I had our people run a security check. There's nothing in his background to suggest any problems."

Alon needed more convincing. "But what have you learned about what he is like to work with?"

"There seems to have been some conflicts in his past. Something happened that no one wants to talk about just before he came to Israel."

"That can't be a good thing."

"Our investigators got the impression that Josh was *involved*, but he wasn't the cause. Still, you're right. Sometimes people invite problems. The background check doesn't suggest this, though. The picture it painted was of a man who tends to work on his own. It doesn't appear that he makes many friends among his colleagues, but he doesn't make enemies either."

Moshe watched as Alon absorbed this information. "I'm still not convinced we should allow him on our team," the younger man said, reluctantly.

Moshe was about to counter when Reverend Smith interjected. "I have a solution. Let's offer to make the American professor an observer. He can watch and be privy to our research and testing. If he agrees, we must of course ask him to sign a confidentiality agreement."

"I'm not sure..." said Michael apprehensively.

Moshe sat up in his chair. "Gentlemen, I have seen the jar. There is an excellent chance it is authentic. We could argue this endlessly, but I suggest we adopt Barnaby's proposal. Remember why we do what we do."

Reluctantly, the rest of the team concurred.

Chapter 7

JOSH HADN'T JOGGED AS MUCH AS HE WOULD HAVE liked since he arrived in Israel. Back home, he did six miles every day regardless of the conditions. Here, on a working vacation, the distractions were too numerous. Given the events of the last couple of days, however, he knew a run would do him good.

As he ran, his thoughts wandered, as they always did, to his adoptive parents. He'd just returned from a run when he got the message that they'd been killed in a plane crash. Since then, he'd never been able to go out for a jog without seeing their faces. In many ways, this was a gift, an opportunity to visit with them in his mind on a regular basis. He'd loved them dearly; he felt that they were the only people who truly understood him. Losing them was a pain he'd never been able to release, but gazing upon them in his mind while he ran was at least a bit of a salve.

Invariably, though, thoughts of his parents led him to thoughts about the people who had given him up. Like so many adopted children, Josh couldn't understand why his genetic parents had deserted him. He often harbored fantasies of seeking them out. He'd made some effort at various times, but came up empty. It seemed ironic to him that, as an archeologist, he could uncover long-hidden antiquities, but couldn't find out who provided him with his DNA.

Eventually he stopped trying. If they didn't want to know him, he wasn't interested in knowing them.

Focusing again on the road, Josh maintained a deliberate pace through the streets of Jerusalem, even though the crowds made this a considerable challenge. The exercise proved restorative, the endorphins released from the effort helping to wash away the tension and wariness he had felt since discovering the scroll.

The good feelings lasted only until he returned to his room—and found it ransacked. Everything in the room was tossed, as though a powerful gust had whipped, dislodging everything in its path. His clothes and possessions were everywhere. His laptop was out of its case and flung on the bed. Just when he'd begun to convince himself that he was being overly paranoid, he realized that he hadn't been paranoid enough.

Feeling angry and betrayed, he spent the next hour restoring order to the room. Remarkably, nothing was missing. Even the cash he'd casually hidden in his underwear drawer was still there.

Of course nothing is missing, he thought. They came for the jar and the jar isn't here.

Josh sat on the edge of his bed. He'd been stupid to relax when his instincts told him to be wary. He wouldn't make that mistake again. Until he confirmed the authenticity of the scroll he would remain as vigilant as he had ever been.

The phone rang and his senses tingled.

"Hello?" Josh answered, voice steady with determination.

There was nothing but silence on the other end of the line.

"Hello?" Josh said again.

"Is this Josh Cohan?" asked a man with a deep, muffled voice.

"It is."

"I want the jar and its contents by midnight tonight. I will call again later with instructions for where to leave it."

When Josh spoke again, he was surprisingly calm. "Who are you?"

"I am the rightful owner of the scroll."

"What are you talking about?"

"You had a role to play in this as well," the voice said coldly, nonchalant. "It was your role to find the scroll. That role is now finished."

A chill ran down Josh's spine.

"You can turn the parchment over to me as I have requested. If you do not, you can be assured that I will use other means to get it."

The phone went dead, but then rang again almost immediately. Josh hesitated—he needed to make sense of this threat, to get his bearings—but he knew he needed to buy himself some time, not to come across as defiant so early in the game. After another ring he picked up the receiver.

"Shalom, Josh; this is Moshe."

There was every chance that Moshe was directly connected to both the break-in and the threatening phone call. Moshe knew more about the jar than anyone other than Josh himself.

"What do you want?" Josh asked sharply.

"I called earlier and left a message. Didn't you get it?" Josh noticed for the first time that his message light was on. Moshe must have called while he was jogging. The last thing Josh thought to look at when he got back was the phone.

"I didn't get it, no."

"I spoke with my colleagues and we have a proposal for you. Can I meet you at your hotel to discuss it?"

"It seems your people have already held a meeting in my hotel room."

"What are you talking about?" Moshe said, obviously confused.

"Are you telling me you had nothing to do with the ransacking of my room while I was out?"

"Your room was ransacked?" Moshe was either genuinely surprised or an excellent actor.

"Maybe you delegated that one out. How about the threatening phone call? Were you more hands-on with that one?"

"Threatening phone call? Josh, what is going on?"

"Who have you told about the jar?"

"Just Danielle—you were there when I did that—and the other members of my team. You knew I was going to talk to them. What is this about a threatening phone call?"

"Someone just called to say he wanted the jar by midnight and suggested he'd go to any means necessary to get it if I didn't comply."

"And you think I had something to do with this? Josh, I swear I know nothing about it."

Josh had promised himself to trust his instincts and, for whatever reason, his instincts indicated that Moshe was telling him the truth. "Someone else knows about this and wants it very badly. If you want to meet, it can't be here. I'm sure someone is watching. I'll sneak out of the hotel and meet you at the entrance of the Citadel in the Old City in an hour."

"Be careful."

"If you weren't involved with this before, Moshe, you are now. I'm not the only one who needs to be careful."

Chapter 8

AFTER HE HUNG UP WITH MOSHE, JOSH DID WHAT HE could to disguise his identity—not much, considering what he had to work with. He never intended to be James Bond. Archaeology was his life, not intrigue. He never would have expected the two to intersect. *There's a reason scholars become scholars*, he thought.

He asked the concierge to lock his laptop in the hotel safe, rode the elevator to several random stops, followed by trips down the stairs and back up, and finally exited through a delivery entrance. He had no idea whether or not he'd eluded the people tracking him, but it was the best he could come up with.

The Citadel stood near the Old City's Jaffa Gate, next to the Armenian Quarter and less than a fifth of a mile from the Church of Holy Sepulcher, the site where Christians believe Jesus was crucified and resurrected.

The Citadel was a strategic fortress built by Herod the Great more than 2,000 years ago and some scholars believed it was the site of Jesus' conviction. Like so many locations in Jerusalem, it was a place of profound historical significance, the weight of which was reflected in its very architecture: David's Tower, one of its five spires, and the only surviving tower, hovered over the Old City like a mysterious force, guarding its past.

The day was cold and cloudy, and rain had begun to fall.

There were very few people on the normally crowded street.
Josh found Moshe waiting outside the entrance to the
Citadel's History of Jerusalem Museum.

"Shalom," Josh said, nodding slightly as he approached
Moshe.

Moshe turned, gave Josh a sidelong glance, and then
walked toward him. "Shalom, Josh. What did you do to your
hair?"

"I was attempting to...oh, never mind."

"What is all of this about threatening phone calls and
people watching you?"

Josh still wasn't entirely certain that he could trust
Moshe, but the expression in the man's eyes seemed genuine.
He guided him toward a secluded corner. "Someone wants
the scroll and he seems to want it very badly. I don't know
why."

"This is crazy. In all my years, I've never encountered
anything like this."

"I have no reason to believe the voice on the phone
today was just trying to intimidate me. This guy was serious—and I'm not sure how far he would go. Are you still
sure you want to be involved with this?"

Moshe looked at him closely. "As you noted yourself, I
don't really have a choice anymore, do I?"

"No, I suppose not," Josh said with a wry smile. He
noticed a glint in Moshe's eyes. They were in this together.
"What did you want to talk to me about?"

"My colleagues and I have agreed that you can observe
our research work. You'll have access to all research procedures and copies of all our findings."

"That means I'll be included in everything, right? I need
access to every procedure, every test, and I need to get all the
same papers and information that you and your colleagues
receive."

"Agreed. If you're going to deal with threatening callers, the least we can do is make sure you are completely involved in the research."

Moshe reached out and shook Josh's hand. As he did, Josh noticed some movement out of the corner of his eye. "Someone is watching us," he said in a sharp whisper.

Moshe's head pivoted. "How do you know?"

"I saw something. Let's go." Josh began walking down the street.

"Where are we going?"

"Away from here. We need to find out if we're being followed."

"I have an idea."

Moshe led Josh through the narrow streets. They stopped at a kiosk and Josh noticed a huge man, dressed entirely in black, stopping no more than fifty feet away from them. When they stopped again, the man was still nearby.

"Why would you send someone that gigantic to follow us?" Josh wondered aloud as they resumed walking. "It's almost as though they want me to know they're watching us."

"They want to make it clear that they're serious."

Josh laughed mirthlessly. "They could have saved themselves the trouble."

Moshe grabbed Josh's arm. "Come on. I can end this now." He led Josh into a store that sold reproductions of artifacts. "The owner is a friend of mine."

Joel was a short man with gray hair and an oval face. He had the look of someone who carried the weight of five hundred pounds of garbage on his shoulders.

"We've got to get out of here," Moshe told him. "Someone's following us."

"Following you? Why?"

"I'll explain some other time."

Joel obviously heard the urgency in Moshe's voice, because he briskly shepherded them to the back of the store. He opened a door leading to a staircase, and the three of them descended. A thick wooden door at the bottom led into a dimly lit tunnel.

"This'll get you out," Joel said, glancing up the stairs. Josh followed his eyes. The enormous man in black wasn't there. Was Moshe right? Was the man's presence simply an attempt to confirm the seriousness of the earlier phone call? If so, it did the trick.

Moshe and Josh walked a half-mile before they came to the tunnel's opening near the Dung Gate. There was no one behind them and no one on the street seemed to be watching. They left the Old City through the gate and Moshe flagged a taxi.

"Can you come with me to the IAA?" he asked, entering the cab. "I want to go over some things with you."

"I can be there in about an hour. I have a few things to take care of first."

Moshe groaned when his secretary reminded him that he had a meeting scheduled with Alexander Paul. Although he was nice enough, and donated huge sums to Israeli museums, Paul expected to be treated like a dignitary. Moshe wasn't in the mood for bowing and scraping today. All he really wanted to think about was the scroll.

A half hour later, however, Paul showed up in his doorway.

"Moshe, good to see you. I hope I'm not bothering you terribly much."

"Never, Alexander, never," Moshe said, rising from behind his desk to greet the benefactor. "I always have time for you. Please...have a seat."

Moshe watched Paul settle into the chair and then sat

back down. The man was certainly a specimen. He was more the six feet tall, with an athletic body and beaming blue eyes. He seemed to be in his late 40s or early 50s, though Moshe knew he was much older. Moshe guessed untold wealth was the closest thing available to the Fountain of Youth.

"Can I get you anything, Alexander?"

"Some coffee would be lovely. I'd especially appreciate a cappuccino if that is possible."

Paul knew it was possible—just not convenient. Getting him a cappuccino meant sending his secretary to the museum's dining room. Moshe called her and sent her to her task. Then he turned back to the billionaire.

"How can I help you today, Alexander?"

Paul leaned forward and pointed his fingers. "The Discoveries from the Temple Mount collection opens at the Israel Museum in a few weeks, doesn't it?"

"Yes it does. The museum is buzzing about it. I hope you're planning to come to the opening night gala."

"Absolutely. Of course. I wouldn't miss it." Paul hesitated. "The problem is the Britons."

"The Britons?"

Paul made the effort to appear embarrassed, which Moshe knew meant he was about to make one of his "little" requests. "My partners on an enormous real estate deal I recently put together. I'm going to make a huge profit from this and you know my favorite thing to do with my profits. I guess in that way it's an enormous deal for *both* of us. Anyway, the Britons are coming to Jerusalem to sign the contracts. I know they would love to see the Temple Mount exhibit, but the *problem* is that they will be here and gone a few days before the opening. Is there any chance you could help me with that?"

Moshe couldn't believe he had to deal with something this mundane when he could be working on deciphering the scroll. Still, keeping someone like Alexander Paul happy made it possible for him to do the interesting parts of his job.

"I'm sure I could arrange something."

"Excellent," Paul said, standing, "I'll have my secretary call you with the details."

Yes sir. Anything you want, Sir, Moshe thought, frustrated, but kept his sentiments to himself. "Please do," he said, instead, playing the role expected of him.

Paul turned toward the door.

"Would you like to wait for your cappuccino?" Moshe asked, already knowing the answer.

"I'm afraid I can't. Please thank your secretary for me when she returns."

Moshe stood to follow Paul out. As they got to the door, Josh started to enter, nearly bumping into the billionaire. The two men stopped within a foot of one another.

"Alexander, allow me to introduce you to Josh Cohan. He's bringing us something interesting. Josh, this is Alexander Paul."

Paul leaned toward Josh and shook his hand. The man had a pneumatic grip, and Moshe saw Josh wince slightly, caught off guard.

"Do I get to hear about this *something interesting*?"

Josh looked at Moshe and then back at Paul. "I'm not sure we're ready to share this yet."

Paul laughed jovially. He released Josh's hand and placed his own on Moshe's shoulder. "My millions don't buy me as much as they once did."

Moshe patted the man's arm. "If this artifact turns out to be authentic, I'll arrange another private showing for you, Alexander."

The man patted Moshe's shoulder and then moved out the door. "I look forward to it. Good to meet you, Josh. Keep on making discoveries."

"Yes, nice to meet you as well. Thank you, I'll try."

Paul smiled, waved, and headed down the hall.

"Alexander Paul helps keep the lights on at some of Israel's most important museums," Moshe told Josh as they watched him leave.

"Does he really get private showings?"

"Considering the donations he makes, he can get whatever he wants. And he never lets us forget it for a second. Come on in. Let's try to do something meaningful."

Moshe's office was as much of a mess as it was the last time Josh saw it. This only barely registered on Josh's mind. "I can't get that call out of my head—and then that person following us. Who would want the scroll that badly?"

"We might understand that better after we have a chance to examine the manuscript. When are you going to give it to us?"

"As soon as I can get it. Is there a phone I can use to call Avner?"

Moshe gestured toward his desk. "Use mine. Hit the third button. I'll be back in a few minutes."

Unfortunately, Avner didn't pick up the phone when Josh called. He deliberated whether it was wise to leave a message, but decided that he had no choice. "Hello, Avner, it's Josh. Things are getting a little scary. You must be very careful. Someone wants the item and I have a feeling they're willing to kill to get it." Josh looked at his watch. "I'll meet you at your place tonight at eight o'clock after the store closes. Don't let anyone in, unless it's me."

Two minutes after Josh hung up, Moshe and another man walked into the room.

"Josh, this is Michael Berg. He's one of my colleagues who will be working with us on our project."

Michael smiled. "Congratulations on your discovery," he said. "When will we get to see it?"

"Tomorrow," Josh told him. "That is, if I'm still breathing."

Michael's eyes widened. "Excuse me?"

"The document inside this jar is a very powerful thing. I am obviously not the only person who feels this way—even though as far as I know I'm the only person who has seen it. Something is happening here that I can't begin to understand." He took a deep breath and considered the obstacles that lay before him. "I only hope I live long enough to figure it out."

Chapter *9*

As JOSH SLID INTO THE PASSENGER SEAT OF THE CAR that Moshe had arranged to take him back to his hotel, he was surprised to find Danielle at the wheel. Dressed in khaki shorts that showed off her long, shapely legs and a loose white blouse, she was unquestionably the most appealing chauffeur he had ever had.

They were not, however, alone. In the back seat sat a dark-haired contradiction of baby face and bulging muscles, a broad smile plastered from ear to ear. Josh got the feeling that this guy knew something he didn't, but his disappointment quickly turned to apprehension when he noticed that the beefcake was holding an Uzi.

Danielle placed a warm hand on Josh's. "Josh, meet Dov. He's with security and he's assigned to protect you."

Josh shook Dov's hand warily. "I appreciate it," he said, "but I don't need any protection."

"Of course you do," Danielle said emphatically. "I know what's going on. Your life is in danger."

When did she learn about the threat? He wondered, and how closely did she work with her father? "I'm capable of protecting myself...."

But Danielle cut him off: "I don't think you understand what you're up against. I'm probably not supposed to tell you this, but we believe someone at the IAA is trying to terminate the project."

47

"That's not exactly news to me."

"Josh, the person responsible for ransacking your hotel room was almost certainly someone on my father's research team."

Did she think he was stupid? "Again, not a news flash. I figured this out already. It didn't take much effort."

Danielle's brow furrowed. "Then here's something you *don't* already know. As I said, I'm probably not supposed to tell you this, but you should know what you're up against. In the past six months, some artifacts have been stolen. We believe it was an inside job. We've put some IAA people under surveillance. These threats to you could be part of something larger and, if they are, defending yourself is not even in the realm of possibility."

If Danielle wanted to ratchet up his anxiety, she was doing an excellent job. "What can you and Dov do for me that I can't do for myself?"

Danielle pointed to the back seat. "Well, fire an Uzi with deadly precision, for one thing. Unless, of course, you're an expert marksman with a store of munitions you smuggled into the country." Her eyes glinted. "Your CV didn't say anything about that."

Josh looked back at Dov or, more specifically, Dov's gun. It would be a nice thing to have on his side. Assuming, of course, it was on his side.

"Josh, you have to trust us," Danielle said, seeming to read his mind.

"Can you give me a good reason?"

"Because we're with you on this."

"How do I know that?" he asked sharply, allowing the tension of the past few days to rise to the surface. He regretted it immediately, though. "Seriously, Danielle," he said in a softer tone, "how do I know that you're really with me?"

Again, she took his hand. "You can know because we

believe in the same things. We both love archaeology. People take archaeology very seriously in this country. It's part of our heritage. Discoveries can change our history, our destiny."

It was a nice little speech, delivered passionately, but it didn't ring true. "If I could innately trust everyone who loved archaeology, I wouldn't be in this situation right now. I assume the 'inside job' you spoke about earlier was done by someone who loves archaeology as well."

Danielle sat back against the seat and exhaled loudly. "You're right, Josh. You can't trust me, Dov, my father, or anyone else at the IAA. Forget everything I said."

He looked back at Dov. The man's smile was gone and he now stared stoically out the window. Josh turned again to Danielle. Could he really trust her? He wanted to for so many reasons. His instincts told him that she wasn't the enemy.

"I've been a little tense lately," he said sheepishly.

She closed her eyes for a moment and then looked at him squarely. "I never would have noticed."

Josh chuckled, wanting badly to change the subject and forget about the danger for a little while. "Let's not go to my hotel," he suggested. "What time does the Church of the Holy Sepulcher close?"

Danielle seemed a little confused by the question. "I think they're on their summer schedule, which means they don't close until eight."

"I think it would be good for me to go there."

"Then we will. Maybe I can even show you one or two things along the way. Have you ever walked the ramparts overlooking the Old City?"

"Many times."

"But you've never seen them from my perspective." She turned the key in the ignition.

"I'm in your hands," Josh said, without really having the slightest clue what that meant.

The Old City walls had been built by Suleiman the Magnificent in the sixteenth century, and were a perfect vantage point for viewing some of the city's most dramatic sights.

Danielle pointed in the direction of the Temple Mount with its towering Gold Dome of the Rock standing guard over Jerusalem. "Beneath all that glitter," she said, "lies the rock where Abraham nearly sacrificed his son, Isaac, and where, in a dream, the prophet Mohammed ascended to heaven on his steed. It is considered holy by the faithful of three religions that have wasted thousands of years and millions of lives in conflict despite this common spiritual heritage. Even the Romans felt the power of the place. After destroying Jerusalem and the Second Temple, they built their own temple on that very site, dedicated to the cult of Jupiter. Later in the sixth century, it became a Christian church. Then, in 638 the Moslems conquered the city and destroyed the church and replaced it in 691 with the structure that you see now. So much destruction and creation right there in front of us...if only we could find a way to make sense of it all."

The information wasn't new to Josh, but hearing the way Danielle expressed it made it feel that way. This city had a very deep meaning to her, something he could only begin to understand. He watched her animated face with admiration, as she continued the tour.

"What interests me most, Josh, is what lies beneath the Temple Mount. I believe there are literally layers upon layers of history under the site, a wealth of archaeological discoveries waiting to be researched. I hope to be able to explore the area someday."

"Why won't you do it now?" he asked. He knew the practical answer, of course, but something told him this woman could talk her way into just about anything.

"I can't," Danielle told him. "It's too political." She pointed to a wall below. "See the holes."

"Yes."

"Those are battle scars from 1967's Six Day War. There are many of them all around the Old City. This place has been fought over more than any city in history. In the last 3,000 years there have been forty wars fought here. Ironically, though, Jerusalem is called the city *of peace*."

With Dov following close behind, Josh and Danielle walked slowly, almost languorously. Given everything that happened in the past few days, it was hard to imagine being so relaxed but, in this place, Josh felt no need to rush.

"I feel elevated here," Danielle said dreamily. He didn't have to ask her what she meant.

He felt an urge to loop his arm in hers. Where was this coming from? Though his heart told him he could trust her, his head told him to stay on guard. Other than Avner, he wasn't sure he could trust *anyone* in this country. Yet he didn't want to stay on guard with Danielle. Every instinct suggested that he cherish this moment, rejoice in her presence, bathe himself in her light. What was that about? Yes, she was beautiful and Josh was hardly immune to the lure of feminine beauty. He'd rarely felt its sway, though. Romance was for people with less to do with their lives. He contemplated love about as often as he contemplated retirement—which is to say not at all. However, it was ridiculous for him to ignore his attraction to Danielle, as perplexing as it was.

"Are you in there?" she asked, smiling up at him and allowing herself to press her shoulder against his arm for a moment. She seemed newly gorgeous to him every time he looked at her.

"Just mesmerized by the sights," he said with a sheep-
ish smile.

She whirled around. "It's magnificent, isn't it?"

They entered the Rampart's Walk that stretched two-
and-half miles around the Old City, through the entrance
near the Jaffa Gate and the Citadel. They could stroll three-
quarters of the walk, which rested on the top of the pale gold
limestone walls, but for security reasons, couldn't cross the
section overlooking the Temple Mount.

Josh gazed at the panoramic view of the city of dreams,
conquerors, and hope. He looked up at Jerusalem's brilliant
blue sky and massive white clouds, and then down at the land
that had witnessed so much bloodshed and conflict. Would
this place ever be what it was truly meant to be?

They stood out on a lookout point where they could see
the glittering gold Dome of the Rock. Like so much of this
city, it was magnificent and the source of endless dispute.

For several minutes, they stared out silently. Josh found
this moment—the Dome, the city, the woman—to be
beyond words. It felt as though time had stopped. He might
have stayed here indefinitely if Danielle didn't turn to him
with youthful enthusiasm.

"Let's visit the Western Wall," she said brightly.

The First Temple was built by King Solomon in 950
BCE and destroyed by the Babylonians in 586 BCE. It was
rebuilt as the Second Temple between 538 and 515 BCE. In
20 BCE, King Herod began enlarging it and making it
more grandiose. He died nearly fifty years before its com-
pletion in the mid-First Century. When the Romans
destroyed Jerusalem in 70 CE, the Second Temple was
reduced to rubble.

The only part left standing was the Western Wall. Two
thousand years of prayer and tradition made this wall the

Jews' holiest site. Jews around the world, no matter where they were, turned in its direction to pray, seeing it as their connection to their past and their hope of the future.

At the wall, in keeping with Orthodox Jewish practice, a black iron barrier divided men from women. Josh looked across it and saw Danielle just a short distance away. She looked radiant, as if the sun had decided to shine on her alone. *I could get used to this view*, Josh thought and then immediately batted it away. *This would be a good time to get a grip on myself.*

Josh looked up at the massive blocks of limestone, more than fifty feet high. Then he touched the wall, closed his eyes, and began to pray. Josh had never felt any certainty about the existence of God. The reason he pursued his life's work was in hopes of finding a definitive answer—at least for himself. More often than not, he felt inclined to believe that the notion of one overarching power that guided the universe was flawed at best. Standing before this wall, though, his heart and mind jogged by recent events, Josh felt there might be some value in sending a message out into the ether to see if anything came back. That was the point of being an agnostic, wasn't it? He might not have all the answers, but he was at least theoretically open to the possibilities.

Show me what I'm supposed to do, he whispered, feeling hopeful and ridiculous at the same time.

He stepped back from the wall and opened his eyes. The first thing he saw was Danielle, smiling at him, coming out of her own prayer. The barrier still separated them, but only for another minute. His first thought when they were together again was to take her hand, but again he resisted. Instead, he turned to make sure Dov was still in view and then they made their way toward the Holy Sepulcher.

The Church of the Holy Sepulcher was one of the most

significant places in the Christian world, yet it lacked the majesty of Saint Peter's in Rome, Notre Dame in Paris, or even Saint Patrick's in Manhattan. Cramped into an area of shops and houses, it didn't tower over its surroundings. It had two domes, the larger of which sheltered the holiest of sites—the tomb of Jesus Christ.

Dov waited outside, Uzi hidden under his coat, while Danielle and Josh entered the church. Josh had visited here several times and it always gave him an uneasy feeling, the sense that something wasn't as it should be. As soon as they entered the holy site, that feeling returned, replacing the peace and pleasure he had felt since they entered the Old City.

They walked across a stone courtyard and entered through a large arched doorway trimmed by a narrow band of pale Jerusalem stone. The church was jammed with tourists, pilgrims, and clergy from six different Christian denominations: Greek Orthodox, Roman Catholic, Armenians, Syrians, Abyssinians, and Coptic clergy. Each group jealously guarded its own assigned territory. Each had a prescribed time for mass, for lighting candles, and opening windows. The various sects were as competitive as the Yankees and the Red Sox. Josh had even read recently about two of the religious groups having a fistfight.

Josh and Danielle walked through the atrium, past Greek Orthodox, Armenian, and Coptic Chapels, and head-ed past Golgotha, the site of the crucifixion. They arrived at the Rotunda, a large dome supported by marble columns and eighteen pillars. In the center of the Rotunda stood the Holy Sepulcher.

Josh and Danielle joined a long line of pilgrims and tourists and waited in silence. Josh felt tense, the uneasiness mounting. Danielle, however, had already given herself over to the moment and to the energy of the place. When he looked at her, she caught his eye and smiled with a deep, knowing look that he found oddly reassuring.

After about half an hour, they entered the small and crowded tomb. Josh looked at the forty-three lamps hanging over the marble that covered the stone slab. It was here that Christ had been entombed, here where he was said to have been resurrected. Many of the tourists and pilgrims were crying, falling on their knees and praying in an explosion of spiritual and emotional intensity.

"It didn't happen here," Josh whispered softly to Danielle. They were the first words he'd spoken in some time; the thought flashed into his head as though placed there by someone else.

"What do you mean?"

"I can't explain. I'm not sure." He shook his head in confusion and then left the Holy Sepulcher, walking toward the Church exit. As he did, he looked through the crowd and noticed a towering figure standing in the shadows, dressed in black priestly garments. Josh was certain it was the man who had chased him and Moshe the day before. The man glared at Josh, and then he reached for something under his clothes.

Suddenly Josh's uneasiness spiked to alarm. He grabbed Danielle's hand and led her quickly out of the church. Dov was there at the entrance.

"Is your Uzi loaded?" Josh asked the bodyguard.

"Of course."

"Good. You may have to use it."

"What's going on?" Danielle said, her voice rising in concern. "Why did we leave so quickly?"

"Someone was there. Let's get out of here."

They ran quickly through the narrow streets of the Christian Quarter of the Old City and ducked into a souvenir shop.

Josh looked out onto the street and tried to catch his breath. "It doesn't look like we're being followed."

"What was that all about?" Danielle said. She didn't seem frightened. In fact, she seemed a little annoyed.

Josh glanced out again to see if it was safe. The threatening giant was nowhere to be seen. He took a deep breath and faced Danielle. "He's gone."

"*Who's* gone?"

"The guy who followed us followed me yesterday as well. He's broken off the chase both times, though." Josh tried to make sense of this. Nothing he'd ever experienced prepared him for what was happening now. "He's trying to scare me. He wants me to know he's around. He's not trying to capture me.

"At least not yet."

Chapter 10

THE MASTER WAITED IN PATIENT CONTEMPLATION IN the dim of the underground hideout. Although his followers' excitement mounted with each new development and revelation of prophesy, he wanted to savor the delicious anticipation of the events about to unfold. It was a position that could be enjoyed only by someone with the upper hand. The Master took a deep breath behind his serpent's mask, inhaling the molecules of thousands of years. The place smelled dank and every bit as ancient as it was. It was invigorating.

After several minutes in silence, he made it a point to arrange his black robes around him, taking time to smooth even the tiniest of imaginary creases before he was done. At last, he regarded his servant.

"Master," the mammoth man said, bowing.

The Master motioned for him to stand erect. "You've done good work. The next group will proceed with more stealth."

"Thank you, Master. I had many opportunities to kill the man, but I didn't because you told me not to. Why do you want him alive?"

The Master took another deep breath, but this time it was intended to calm himself. The giant was valuable even if he was almost absurdly stupid. "He needs to be alive in order to lead us to the artifact. Once we have it, he will no longer have any reason to live."

Slowly, as if absorbing some deep and esoteric wisdom, the giant nodded his huge head. "Thank you, Master," he said. "I understand now."

The Master found it ironic that such an enormous cranium should hold such a small brain. But then, intelligence and independent thinking weren't necessarily the most desirable traits in a devotee. Righteous belief and brute strength were all that were required. The Master worked to establish a delicate balance for his followers, with just the right combination of dependency and entitlement to stoke the flames of their faith. As for the muscle, this one was more than qualified.

"I want you to go to the Dung Gate," the Master told him. "There you will meet some of our brothers. I have a plan that should help us get the ancient document. You should enjoy it, I think. It involves a very captivating young woman."

"Is this woman one of ours?" ventured the servant, obviously impressed by his own deductive reasoning.

"Not technically, no." The Master grinned. "Not yet."

Chapter 11

On their way to the car, Josh looked at his watch, saw it was 7:45, and decided to change his plan. He touched Danielle on the shoulder. "Are you armed?"

Danielle seemed startled by the question. "No, of course not."

"I think it's better for you to get the car and meet me at 8:15 at the entrance of the Dung Gate. Be extremely careful, though. If you think you're being watched or followed, call for help and get out of the area."

"I don't understand. Why are we splitting up?" she asked, somewhat irritated and more than a little bit disappointed. "I'm the one who came with security, remember?"

"You'll be safer if you aren't with me where I need to go."

Danielle's eyes opened wider. "You're going to get the jar?"

A voice in Josh's head told him to run away with her—to simply forget everything going on and head out of Israel with this woman. Of course, he paid it no heed. "You'll be safer if you also don't know where I'm going."

Danielle tilted her head. "Josh, this concern of yours is very nice, but I haven't accepted coddling since I was eight years old."

"I'm not coddling you. I'm doing the prudent thing. The fewer people who know about this the better."

Danielle seemed about to protest, but Josh held up a hand. "This isn't about trust."

Danielle glowered. "It certainly seems like it."

Josh shook his head. "Believe me, it isn't. I trust you. I genuinely do."

Danielle seemed to contemplate continuing the debate and then her expression softened. "You're taking Dov, right?"

Josh looked over at the bodyguard. "You never know when you'll need an Uzi."

Danielle reached up and kissed Josh tenderly on the cheek. The kiss was only a whisper, but it reverberated in his soul. "Be careful," she said.

Josh took a deep breath. "I will be. I'll see you in a little while near the Dung Gate."

Josh spotted the darkened entrance to Avner's store. No one was following them. At this point, he was certain he'd be able to tell because his pursuers made their presence intentionally obvious. He knocked on the door and saw Avner peering through the peephole. Immediately, he heard the door's locks turning.

When Avner opened the door, his normally jovial face was tight. "That message you left on my machine practically scared the shit out of me. What's this about killers? I've been looking over my shoulder all afternoon." He noted Dov and eyed him suspiciously. "Who's this?"

"This is Dov. He's one of the good guys. He works for IAA security and is assigned to protect me."

Avner ushered them in and locked the door once again, trembling as he double and triple checked the bolt. He quickly headed toward the back of the store. "I hope you know what you're doing with this thing, Josh. People in your business aren't supposed to get involved with killers. Neither are people in my business."

Josh had never seen his friend act so nervous. He felt bad for putting him through this, but at the time he brought the jar to him, Avner was the only person in the entire country he knew he could trust.

Avner stepped into his office and returned with the backpack, holding it out to Josh as though it was a ticking bomb. Josh took the pack and smiled at his friend. "I suppose I owe you more than drinks now, huh?"

Avner chuckled, though he still seemed unnerved. "The best dinner in Jerusalem would be a start—but only a start."

"You got it. Just as soon as all of this is over. You name the place."

Just then, Josh felt a cold spike from his spine to the back of his neck. What was that about? Certainly, this was a tense situation on top of an already tense situation—and Avner's apprehension didn't make things more relaxing—but his warning system was suddenly on overdrive. He needed to get the scroll to a safer place. He wouldn't feel a moment's comfort until he did.

"Are you in there?"

Josh snapped out of his reverie to see Avner staring at him.

"Sorry," he said. "My mind has been wandering a lot lately."

Avner snorted. "Oh, I get it. That's the excuse you're going to give me when your mind wanders and you forget to buy me that expensive dinner."

The big man's cajoling put Josh at ease. "I'll remember, don't worry. We'll go somewhere extravagant. A coat-and-tie place. You do own a coat and tie, don't you, Avner?"

Avner pretended to be baffled by the question. "Gee, I don't know. I'll have to check the back of my closet."

"You do that. And we'll try to get together next week."

"You're on."

Josh smiled. He looked forward to the dinner. It would be nice to relax with an old friend after the craziness of the past few days.

It took less than ten minutes to reach the entrance to Dung Gate. The gate was always heavily guarded because it stood between the Jewish Quarter and an Arab neighborhood. At this time in the evening, the bus terminal just inside was deserted. Josh looked for Danielle's car, but it wasn't there. He checked his watch; it was 8:15. He was sure she'd be here any minute.

The icy sensation that had come over Josh in Avner's shop had receded a bit, but now he felt another spike. What were his nerves doing to him? He motioned to Dov to follow him and they walked through the terminal to see if anyone was watching them. There was no one in sight, but who knew what the shadows held?

Suddenly, a rush of air to his left kicked Josh's senses into overdrive. He stopped in his tracks, but before he could warn Dov to be careful the bodyguard collapsed, a dagger piercing his neck. As he went down, blood gushing from his throat, Dov managed to pull the Uzi from its holster and fire off a few rounds, the shells clattering to the ground and bouncing into the shadows.

Josh had no idea where the assailants had come from or where they had gone, but there was no time to take precautions. He rushed to Dov's side and was doused with blood. That dagger had been thrown at him, he knew it. But Dov had been caught off guard. Why hadn't Josh been attacked once his bodyguard was down? Had something gone wrong?

The squealing of car tires drew Josh's attention to the entrance of the gate. There, two men in long black robes rushed toward a slow-moving vehicle. Before he could even think about pursuing them, the men were in the car and speeding out of sight.

From the opposite direction, Josh could hear shouting and the sound of boots echoing through the empty terminal. As Israeli security ran toward him, Josh turned back toward Dov.

Gurgling and in spasms, Dov was obviously in trouble. Dov had pulled the dagger out of his neck and the blood spurted as he tried to contain it. Josh was well versed in first aid, but this was way beyond anything he'd encountered before. He grabbed a cloth from his backpack and applied pressure to stop the bleeding, though he knew the effort was futile.

Maintaining the pressure, Josh closed his eyes and wished for help. In his mind, he imagined the blood flow stopping and Dov getting much needed air into his lungs. Josh felt lightheaded; the insanity swirling around him was overwhelming. *Concentrate on Dov!* he ordered himself. Josh opened his eyes to see if he was making any progress and found the bodyguard looking at him. He was no longer struggling. In fact, he seemed at peace. Was that because he was about to die? The man's breathing was easy, almost relaxed.

Josh lifted the crimson cloth. The flow of blood from the wound had slowed to a trickle.

Three Israeli policemen ran to his side, firearms drawn. Josh indicated that he was unarmed and pointed to Dov's Uzi lying on the ground ten feet away. One of the policemen picked up the gun and then the others lowered their weapons.

"We'll call for an ambulance," one of them said. "Let me see your identification."

Josh pulled it out and told them what happened. Within minutes, he heard the sound of an approaching ambulance.

The Israelis were by necessity well prepared for sudden tragedies.

"Do you want to go to the hospital with your friend?" one of the officers said.

But Josh wasn't listening anymore. He had just realized he knew the car in which the assailants had escaped. It was Danielle's.

A policeman wrote down Josh's hotel information and said, "Come down to headquarters tomorrow. We'll need you to answer more questions." He wrote down his address on another piece of paper and handed it to Josh.

Josh stood by while paramedics dressed Dov's wound and loaded him onto the ambulance. Amazingly, Dov was conscious the entire time. The man should have been dead.

What had happened while Josh held his hands over the bodyguard?

The answers to those questions would have to wait. He had too many other questions to answer first.

Chapter 12

JOSH DIDN'T ACTUALLY SEE DANIELLE WITH THE MEN who drove off in her car, but he knew that she was with them. Had she been abducted…or was she in on whatever plot he had stumbled into? It was impossible for Josh to believe that she could have anything to do with whoever was stalking him, but there were so many incongruities here. If she were involved, then this adventure had taken its ugliest turn yet. If she weren't involved, though, she was in serious trouble.

The only thing Josh knew with certainty was that he needed help. He believed he could take care of himself, but he couldn't identify his adversaries and rescue Danielle—if she needed rescuing—alone. He had begun to trust Danielle and even feel comfortable with Dov. With both of them gone now, though, there was only one other person he knew in the entire country that he could turn to. He'd asked a lot of Avner, but he was going to have to ask more. He was going to owe him a hell of a dinner when they finally got through this.

Josh walked alone through the dark and narrow streets. He looked at the old stone and mortar buildings that surrounded him and felt as though he had stepped back in time. *Funny*, he thought, people tend to think of the past as a more innocent time. *That wasn't true here, was it? When was the last time this land was truly innocent?*

Josh turned the corner and saw Avner's store. The light was on and the front door open. Immediately, his nerves tingled. It didn't make sense for Avner to have the store open at this hour, especially after their last conversation.

Cautiously, Josh entered the store and walked toward the back.

"Avner?"

There was no answer. There was, in fact, no sound at all. The store had an unnatural stillness to it—something that Josh had never experienced in Avner's presence.

"Avner, it's Josh. Are you back there?"

Josh's senses were on full alert—something was very wrong here. Yet as he moved cautiously toward the back office, a part of him was centered in that strange calm that he had experienced before, when he first began to decipher the text of the scroll. Where there would normally have been panic, Josh felt certain knowingness, along with something else. It was almost like an unbearable sadness, but an unspecific, and almost non-personal emotion. He felt as if his heart was about to tear open with compassion.

Until he opened the door.

But nothing could have prepared him for what he saw, and as inexplicably as that calm had come over Josh, it was gone.

Avner had been stripped naked and nailed by his hands to the back wall. Guts and gore pooled at his feet, spilling out from the cavernous hollow of his pale belly, and where his star of David necklace had hung since childhood, his chest was now emblazoned with an elaborate drawing of a serpent entwined around a cross. His face was frozen in death in an agonized grimace.

Josh collapsed to the floor and vomited. He wailed in mourning for his dear friend. He cried until he felt the weeping would overcome him.

"I'm so sorry, Avner," he wailed. "I never knew this would happen. I never would have involved you."

He forced himself to look at Avner's face, frozen in death

in a mask of agony. He would gain fury from the image, and from that fury, resolve. He stood and fought back his revulsion, then kissed the burly man on his cheek. "I will not let your death mean nothing."

When he pulled back, there was blood on his hands.

The police arrived only minutes after Josh called them. One thing you could always count on in this city was a quick response from the cops.

"This looks like a ritual killing," one officer said when he examined the body. Josh could tell that, even with all this policeman had probably seen in the line of duty, this appalled him.

"It was," Josh said.

"What do you know about it?"

"More than I'd like and not nearly enough."

Josh spent the next twenty minutes explaining what happened. A second officer searched Josh's backpack and pulled out the jar.

Josh carefully took it from him. "That's a jar I discovered in a cave near the Dead Sea. I've made arrangements to deliver it to the Israel Antiquities Authority."

One of the policemen went to the front of the store, pulled out his cell phone and dialed. He returned five minutes later. "I just spoke to Moshe Ben Daniel and he confirmed your story. After we finish our investigation here, we're to escort you to the IAA."

Josh nodded listlessly. He kept flitting between shock and anger. At the moment he felt exhausted.

"Maybe you should sit for a while," the first officer said.

"I want to help."

"You can't help here. Please go sit somewhere; you look very shaky."

Josh nodded again and sat in a chair behind one of the counters. An ambulance arrived with a body bag. Josh simply watched as everyone did their jobs, wondering what job he would next be called to do.

When Josh arrived at the IAA, Moshe and the archaeological team were there to meet him at the front entrance. They ushered him inside.

"Are you all right?" Moshe said.

"One of my closest friends was murdered over the contents of this backpack. Is there any conceivable way I can be all right with that?"

"I'm very sorry, Josh."

"That isn't all. We need to talk privately."

Moshe turned to the other men in the group. "We'll be right there."

A couple of the archaeologists seemed miffed at the dismissal. Josh didn't care.

"What do you need to tell me?"

"Dov is in the hospital and Danielle is…gone."

Moshe's face stiffened. "What do you mean she's gone?"

"She was supposed to meet us at the Dung Gate. She never showed up, but I saw her car. The men who attacked Dov sped away in it."

Moshe's expression turned to one of alarm, his gaze distant.

"Moshe, how well do you know your daughter?"

Moshe stared at him sharply. "I know her as well as any man can know his adult child. What do you mean by that question?"

"Is there any reason for you to believe she might be tied up in this?"

"Are you asking me if I think my daughter is a criminal and a murderer?"

Josh waited a moment to still the tension between himself and Moshe. "I'm asking if she might be an unwitting accomplice."

Moshe shook his head. "Danielle isn't unwitting about anything."

"Then she might be in very serious trouble."

Moshe closed his eyes for a long moment, and Josh wondered if he was praying.

"You don't need to worry about Danielle," Moshe said, opening his eyes. "She can take care of herself. In fact, she's probably far more than you can handle, Josh."

"With all due respect, Moshe, I don't think you understand...."

"No, Josh, I think it's you who don't understand. I should have explained this to you earlier, when I first noticed that look in your eyes. I'm sorry, but my daughter is very...passionate. She has a certain energy about her that attracts many men; but she is also very independent and in some ways impulsive. If I know Danielle, she is off chasing a lost thread of history or plunging headlong into some new experience. She'll turn up in a few days. She always does."

Josh was taken aback, but something deeper than his pride told him that Moshe was wrong this time. "Look at what they did to Avner and to Dov. Danielle could be in serious danger right now. We have to do something."

"My daughter is fine," said Moshe, resolved. And then, more quietly, dropping his head, "She has to be. She's all I have."

But then he shifted abruptly and changed the subject, as if the moment before had been a mere trifle.

"Let's go examine the jar," he said. "It is surrounded by so much horror...we need to learn why."

Josh clapped a hand on the older man's shoulder, following him into the IAA offices. *We'll find her*, he thought. *I'm not sure how, but we will.*

Chapter 13

THE ARCHAEOLOGISTS HAD GATHERED AROUND THE JAR, their excitement palpable.

At least one of these men was involved in Avner's murder and Danielle's kidnapping, Josh thought. *Yet now they look like boys at play.*

"It looks similar to pottery from the first century," said Jonathan, practically shouldering his way past the other members of the team to get a closer look.

But the older and more experienced Father Andre wasn't about to break protocol, excitement or not. "Has the pottery been soaked in clean water to make sure soluble salts have been removed?" he questioned, only the slightest hint of chiding in his voice.

Josh scrutinized each man carefully. It seemed amazing to him that only a few days ago the thought of this moment would have filled him with the same thrill. He had the feeling nothing would ever be that simple again.

Reverend Barnaby Smith, a man who was so skinny and awkward looking that he resembled Ichabod Crane, returned with first century pottery taken from the museum's collection. He put the jars side by side.

Josh recognized the procedure as typology. Through this process they would classify the new jar based on a series of attributes, comparing it to other pieces from the same period. This was the first step to dating it and determining its authenticity.

The archaeologists gathered around the jar. They weren't allowed to touch the artifact; they had to rely on their naked eyes. The eye could be a powerful tool when evaluating and analyzing pottery. The team studied the size and shape of the jar and scrutinized the outside surface details. They observed the cross section of the vessel, which indicated the degree to which the clay was worked and the nature, size, and quantity of temper added to the clay to improve its firing qualities. All these attributes would assist the archaeologists in determining the period and locale of the jar's creation. Later, they would test the scroll by putting it through radiocarbon dating, which would determine the scroll's age within fifty years.

It was two o'clock in the morning when Moshe finally suggested that they quit for the night and reconvene at noon the next day. "Can you all be here?" he asked.

It was a rhetorical question, but despite their exhaustion, everyone nodded enthusiastically. Except Josh. "I have an appointment at ten," he said, his mind racing with thoughts of Avner, Dov, and Danielle, "but I'll try to be here on time."

Father Andre was the first to say goodnight to Josh. "I understand this discovery has come with a terrible cost for you already. I'm very sorry for your loss. I apologize if this seems indelicate, but I'm finding this very exciting. If the jar is authentic, the scroll could be a real breakthrough."

Josh nodded and studied the man closely, looking for what poker players called a "tell," an indicator that would reveal what game, if any, he was playing. "Thank you for your condolences."

Father Andre left without another word, followed soon by the others. Only Josh, Moshe, and a security guard remained in the room.

Moshe carefully lifted the artifact and put it in a safe.

"Is that secure?" Josh asked.

"As secure as anything on the premises."

"Why doesn't that make me feel better?"

Moshe looked at Josh and then dropped his eyes.

Josh fought back a sudden swelling of anger. *Remember*, he told himself, *he's as anguished as I am.*

"We'll learn more tomorrow," Moshe said uneasily. "Where will you stay tonight?"

"At my hotel. Where else would I stay?"

"Do you really need to ask that question?"

Josh hadn't given much thought to his personal safety in the past several hours. "What do you suggest?"

"We have facilities here. We can keep you under guard at least until we can make better arrangements. The accommodations are relatively comfortable."

Josh snickered. The concept of "comfortable" seemed utterly alien to him.

Chapter 14

DANIELLE WAS COLD. SHE LAY ON A STONE SLAB, NAKED except for a light robe. In the darkness, she could discern nothing about her surroundings or whether she was alone. She knew only that there were ropes bound tightly around her hands, arms, and feet.

After some time Danielle heard voices and tried unsuccessfully to turn her head toward the sound.

"What are we going to do with her?"

"Wait for the Master's instructions."

"If I wasn't celibate, you know what I'd like to do."

"We are holy men. We must not think impure thoughts."

Danielle closed her eyes, trying to suppress the anxiety that rose at these words. In her experience, impure thoughts precipitated impure actions, regardless of one's training.

She opened her eyes again and tried to see something. She'd adapted to the limited light but everything still seemed formless. From the echoes and the stone beneath her, Danielle suspected she was in one of the ancient tombs that surrounded the Old City. There were hundreds of them, some dating back nearly 3,000 years. It would be difficult for anyone to find her—if anyone was actually looking. She wondered if her father even realized she was gone. She'd disappeared for days at a time before, often with some man who briefly excited her. Her father never approved of these excursions, but by this point, he'd become accustomed to them.

What about Josh? Something happened between them last night, something that didn't happen with Danielle very often. She had no desire to rush off with him, but she definitely wanted to be with him. But it was difficult to tell whether he felt the same way—which was odd since she always knew when a man was interested. What did he make of her disappearance? Was he worried for her, or did he just think she ran away from him?

If neither her father nor Josh realized that this time was different, she had no one to help her but herself. She tugged against the ropes and instantly understood that helping herself would be nearly impossible.

Chapter 15

Josh entered the police station near the Old City.

"Can I help you?" asked an overweight policeman who was seated behind a huge wooden desk said.

"I was told to come here this morning for an interview," Josh told him." "The officers never told me their names, but they gave me this."

The cop reached out for the piece of paper, not bothering to get up. He examined it halfheartedly, then picked up the phone and dialed. In less than a minute, the two familiar policemen appeared and escorted Josh back to an office.

"How is your security man doing?" asked the taller one, who introduced himself as Yosef.

"I called the hospital two hours ago and they said he was stable. It looks like he's going to make it."

"He can thank you."

"No, he was just lucky."

The shorter one, Avraham, said, "Not like your other friend."

"No," Josh said, his voice barely a whisper.

Yosef pulled out a black dagger. "This is the dagger they used in the attack on your bodyguard last night."

Josh examined it closely. "It's only a copy, but it looks like a knife used by the Sicarii about two thousand years ago."

"By the who?"

"The Sicarii. They were a First Century group of revolutionaries. Some called them assassins. They carried daggers like that one under their garments and used them to attack Roman Forces and the Jews who supported them."

"Well," said Avraham, "it appears that both the security guard and your friend who was killed…"

"His name was Avner," Josh said, more defensively than he meant to.

"Both of them were attacked by the same group."

Josh nodded. "I assumed the same thing."

"Do you know who they are?"

"No, but I'll find out."

Avraham leaned toward him. "That's not your line of business, Mr. Cohan."

Josh fixed the man with an unwavering gaze. "That isn't really the point anymore."

"This is a very dangerous city, as you should well know by now. Let us address this investigation."

"I appreciate your help, but I won't simply stand by. I owe Dov and Avner more than that."

Josh hadn't mentioned Danielle. He honestly didn't know what to say about her. He also had no idea how to look for her, but still thought it better to keep the police out of it.

He hoped he wasn't making another fatal mistake.

Josh was the last to arrive at the IAA, and when he hurried into the lab the other archaeologists were already staring at the red jar on the table.

"It's in such good condition, it's hard to believe that it's ancient," Father Andre said.

The others agreed enthusiastically.

Alon, one of the four Israeli archaeologists in the room, eyed Josh suspiciously, "Have you opened the lid?"

"Yes, I opened it briefly, took the scroll out, and examined its condition."

"I'd hoped you hadn't," Reverend Barnaby said.

But Josh reassured them that he knew what he was doing. "I handled it very carefully. I wore surgical gloves so I wouldn't leave any marks, and put it back exactly the way I found it." He decided not to mention photographing the scroll before he re-sealed it.

"Then you read it," Smith said. It wasn't an accusation, but more of a resigned assumption.

Josh could tell that some of the team members were still wary of his involvement here, and he didn't want to make any more enemies than he already had. "I read a very small piece of it. As you know, this kind of translation takes a huge amount of time."

"What did it say?"

"I think you'll want to discover that yourself."

"If you did it already, why not tell us?" Alon snapped.

"Because you need to read it to believe it."

"Do *you* believe it?" Reverend Barnaby asked, giving Josh the floor and putting the younger archaeologist in his place.

"I'll wait till the C14 tests are finished," Josh said, but he didn't really know whether he meant it.

The discovery of radiocarbon dating had been a monumental event in the history of archaeology. Its discoverer, Professor Willard F. Libby, had won the Nobel Prize in 1960 for figuring out that because C14 decayed at a steady and measurable rate, it was possible to test the remaining C14 in any specimen, then compare it to a baseline measurement in order to determine the approximate age of the sample. The discovery shook the world of archaeology to its foundations by answering the key question: how old?

But it couldn't tell them anything about the author of the scroll. Despite all their training and access to technology, and regardless of who died along the way, Josh knew that belief or disbelief would ultimately come down to faith. It made the scientist in him extremely uneasy. Still, there was that persistent sense of calmness and knowing. At this point he didn't know what to make of any of it—but he was in a lab surrounded by other archaeologists, so the choice, for the moment, was simple.

As if on cue, a wild-haired man in his fifties entered the room, looking more like a symphony conductor than a scientist.

"This is Steven Fishman," Moshe said to Josh. "He's our radiocarbon specialist."

"Let's see what we have," Fishman said enthusiastically, making a beeline for the artifact. "Is it all right to open the lid?"

Several archaeologists nodded eagerly.

Carefully, Steven opened the jar and slid out the scroll, touching it only with surgical gloves. He unrolled the scroll and stopped at the first sheet. "It looks like sheepskin."

"It's written in Aramaic," Father Andre said, leaning over it. He studied the document carefully. Josh guessed he was translating. Suddenly, the man stopped, his face white.

"I don't think we should start translating until Steven is finished testing," Father Andre said, his voice quivering.

"That should only take a few days," Steven said. He cut a tiny piece off the end of the scroll. "I plan to ask the permission of the authority council to use the accelerator mass spectrometer so that we can get results as quickly as possible. I'll still have to take my time preparing the sample, though, since any contamination could invalidate the results altogether. I'm as eager as any of you to see how this pans out, but it just isn't worth the risk to rush."

Moshe turned to the others. "Should we wait?"

"No!" Alon said impatiently. "Let's at least take a look at the condition of the writing."

Several archaeologists gathered around the scroll. Josh stayed on the periphery, already well aware of the contents.

"It's going to be a challenge for us to translate all the words," Jonathan said.

"It may take more time than we planned, but we'll get it done."

Father Andre looked up from the document. "If this scroll is truly from the Second Temple period, this is a stunning discovery."

He locked eyes with Josh, who could only begin to guess the meaning in the priest's gaze.

Chapter 16

Hours had passed and Danielle was hungry and thirsty. Bound in place and uncertain if she would ever see the light of day again, her mind began to play tricks on her. She was sure she heard things skittering around her. Then she began to imagine disembodied heads hovering over her, leering. Her skin began to feel as though it was being pricked with thousands of tiny needles. The pain rippled through her, attacking her everywhere at once—and she couldn't move. She wanted to scream, but somehow she couldn't do that either.

Suddenly, the pain eased. She felt the stone slab again and for a few moments, she thought about surviving this, about somehow managing an escape. Then she shifted, felt the ropes that held her down, and her anxiety spiked.

Danielle's vision turned to white and she couldn't see anything at all. Her heart raced as she tried to contend with this latest hallucination, but as images began to return she realized that this wasn't the product of her tortured mind but of a bright light shining in her face. Slowly, her eyes adjusted and she saw where she was—a claustrophobic space cut into a stone wall. As Danielle had guessed, and feared, she was in a tomb.

The light ran the length of her body with excruciating slowness. At last, the man behind the light spoke. "I'm going to untie you," he said in a deep voice. "Do not attempt to run or I will be forced to hurt you."

The man approached and with huge hands loosened her bonds. As she tried to get some circulation into her limbs, he pulled her out of the enclosed space.

He suddenly turned on another light, once again temporarily blinding Danielle. A minute or so later, she saw him for the first time. He was dressed in a black robe. A veil covered his face, but his piercing yellow eyes glowed from his head. She knew him. She'd seen those eyes before. But where?

"You're a mess," he said darkly. "Take off your robe."

Slowly she complied until she was completely naked. She felt vulnerable, humiliated, and helpless. Danielle had always despised these emotions and the combination caused her anger to surge. She couldn't do anything with this anger, though. The man was easily a foot taller than she was and probably twice her weight. All she could do was watch him watch her. His thoughts were painfully transparent. What would she do if he attacked her? What *could* she do?

He handed her a heel of bread and a cup of water. "Drink. Eat. Now."

She did as he instructed while he molested her with his eyes. She was so famished that she barely noticed, but as her hunger and thirst subsided, her sense of revulsion returned. She hated this man. She would kill him if she could.

He seemed oblivious to any of this. He pointed to a spot in the corner where there was a hole in floor. She hesitated, then went over and relieved herself. He gave her soap and a bucket of water and she washed. He didn't say a word; he just watched.

At last, it occurred to Danielle that this giant of a man was the one who followed Josh, Dov, and her out of the Church of the Holy Sepulcher. The man had followed Josh before that as well. Who did he work for? What did he want? What were they planning to do with her?

The man came closer to her, so close that their bodies touched. He ran a callused hand over her shoulder, down her arm, and around to her buttocks.

Don't let this happen to me, she pleaded silently. *Please don't let this happen to me.*

Abruptly, he stepped back. He turned and retrieved the robe she had worn before. "Put this on again," he commanded.

Danielle quickly did as she was told, for the first time happy to comply. She knew he was aroused and she knew that she was powerless to stop him, but still he restrained himself. Did that mean that her captor had a whisper of decency? Or was he simply drawing out her torture?

She couldn't go on like this. She needed a plan, some way to get free. Danielle decided that she would speak with him. Maybe if he believed she liked him, he would let down his guard in some way.

"What's your name?" she asked, hoping to keep the anguish from her voice and actually sound friendly.

"Alu," he said gruffly.

Danielle tried a smile. "What an unusual and interesting name."

He huffed. "Do you know who Alu was?"

"No."

"He was the son of a Semitic woman and the devil."

His laugh chilled her to the bone.

Chapter 17

JOSH COULD BARELY CONCENTRATE ON WHAT THE other archaeologists were saying. Even the scroll itself was an afterthought. All he could think about was what had happened to Avner, and what he could only guess had happened to Danielle. Josh was more convinced with every hour Danielle was gone that she'd had nothing to do with the attack on Dov. She had been kidnapped; he knew this with certainty. But why? What did her captors think she knew about the scroll? Certainly, if the person who had ransacked Josh's room and threatened him over the phone was a member of the IAA, he also knew that Danielle had little or no information to offer.

I'm not cut out to think this way, Josh thought. *These aren't the mysteries I'm supposed to solve.*

Despite several hours' worth of theoretical debate, the archaeologists really couldn't do much until the results of the radiocarbon dating came back, and by mid-afternoon they agreed to break until the following day. The end of their meeting couldn't come quickly enough for Josh. It was insane, he thought, that they had wasted so much time when Danielle was still missing. If that wasn't a priority for all of the archaeologists, it absolutely should be for Moshe. The man seemed stuck in quicksand, though. Was he so stunned by his daughter's disappearance that he couldn't act, or was there something else behind his apparent lack of

concern? Josh just didn't know what to think about anything.

For his own protection, museum security had moved
Josh to a condo less than a mile's walk from the Old City.
Only Moshe and Josh's new bodyguard, Ari, knew his new
address. It was now well past the deadline he had been given
for turning over the scroll, but he was still alive. At least
something was working properly.

Josh was exhausted, running on fumes. He just needed
a few minutes to regroup and then he'd set off in search of
Danielle—even though he had no clear plan how to find her.
Josh practically stumbled through the front door of the safe
house, tossed his key on the counter, and made for the couch.
He needed to rest for a few minutes, to plan out his actions.
Within seconds, he was asleep.

*He is standing before the Citadel, the imposing form of
David's tower rising high above the magnificent fortress. In the
distance, Josh can see the dome of the Church of the Holy
Sepulcher. . .*

*He is present on the scene, but removed from it at the same
time. As he watches, unseen and unable to interact with anyone
around him, armor-clad Crusaders are rounding up Jews—
men, women, and children—and herding them toward the synagogue. Josh can feel the people's fear and he knows that their
lives are in grave danger. He knows that they, too, are helpless
to save themselves, and he can feel their suffering and loss of
hope.*

*When all of the people are inside, the Crusaders lock the
building tight. Then, dispassionately, as though this is all in a
day's work, they set fire to the synagogue. Josh wants desperately to help, to find some way to free the innocent victims, but he
cannot move.*

The sound of screams fills the air and there is only billow-

ing black smoke and flame, reflecting brightly off of the
Crusaders' armor and casting long, terrifying shadows over the
sign of the cross emblazoned on their standard.

Josh can only watch the building burn, unable to avert his
eyes. Eventually the screams subside and the building turns to
ashes.

Josh awoke from the nightmare, his heart racing. Instinctively, he took out a copy of the New Testament and turned to Matthew 10:34.

> *Think not that I come to send peace on earth. I come*
> *not to send peace, but a sword.*

The Crusaders had used swords to kill thousands of Jews. Did they do this in the name of Jesus the Jew?

Based on everything Josh had read about the historical Jesus, he had been a man of love. How could things have gone so wrong? Although there was no empirical evidence that he had ever existed, by all accounts Jesus had preached good deeds and proper actions yet others who did not know him had distorted his message. Would whoever was trying to steal the scroll pervert the newly discovered words in the same way—and leave the same legacy of violence?

Chapter 18

A<small>LU NEEDED TO WALK</small>. H<small>E NEEDED TO FIGURE OUT</small> what was going on in his head. He was a deeply religious man—far more religious than so many so-called "pious" people were. He took his commitment to the Master seriously and, along with that, his vow of celibacy. Never once had he disobeyed an order, and this time should be no different. But the plan had gone wrong.

Israeli security had shown up at the Dung Gate before the others had been able to complete their part of the mission, and in order to escape they had hijacked a car with the woman still in it. They had wanted to kill her immediately, before the Master could find out how careless they had been, but once Alu laid eyes on her he couldn't let them do it. Instead, he had taken her to the tomb and hidden her away until he could figure out what to do next.

He couldn't explain his actions, even to himself. But there was something about the frightened look in her eyes mixed with...was it kindness? Tenderness, even? It reminded Alu of someone—and something—he had long tried to forget. Now, as he hurried through the streets to stay one step ahead of his panic, he was taken back to another time, long ago, when he had first learned what it was like to be alone. He could still see the moment as clearly as if it had just happened.

He was twelve years old, still a child, and usually sat in

the back of the car. On this occasion, though, his mother had insisted that he sit beside her in the front passenger seat.

"You are as attractive as a movie star," she said to him, brushing a lock of his hair.

Alu blushed and squirmed. "You're just saying that because I'm your son."

"Not at all. Don't you notice the way girls stare at you?"

"No." He was shy, and still awkward in his recently acquired adolescence. He wasn't used to taking up so much space, but it felt good to be doted on like this, like a man.

"You are so tall for your age and you have such a strong chin. This has nothing to do with my being your mother. Even if I weren't, I would still find you handsome."

Alu smiled and stared at his mother's beautiful face.

It was the last peaceful image he would ever have.

Suddenly, a pick-up truck slammed into the back of their small car and they were engulfed in flames. Alu didn't remember what happened next. He was told later that he had gotten out of the front passenger door and collapsed on the street, severely burned and in shock. His mother had been trapped inside the automobile, incinerated as she struggled to free herself from the wreck.

Alu was left scarred both physically and mentally. He still looked like a movie star, only now it was the star villain of a horror movie that he resembled. With half his face disfigured and his cherished mother gone, he withdrew from the world. Only the Master didn't shrink from him or call him names. Only the Master took him in and showed him the true light of God. Alu was bound to his savior by far more than simple gratitude.

The woman, though—she did something to him.

When he first gazed at her, long forgotten memories burst forth. Alu saw Danielle, and in his mind, he saw his mother reborn. She had the same beautiful soft mouth and raven hair. And she looked at him with something like the fondness that had once been in his mother's eyes. His heart went out to her. Maybe she could even care for him.

When Alu gazed at her naked body, his own body stirred with a kind of lust he had never felt before. The woman was magnificent; when he touched her, it was like touching fire. Unlike the fire that had disfigured him years before and forced him to wear a veil, these flames were delicious. They didn't consume him, but made him feel stronger.

He wanted her so desperately that he was ready to deny his vows and force himself on her if necessary—which he knew it would be, since no one would willingly make love to so hideous a monster. His passions overwhelmed him, but when he moved to take her, he saw the fear in her eyes and it stopped him cold. He couldn't hurt her.

Then she had talked to him, not as someone she feared, but as a friend. She liked him. Maybe she even appreciated his restraint. He had scared her with that story about his name because he, himself, had been frightened by the confusing rush of emotions. But something had happened between them. He knew it as well as he knew anything in his life.

Alu hurried down Via Dolorosa, his mind racing as quickly as his hulking body. It wasn't until his cell phone rang that he finally stopped to catch his breath.

"Yes?"

"How is the girl?"

"Master, I can explain...."

"The others have already been punished for their recklessness and insubordination. What concerns us now, Alu, is whether our mission has been compromised by this indiscretion."

"The girl is fine. She's frightened and confused, but she is unhurt. After I fed her, I tied her up again and put her back in the niche."

"When are you going back there?"

"I'm on my way there now."

"When you get there, kill her."

Alu's heart skipped several beats. "But, I thought…"

"Are you questioning the Master? That is never your function. You will follow my orders." The line crackled in silence for a moment.

"Master, may I please speak? I have never questioned you and always carried out every command you have given me."

"Yes, you have. That is why you are still alive."

Alu bit his lip. To say one more word could be suicide. But he thought of Danielle's beautiful face and his heart yearned for her. There had to be something he could do. "Master, after all my years of loyal service to you and our cause, I ask that you hear me out this one time." He had to think quickly.

There was another pause and then the Master spoke. "You realize the price if I don't like what I hear."

Alu responded carefully, "I understand. Thank you, Master. I will always be your humble servant." Alu could barely get the next words out; his heart was beating so quickly. "I think it would be wise for us to spare the girl."

"Impossible. She knows too much."

"Master, I questioned her at great length." He was lying, but he had no choice. "I do not believe she has knowledge of anything that can harm us. Perhaps we could trade her for the artifact?"

"She's aware of the location of one of our meeting places."

"She knows she's in a tomb, but she doesn't know where it is located. When we kidnapped her, we blindfolded her and didn't take the blindfold off until she was in the niche of the wall."

Seemingly from nowhere, the Master laughed cruelly and mockingly. "Are you smitten, Alu? Do you think she likes you as much as you like her?" The Master laughed long and hard and hearing it pained Alu greatly. However this pain gave him the courage to continue speaking his mind.

"Master, if you want her killed, I will kill her, but I see no harm to us if we let her go. We've spilled enough blood."

"If the artifact is authentic and what it says is harmful to our cause, there will be enough blood spilled to feed a league of vampires for generations." The Master laughed again.

The laughter abated slowly. "You are right, Alu; you have been a loyal servant. If you want to keep this girl to feed your fantasies a little longer, I will be magnanimous. I'll let you make the decision when to kill her. If it turns out being a wrong one, however, your death will be your own doing."

"Yes, Master," Alu said thankfully. The Master cut the connection and Alu stared at the phone. He'd never before known anyone to convince the Master to change his mind.

Would it cost him his life to be the first?

Alu felt powerful and terrified at the same time. He needed to get out of his own head and ask God for guidance. There was only one place where he could go.

Bathed in myth and legend is the Mount of Olives where many pious Jews believed the Day of Judgment would take place, when the dead would literally rise. It was also the location of Gethsemane, where Jesus and his disciples came on the night before his arrest and trial. Although he was only a lowly initiate and nowhere near as wise or holy as the Master, Alu always felt the thrill of God's righteous judgment when he came to this spot. Here on the steep hillside, looking out over the Old City wall east of the Temple Mount, amidst the ancient Jewish cemetery and many tombs, he could always throw off the temptations of the world and find his faith.

As Alu moved through the deserted hillside, however, he became cautious. Two men seemed to be following some fifty yards behind him. He decided not to take any chances, turned around, and headed back to the Old City. He went through St. Stephen's Gate, the main connection between the Moslem quarter and the Arab neighborhoods to the east. Alu headed along Sha'ar Ha'arayot Street, passing the Monastery of the Flagellation where, according to tradition, Jesus received the cross and was scourged. He rushed down a bustling, narrow street into the heart of the Moslem quarter and disappeared into the crowd.

Only in the darkness of the night did he return to the tomb where he kept Danielle captive. She had been there twenty-four hours, eating only that one bit of bread and water. He went to the niche, pulled Danielle out, and untied her. This time he gave her some cheese to go with the bread. When she took it, she thanked him with a smile that suffused him with warmth. Neither spoke while she ate hungrily and then relieved herself.

When she returned, she stood before him. Draped like an angel in her thin, white robe, her beauty seemed to cast a light even in this cold, dark tomb. But the light was fragile, and her face suddenly crumpled as she burst into tears.

"What's wrong?" demanded Alu, unsure how to react. He meant to be gentle, but his voice was too loud, his big hands rough and clumsy rather than soothing as he tried to stroke her hair.

"I'm scared," she said, sobbing. "I miss my father. I miss my life. I know you're going to kill me."

Danielle's body rocked with sobs and Alu's heart went out to her. Surprising himself, he reached out and took her in his arms. Even more surprisingly, she didn't resist. In fact, she seemed to welcome his comfort.

She likes me. She doesn't think of me as a monster.

"I'm not going to kill you," he said softly.

She looked up at him, rivulets of tears streaking her cheeks. "How can I believe you?"

He pulled her close again, feeling his body respond to hers. He forced himself to keep his lust under control. "You can believe me because I'll never do anything to hurt you," he told her.

She rested her face against his chest. "Then let me go."

She started crying again, and Alu was struck by how very small she seemed to him now. Her pain tore at him. He wanted to protect her, and yet the Master would kill him if he set her free. If he didn't release her and she came to harm—maybe even at his own hands—he would live the rest of his life in torment.

"Danielle," he said, the words speaking themselves before his mind could protest any more, "do you know where you are?"

She sniffled and took a moment to gather herself. "I'm in a tomb." She was quiet for a second and then said, "There are hundreds of them in and around Jerusalem. I've been in other tombs but from the inside they all look the same."

Alu knew that she was telling the truth. He had been in many of the tombs himself, and they were impossible to distinguish from one another without seeing them from the outside. He felt suddenly elated at the realization that he could commit an act of kindness without compromising the Master in any way. "If I let you go," he said, "I need your word of honor that you will not tell anyone where you've been."

She looked up at him again. Her glistening eyes made him want to hold her forever. "I swear I don't know where I am."

"No one can ever know."

She nodded slowly. "I promise."

Alu closed his eyes, understanding the consequences of his next words. "Then I will release you."

There is still time to change my mind, Alu thought as he blindfolded Danielle, took her hand, and led her out of the tomb. *The Master need never know. I'll tell the driver there was a change in plans.* But Alu knew he wouldn't change his mind. He had lost the power to harm her when she first looked at him with such knowing and compassion. Danielle had never seen his face, but Alu was convinced that she saw him in a way no one in the world ever had before.

They walked a hundred yards and then Alu told her to stop. "I'll be right back," he said. "Don't do anything. I don't want to hurt you."

"I'll wait for you," Danielle said.

A few minutes later, Alu returned and led Danielle down the hill. A waiting car took them to a deserted part of Eastern Jerusalem.

As he led her out of the car, Alu told her not to take the blindfold off for five minutes.

Danielle nodded.

"And remember—you must never speak of where you were."

"I promise," she said, smiling warmly. "I never will."

Alu wanted to kiss her, or at least to hold her one more time. How would he explain this to the driver, though? He had to resist. He stared at Danielle a moment longer, knowing that he may never see her again. He wanted to memorize every detail of the vision.

"Never speak a word," he said, and then got back into the car. The driver sped off, but Alu looked back through the rear window, watching Danielle until she was no longer visible.

Chapter 19

Searching for Danielle was hopeless. The city was simply too big. There were too many places to hide her, and Josh had virtually no clues. He felt frustrated and angry with himself. He should be able to do more for the people he cared about. Was she okay? Was she even alive? Danielle was already a victim of his discovery, but if she died because of it, he was certain he'd never be able to make peace with that.

Knowing he would drive himself crazy if he didn't do something, Josh sought solace in the images of the scroll he had stored on his laptop. The scroll itself consisted of nine sections, all written in the same Aramaic script, some of which was barely visible. He skimmed through the text, trying to concentrate, to find some sign as to what he should do next. His mind was restless and the glare from the screen was giving him a stabbing headache. Still, the promise of the scroll's secrets had a hold on Josh and wouldn't let him go.

He wondered how the IAA would handle his discovery. Would they think it genuine, or just another of the hundreds of fake artifacts they handled? Even if they decided it wasn't authentic, would it really matter? There had been controversies before, like the one surrounding the James Ossuary—the stone burial box of James, son of Joseph and brother of Jesus. The Israel Antiquities Authority considered it a fraud, but some experts disagreed.

He understood their dilemma: Israel's antiquities black market was booming. A few of Israel's biggest antiquity dealers were under investigation for fraud and illegal dealing, and many of the nation's artifacts had turned out to be fakes. The IAA had their hands full; still, it was incumbent upon them to take every discovery seriously. In many ways, they were the keepers of civilization's history.

Josh had an uncanny feeling that his discovery was authentic, though none of the carbon 14, paleographic, or typographic tests were yet complete. This was only the first step and, in many ways, the easiest. Dating the scroll was the easy part; but determining the identity of its writer was nearly impossible. Yet Josh had a deep conviction, which he couldn't explain, that he knew who wrote the scroll.

He had previously translated part of the first section and now began to look at the words that followed. Josh once again read the author's name: Yehoshua ben Yosef—Joshua, son of Joseph. It was the Aramaic name of Jesus of Nazareth. To millions, he was God. To others, he was a prophet or holy man. To some, he was an enlightened rabbi. There were others who thought him a mortal man and still others who thought him a mere myth.

Josh himself was a maximalist, seeking the historical truth in Biblical narratives. In many cases, Josh doubted that the authors credited were the original writers. In fact, he was convinced from his studies and research that the majority of the Bible was based on myths and legends. Yet, even though he questioned who the real authors were, he enjoyed reading its teachings and found great wisdom and valuable lessons in the book.

The archaeologists had agreed to wait until the dating tests came back before continuing their translations of the scroll—but, of course, they didn't know that Josh had these images. He decided to press on now, knowing that it was the only thing that would tamp down his anxiety over Danielle. As before, the translation was painstaking and slow, the already cumbersome task made even more difficult by broken and faded characters. Deep into the night, Josh worked to complete another passage:

> *I was a young child when I discovered that I was different. I was playing near a stream when another child threw a stone that hit me on my right arm, causing a throbbing pain. Anger raised inside me. I wished the assailant harm, and to my surprise, he fell down and appeared dead. Guilt overwhelmed me and I ran to the lifeless boy, touched him, and wished he would open his eyes. He did. From that day on, I realized I must control my anger.*
>
> *When I was six, my mother, Miriam, told me that she had a secret she would share with me when the time was right. She never told me what it was. I had heard some of the villagers gossiping that my real father, Joseph, wasn't really my father. They also whispered other malicious things about this.*
>
> *I was mischievous and always in trouble as a child. As a young man I began to conquer my inner demons. I studied Torah and prayed every day. I experienced the pleasures of the flesh but eventually realized that it was an impediment to my mission. For this reason I chose to become celibate.*
>
> *From the time I was a child, I felt my life had a bigger purpose. I was thirty when I discovered what this purpose was. Bright sunshine illuminated the water of the Jordan River and there appeared John. He was called the Baptist. John the Baptist looked at me as though he had always known me. He immersed me in water and screamed of repentance,*

for the end of days was at hand. "*Repent,*" *he yelled in a booming voice, and the crowd around him was enthralled by every word he uttered.*

John gazed at me and a smile appeared on his serious face. His dark, brown eyes seemed to penetrate my soul and he said, "You are the one." I didn't know what he meant, but that night I had a dream. I would be a shepherd to the poor, the downtrodden, the frustrated, and the hopeless. I would be their rabbi, their teacher, and their healer.

With each word he translated, Josh became more convinced of the scroll's authenticity. This wasn't the Jesus of children's stories or books written hundreds of years after his death. These were words written by a man who knew of life, who understood the times he lived in, and who was confused by his gifts. He was a man who spoke of the pleasures of the flesh and of battling his anger. In other words, a real man, not a myth or symbol.

Josh had been fascinated with Jesus for his entire adult life. As he brought these words into this century, however, he felt closer to this man than he'd ever felt before. It was both exhilarating and a bit perplexing.

Physically exhausted, but feeling a sense of accomplishment for the first time in days, Josh fell into a dreamless sleep. Tomorrow he would find a way to rescue Danielle. He was certain of this.

Josh awoke to the ringing of his phone. He could have sworn that he had just shut his eyes, yet daylight streamed in through the bedroom window.

"Josh, this is Moshe. I have wonderful news—Danielle is free."

He bolted up in bed. "She's free? Is she okay?"

"She's shaken, but physically unharmed. We have her sedated right now and I'm sure she's going to need some help; but she's safe, thank God." The emotion in Moshe's voice revealed for the first time how frightened he'd truly been about his daughter.

"Do you know anything about what happened to her?" Josh asked, trying to be delicate.

"She was abducted by a gigantic man named Alu and held captive in a tomb. Somehow she managed to convince this man to release her." Moshe chuckled softly. "He'd probably never matched wits with anyone like Danielle before."

Josh instantly remembered the giant in black who he had twice spotted following him. But he knew that there had to be others that were involved with this, too. The two men who had attacked Dov were much smaller.

"I thought you'd want to know," Moshe said, bringing Josh back to the present.

"Yes, absolutely; thank you for calling me." As the news of Danielle's safety settled on him, Josh allowed himself to feel for the first time all the despair he had pent up over her loss. It was nearly as overwhelming as the magnitude of his joy at knowing she was okay.

"When can I see her?" he asked eagerly.

"We need to give her a little time. Let her come to terms with this."

"I'd like to help her."

"You will," Moshe said, keeping his distance. "Just give her a little time."

"Of course," Josh said. After all, Moshe had a right to be his daughter's protector at a time like this. Despite his own feelings, he knew that they would want some time alone together. "Moshe?" he asked.

"Yes?"

"I'm happy for you."

Moshe was quiet for a long moment. "Be happy for all of us, Josh," he said with a catch in his throat.

Chapter 20

DANIELLE OPENED HER EYES TO DISCOVER HERSELF ON a firm, comfortable mattress, lying beneath a quilted blanket. It was her childhood bed, one of the safest places she had ever known.

She sat up slowly and rubbed her forehead. Alu had released her for a reason she only partly understood. She remembered being blindfolded in the car and then finding herself on an unfamiliar street when the car sped away. She didn't remember much after that, but obviously she'd made it to her father's house. It was now light outside, but she was unsure what time. Glancing over at the clock in the room, she saw that it was early afternoon.

Danielle moved to get out of bed, but when she drew back the covers, she felt a chill run though her body, as though she was racked with the flu. She hated that this was happening to her—first the abduction, and now even her body felt weak and vulnerable. It wasn't a feeling she was used to, and she considered fighting against it. After sitting on the edge of the bed for a moment with her limbs like lead weights and the blood throbbing in her head, she finally relented and curled up under the quilt again. Maybe it was best to let herself be taken care of, just for a little while, just this once.

Several minutes later, her father poked his head in through the doorway to check on her. When he saw that she was awake, he entered the room, came to her bedside, and kissed her gently.

"How are you feeling?" he said.

"Not as well as I would like."

Her father sat on the edge of the bed and took her hand. "You've been through a terrible thing."

"I've been through terrible things before," she protested, still finding it hard to let go.

Her father squeezed her hand. "Not like this."

Danielle closed her eyes briefly. She didn't like what she saw. "I thought he was going to rape me," she whispered. "I thought he was going to kill me and leave me there to rot."

"He will pay, my love. We'll find some way to make him pay."

She looked deep into her father's eyes. He'd always been so protective of her, even though she proved long ago that she could take care of herself. "To be honest, Dad, I'd be just as happy forgetting that he ever existed."

"Maybe that will be possible as well," Moshe hesitated. "But it might not."

Danielle knew that it was true and that this was not a trauma she could force to the back of her mind. "This obviously had to do with the scroll Josh found and the threats he received...." Then a thought struck her for the first time.

Her father saw the color drain from her face and spoke calmly to reassure her. "Josh is fine. He has been very worried about you, but I telephoned him earlier to let him know that you were all right."

Even in the midst of her trauma and exhaustion, Danielle was surprised by the intensity of the relief she suddenly felt. Still, she knew better than to think that the whole thing was over with. Josh might still be in serious danger. One thing puzzled her, though. "Do you know what they wanted with me?"

Moshe patted her hand absently. "I don't know. They never contacted us about you at all." He let out a brief chuckle. "I even allowed myself to hope that you'd gone off on one of your *adventures* again.... The only thing I can think of is that you managed to get free before they used you for whatever ends they had intended."

Danielle grasped her father's hand and they locked eyes in silence for a long moment. Then she released his hand and moved to get up again.

"You should stay in bed," he said in a typically fatherly fashion.

Danielle swung her legs around. The chill stayed away this time. She knew she could stand. "No, I shouldn't. Believe me, the last thing I want to do at this point is lie down. I want to see Josh. Can you take me to wherever you've hidden him?"

Her father tipped his head. "No need. He's been in the living room for hours."

Chapter 21

JOSH FELT THE PULL OF THE DEEP MEDITATIVE TRANCE he'd put himself in. This was where he went to think, where he went to ask the questions he couldn't answer any other way. Josh used meditation in different ways. When in a deep trance, he visualized his body's energy fields and tried to control them. At first, he had failed; but after countless attempts over the course of several years, he had learned enough to achieve some palpable success. He began to work with what seemed to be twelve major energy fields. After some time he discovered a book on Chinese medicine and realized that these were the same fields used by acupuncture practitioners. Of course, they used needles; Josh used his mind. He practiced regulating the blood flow to different parts of his body and manipulating the energy.

The first time Josh had become aware of this special gift was when he was five years old. Avner had crashed his sled and was knocked unconscious. Instinctively, Josh placed his hands over his friend and felt his own life force radiating outward, and within moments Avner was upright and wondering what had happened. The other kids thought that it was weird and even Avner seemed uncomfortable with the event. Embarrassed by that episode, Josh had kept his practice to himself and never used that gift on another person until the incident with Dov at the Dung Gate.

Now, as he concentrated on his breathing, he prompted himself with questions about the scroll, Danielle's abduction, and why someone had resorted to violence, kidnapping, and murder to take what he'd found. In his mind's eye he saw snippets—a serpent and a gold chain—but the answers remained elusive.

Then, without any grand climax to his visions, Josh felt compelled to exit the trance. All of his meditations ended this way and he never fought it. Each session lasted only as long as it should.

When he opened his eyes, Josh saw Danielle looking down at him. Somehow, after what she'd been through, she was still radiant.

"Taking a nap?" she said playfully. "It's good that you weren't too worried about my condition."

He grinned. He'd missed her voice. "I figured I didn't have to worry too much about anyone who could talk her way out of a tomb guarded by an awful giant."

She laughed at that and his heart leapt. He leaned toward her. "Are you okay?"

She sat next to him on the couch. "I'm going to be."

Before he could prevent himself from doing so, he reached out and took her in his arms, bringing her toward his chest and holding her there as tightly as he'd ever held anything in his life. He wanted to breathe strength into her and let her know that he'd do everything he could to prevent her from experiencing further anguish. At the same time, though, he sought her strength—the strength she could offer just by being present in his life.

"I was unbelievably worried about you," he said in a surprisingly raspy voice, "and I couldn't figure out what to do. I tried to find you, but I didn't know where to look."

Danielle nuzzled against him closer. "I'm back. I made it."

"I never meant for you to be hurt by this. It has changed everything for me."

She lifted her head up. "It can't change everything for you. We need to learn all that we can about the scroll. We need to find out why someone wants it so badly. You can't back off now. You..."

Josh interrupted her, smiling. "No, this was what I meant." He brought his lips to hers and kissed her gently, then with a sudden, desperate passion. Kissing Danielle was like entering another form of trance. He felt himself lifted, almost as though he'd left his body. At the same time, though, he'd never felt more grounded in his life. There were answers here as well, to questions he'd never even thought to ask.

Chapter 22

THE GUARDIANS WERE ASSEMBLED DEEP BENEATH THE Old City, in their underground hideout. The sect had been headquartered here for more than seventy years, since before the establishment of modern Israel. Dressed as Catholic priests, they were able to move around the Christian Quarter without attracting the attention of Israeli soldiers and police, who were accustomed to seeing holy men in clerical garments. The subterfuge was almost effortless, since the clergy was considered above reproach and nobody bothered to look close enough to distinguish the particular differences in the garb of the Guardians—differences like guns and knives hidden beneath their robes.

Torchlight from ancient wall sconces cast long shadows across the gloomy meeting space. The twelve Chosen Ones sat on stone benches that dated back to the first century, awaiting the arrival of the Master. Though they were outwardly silent, they chanted as one through their inner voices.

All praise to the Creator God.

We thank you for your vessel Paul, for only he speaks with the True Voice.

Grant us the power to resist the false prophecies and the Demiurge, the lesser god of Genesis.

Let us carry your message until the End Days.

They repeated the Four Proclamations for countless minutes while they waited.

When the energy of the inner voices reached the critical pitch, the Master allowed the Chosen Ones to share his presence, making his entrance in full regalia. He was dressed in the same priestly garments as his minions, but on his face was the sacred serpent mask. Around his neck, he wore the symbol of their sect: the snake entwined around the crucifix.

"I have many things to discuss with you," the Master said in a sonorous tone, "but first I must tell you about one of our brothers who has failed us and must be tried."

The Master held his followers in silent expectation for several long moments, allowing the impact of his words to sink in.

"All of you understand the gravity of our calling. Each of you knows how critical it is that we stand tall against the blind believers of the false god. It is our privilege and our sworn duty to ready this sickly world for the coming rapture. You have been chosen for this task and I have been chosen to lead you. As your Master, I must be obeyed—absolutely. Yet one of you has chosen to act alone, abandoning the righteous path. Today, you must assist me in judging one of our members who has faltered."

"Yes, Master," said the Chosen Ones in unison.

The Master turned to the giant among them, fixing his gaze while the enormous man squirmed. "Stand up, Alu."

"Yes, Master," the giant said, standing warily.

"Do you wonder why I have asked you to stand?"

"I do not, Master."

The Master stared holes into the back of the man's head. "Are you saying that you wittingly disobeyed me?"

The giant shook his head rapidly. "I didn't intentionally disobey you, Master. I didn't mean to do anything of the sort. But the Jewess was so enchanting, so irresistible. I couldn't help myself."

"So you let her escape."

Alu's eyes darted. Had he just revealed more than the Master had already known? But there was no turning back. "Yes, Master," he said, knowing all too well what those words might bring.

"You have complicated our plans unnecessarily, Alu, and in your weakness, brought potential danger to your brothers and our entire mission. And for what? A Semite whore? I have treated you like a son. When no one cared for you, I took you in and accepted you as one of my own. This is how you repay me?"

"I'm sorry, Master," Alu muttered, face hot with shame beneath his veil.

"Do you have anything else to say for yourself?" the Master demanded, unrelenting.

The blood pounded in Alu's head and his vision became hazy with a conflicted rage. But the emotion turned in on itself and drained him of any lingering bravado. For several moments, he said nothing. When he finally spoke, the words barely left his lips.

"She liked me, Master."

The Master spun away from Alu and turned toward the others. "Alu is possessed. Brothers, we must help him. We must get rid of the demon inside of him."

The Chosen Ones nodded.

The Master looked back at Alu. "Take off your garments," he spat venomously.

Quickly, Alu stripped to his underwear.

Each of the Chosen Ones reached for a whip and began striking the giant. Alu suffered in silence as the sounds of cracking whips reverberated off the stone walls of the chamber.

After dozens of lashes, the Master called for the flagellation to end. Alu slumped back against a nearby wall.

"Are you ready to repent your sins, my son?"

Alu was a bloody mess. "Yes, Master," he said, sweating and heaving, his voice replete with agony.

"If you ever disobey me again, you know what the consequence will be."

"Yes, Master."

"I am not without mercy, but do not dare to think that I would spare even our best assassin from the punishment meted out for heretics by holy law."

As if at some invisible signal, two acolytes entered the chamber and escorted the fallen behemoth out of the meeting room. When they had dragged him away, the Master addressed the others.

"We have waited more than nineteen hundred years for the prophecy's fulfillment, and, brothers, the time is at hand. Even now the Israel Antiquities Authority is in possession of the sacred document that will validate the conclusions of our first master and the secret letters of Paul.

"As prophesied, this document will ignite the holy spark of judgment, inspiring the Battle of all Battles and the destruction of all evil in the world. This confrontation will usher forth the Second Coming of the Spirit of Jesus told to us in our sacred scriptures. You must prepare yourselves; when the scroll has been authenticated, we will make our move."

Chapter 23

JOSH HELD DANIELLE AS LONG AS HE COULD. THEY'D kissed passionately for several minutes, the heat rising between them precipitously. There was no question in Josh's mind that he wanted to take this further—being with Danielle released something both primal and exalted in him—and he could tell she felt the same way. But this wasn't the place for it. Not on her father's couch, with Moshe recently off to run some errands. Instead, Josh kissed her until he felt all of his resolve slipping and then he gently pulled her back and laid her head on his chest. Danielle didn't understand at first and began to tug at his shirt, but with a kiss on her forehead, he sent her the message. After that, they lay wordlessly—as though words could possibly be necessary—and basked in the moment.

"The last few days have been quite a roller coaster ride," she said after several minutes of silence. Her voice danced on top of the quiet.

"I could have done without the steep drops."

Danielle patted Josh's chest. "Me too. The climb is incredible, though." She arched her neck upward and kissed his chin. "I like the view from here."

He snuggled more tightly against her. "I don't know when this ride stops, Danielle. I have no idea what your captors want. It's obviously related to the scroll—it has to be—but I can't guess what they're planning."

"I wish I could have learned something while they kept me."

Josh searched his thoughts. "They know who the author is, or at least who the author claims to be. If these are really the words of Jesus, they'll have incredible ramifications. Some people wouldn't want those words to get out, but how would they know that before we authenticate and translate? What if he says something completely different from what we think he would?"

"That's not a chance worth taking for some people."

"You're right...different religious groups would have differing interpretations of the scroll's message." Josh's face grew pensive. "Catholics and traditional Christians will be upset if Jesus doesn't declare that he's the messiah. Or worse, doesn't mention his divinity."

"Josh, you must be aware of the potential controversy the scroll could cause. You may be in the center of a hurricane."

"Let's assume the scroll doesn't mention that Jesus is God. In the first words of the scroll, the author says that he's writing two weeks before he meets his fate. That means the major event in Jesus' life—the passion—hasn't happened yet. Many incidents could have occurred in those two weeks."

"I still think that the scroll will create heated controversy."

"Not necessarily. What I've translated thus far is not a depiction of the Jesus of faith, but of the historic Jesus. Many people will be brought closer to him because of his very humanity."

"You don't believe that Jesus was God or the Messiah... do you?"

"No," he said, realizing the strength of his conviction only when he spoke the word. "I guess not."

Danielle looked up at him wordlessly for several long seconds. Then she tucked her head back into his chest.

Josh squeezed her tightly. If not for the scroll, he never would have found her. At the same time, though, she wouldn't be in danger now, either. Life was so often too baffling to comprehend.

Slowly, he moved as if to rise from the couch.

"Are we leaving?" Danielle asked.

"I am, unfortunately. Your father and I have plans to meet the other members of the team to discuss our next steps." All Josh really wanted to do was hold her the rest of the day.

Danielle sat upright, separating from him. "I'll go with you."

"Please don't. You're safe here. I don't know how safe any of us are out there."

She smirked. "So it's okay for you to be in danger, but not for me? Is this supposed to be some form of chivalry?"

"You don't think you've been through enough the past few days?" he asked, both surprised and impressed by her resilience.

Her expression dropped as she gave in to his common sense. "Maybe you're right."

He kissed her on the forehead, and then more lovingly on the lips. "Rest. You're supposed to be recovering. You may feel fine now, but nobody gets over something like what you've been through that quickly."

Danielle nodded. "When will you be back?"

"I'm not sure." He smiled. "Some of these archaeologists can really prattle on."

She kissed his cheek and pressed her face against his. "Just make sure you do get back."

Josh would absolutely make sure of that. He knew with a certainty that he'd never felt before that nothing could keep him away from this woman.

Chapter 24

When Josh and Moshe arrived at Café Chagall, on Ben Yehuda Street, Andre, Alon, Barnaby, Jonathan, and Michael were already seated at a large circular table, talking and drinking coffee. Remnants of bagels and pastries littered their plates.

"How's Danielle?" asked Father Andre.

"She's remarkable," Josh said spontaneously. Moshe tossed him a sidelong glance and Josh felt immediately embarrassed. "What I mean is that it's remarkable that her recovery is moving along so quickly. She's very resilient."

"She's doing as well as can be expected," Moshe said firmly. Josh had met Moshe a block from the café. When Moshe asked him how he thought Danielle was doing, Josh was certain that Moshe knew what had transpired between them. Still, neither man said a word about it. It was yet another complication—albeit a much easier one to contend with.

Moshe signaled the waiter and ordered coffees and croissants for himself and for Josh.

"Any news about the scroll's test?" asked Alon, getting back to the question of the hour. The group's energy shifted palpably as the men leaned forward in their seats, all casual chitchat abandoned.

"Not yet," Moshe told them. "Steven and his team require a few more days, and the paleographers are continuing their examinations of the scroll's inscriptions. An initial report is expected by Tuesday."

This was not the answer that they were hoping for, and Jonathan groaned with frustration. The older members of the team were used to the waiting game, though, and nodded their resigned approval.

The Reverend Barnaby turned to Josh. "Do you believe that the scroll is authentic?"

"I don't know," Josh ventured carefully. "But I have a very strong feeling that it is."

"And you think the author is Jesus of Nazareth?"

"That's who he says he is."

Barnaby closed his eyes. It was almost as though he'd retreated into silent prayer. When he opened them, he had a look of abiding calm. "I've searched for years for some historical evidence of our Savior's existence. Official confirmation of the document's authenticity would mean that my prayers have been answered."

"What if it contradicts the gospels of the New Testament?" asked Alon, too excited by the theoretical to bother with tact. "Will it change your beliefs?"

"It won't matter," Barnaby assured him. "Faith doesn't come from the head; it comes from the heart. My belief in Jesus has given meaning and purpose to my life. Still, to hear his thoughts and have insight into the historic Jesus would enhance my work and my existence."

Michael interjected, pointing with a stub of bagel. "The Gospel according to Mark was written around 70 C.E., forty years after Jesus was crucified. Matthew was written around 80 C.E., Luke around 90 C.E., and John around 100 C.E. Their gospels don't always agree with each other. None of them knew Jesus personally, so they are bound to have some inconsistencies."

Father Andre broke in. "The Gospels are the word. I

believe in them with all my heart. Jesus is my Lord and Savior. He died on the cross to save mankind, and if men followed his teaching, the world wouldn't be in the condition it is."

Josh couldn't help but feel skeptical about such an out-pouring. "Do you follow all of his teachings?" he asked. "Do you love your fellow man, particularly those whose beliefs are contrary to yours?"

Andre's brows narrowed. "I care for mankind and have sympathy for those who do not believe in our Savior—even though they will ultimately burn in hell."

Josh took a sip of coffee to conceal his distaste for Andre's view of the world.

"What do you believe?" Andre asked pointedly.

"About what?"

"About God and religion?"

"Religion is a sensitive issue and there are obviously many different opinions. I don't want to offend anyone."

"I don't think you would offend any of us if you shared your beliefs," Alon said.

Josh noticed the other archaeologists nodding in agreement. Although he wasn't comfortable discussing his personal beliefs, Josh felt compelled to answer them. "There is reason to believe that a larger power governs the universe. However, I think it is possible that it is beyond our comprehension to know who or what that power is."

"Sounds to me like you're an agnostic," Jonathan said.

"I think agnostics are more comfortable with their ambivalence than I am," Josh admitted. "I really do want an answer—though I don't have a vested interest in what that answer might be. I'm confident that the day will come when I'll find it." He thought he was finished speaking, but new words came unbidden. "I have to tell you that I can't stand fanatical people who believe their way is the only way. It's like saying God is in one room and not in another. Religious

intolerance—especially from people who claim to be pious—
is the worst form of hypocrisy."

Josh felt his emotions rising. Now that he'd opened his
mouth, he had a lot more to say on this subject. His voice was
stilled, though, by the terrifying sound of an earth-shattering
explosion.

The archaeologists ran outside the restaurant and saw
dead and injured people everywhere. Josh looked at the bodies of men, women, and children and felt shaken to his core,
tears welling in his eyes. Had he somehow brought this on
with his rant? Did the world really need another example of
the intolerance he had just railed against?

Dozens of people were injured. Josh had to help, but he
wasn't sure what to do first. As if in answer, a young girl's
wails cut through the din. Josh went to her side immediately. She was bleeding badly.

The image ignited the painful memory of an event that
had occurred many years before, when Josh was a carefree,
extroverted five-year-old. It had just snowed six inches and
Josh and Avner joined a group of other children who were
sledding on Franklin Street in North Philadelphia. The narrow street was lined with old three-and four-story apartment
buildings dating back to the nineteenth century. Unused,
rusting trolley tracks ran down the middle of the street. The
snow was blinding and Josh lost sight of Avner.

Suddenly, he heard a scream. Josh left his sled and
sprinted in the direction of the sound. A group of children
surrounded Avner as he lay on the ground, unconscious and
shallowly breathing. He had an egg-sized bump on the right
side of his head and was bleeding from a nasty cut on his left
temple. His sled, damaged from the collision with an apartment house's stone steps, lay on its side.

Josh darted to Avner. Acting intuitively, as if possessed

with magic, Josh closed his eyes and touched Avner's bleeding head. A few seconds later the bleeding stopped and Avner opened his eyes.

The other children gazed at Avner in surprise. Then Seth Feinberg, a big, pudgy bully with scarlet-hair and alligator skin, shouted, "You're a freak."

As if he were leading a band, the other children joined in.

"You're weird," they taunted. "Stay away from us, freak." Heart pounding, Josh helped Avner to his feet and ignored the jeers.

"You shouldn't have done that," Avner said defensively.

Josh was stunned. "I helped you," he stammered. "You're my best friend."

Avner's looked away in confusion and maybe a little fear. "I don't know what you did, but you shouldn't have." He then picked up his sled and walked away.

Humiliated, Josh vowed never to use his unexplained power again. Here in Israel, though, he found it impossible to keep that vow.

Josh looked at the bleeding young girl and decided to take action. He ripped off part of his shirt and wrapped it around her right leg, holding the cloth in place to staunch the flow. As he had with Dov, he concentrated on the wound, praying—if that was the right word—for it to heal. A minute or two later, he lifted the cloth to examine the wound and saw that the bleeding had slowed considerably.

At a calmer time—if that ever happened again—Josh would try to make sense of how this was possible. There was no time to question now.

"You will be all right," Josh said. "The ambulance will be here soon and take you to the hospital."

The girl wailed again. "It hurts so bad."

Josh felt her pain as though it racked his own body.

Wanting to help her any way he could, he placed his hands on the sides of her head and said, "It will be better soon."

For several seconds, the girl continued to grimace and writhe. At one point, though, she opened her eyes and looked directly at Josh. At first, she simply stared at him. Then the tension in her face eased and slowly her eyes drooped closed. Her breathing became more shallow and relaxed.

Moshe put his hand on Josh's shoulder. "How did you do that?"

"I didn't do anything special. I just removed her fear."

The sounds of ambulances filled the air.

Josh stood. "Moshe, please make sure the ambulance takes her immediately. I'm going to see what else I can do to help."

He scanned the area for others in need. About thirty yards away, Josh spotted three priests. They were not assisting the wounded, but simply observed the scene with a detached half-interest. When they saw Josh staring at them, though, they fled, disappearing into the crowd.

Josh knew that this was connected to the scroll, Avner's murder, Danielle's kidnapping…but the whos and whys didn't matter for the moment. He turned his attention back to the injured, now being taken away in ambulances as Orthodox Jews piously collected body parts of the dead.

Alon approached him. "It's under control now. The paramedics know what to do. We should reconvene our meeting."

The notion of discussing archaeology in the face of this carnage seemed ludicrous to Josh. "Maybe we can get together tomorrow at the museum."

Alon's eyes narrowed. "We have important things to discuss. If you weren't American you would understand that it is our mission to make sure life goes on in the face of this."

"I'm not going to apologize for being American, Alon. Just as I'm not going to apologize for my compassion."

Alon glared at him. Josh's nerves were frayed. He wasn't sure he'd be able to control himself if Alon challenged him again.

Moshe and the others were now nearby. "Josh is right," Moshe said.

The rest agreed, some more reluctantly than others, and soon dispersed, leaving Josh to watch until every victim was removed from the scene.

Chapter 25

JOSH SPENT AN HOUR WALKING THROUGH THE OLD CITY trying to make sense of what he had just seen. As an archaeologist and a student of history, he knew more examples of intentional human atrocities than he cared to remember. Still, what he'd witnessed over the past few days left him shaken to the core. He'd seen so much hatred—directed at him, directed at people he cared about, directed at people he never knew—that his basic survival instincts were telling him to get as far from this place as he could.

Josh knew that he couldn't escape. He needed to learn more about the scroll and whether the author was Jesus himself. He needed to be here when the analysts confirmed what he already felt in his heart—that the scroll was real.

And realistically, there was no escape. He was in the middle of this now. The deadline his unknown enemies had given him for turning over the scroll had long passed, but Josh didn't think for a second that they had rescinded their threats. They were biding their time. Josh just didn't know why.

After his walk, Josh grabbed a cab back to his new residence. He was surprised to find Danielle in the living room, along with several men he didn't know. His first impulse was to protect Danielle, but she seemed far too relaxed to be in any danger.

"What are you doing here?" he asked.

"It looks like we're roommates now," Danielle said with

a glint in her eye. "They moved me here for safety this afternoon."

"Who did?"

"My father and the authorities."

"Your father moved you *here*?"

"He knew I could be protected here." Danielle grinned
seductively. "And there are *multiple* bedrooms."

"Right," Josh said, reddening slightly. "Multiple bedrooms."

He looked at the four new men in the room. "Want to
introduce me to your friends?"

Danielle pointed to a wiry man sitting on the couch.
"This is Ethan, my personal bodyguard."

The man nodded at Josh, who smiled at him in shy gratitude.

"These men," Danielle said, gesturing toward the other
people in the room, "are Israeli security people. They're
meant for both of us."

Danielle didn't mention their names. It was entirely
possible that they hadn't told her. Josh guessed they were
IAA inspectors or Shin Bet agents, the equivalent of
America's FBI. That meant the government was aware of
what was going on and understood the consequences. Josh
hoped that was a good thing.

The Scroll could be a political bombshell for Israel, a
small country the size of New Jersey that had more of the
world's media attention than most countries many times its
size. Israel would be right to be nervous about the scroll,
which had the potential to spark bitter debates in Christian
and Jewish circles alike and could present serious political
problems.

"Things just keep getting more interesting," Josh said
to no one in particular. He locked eyes with Danielle. The
last time they had seen one another his body had longed des-

perately for her. Though the feeling was still strong, it would likely be some time before they were alone again. "So we're roommates."

"Seems so."

"Just you, me, and four of Israel's finest."

Danielle rolled her eyes. "Yeah."

Josh took a deep breath. "I think I'm going to go to my room for a while. It has been a very full day."

Josh closed his bedroom door. He knew that sleep would help after such a tumultuous day. He also knew that sleep wasn't an option right now. Not with Danielle sitting just outside. Not after what happened between them this morning. Not after the explosion, the incident with the little girl, and then the sight of those three priests watching him.

He went to his closet. Buried under a pile of dirty clothes was his laptop. He took it out, typed the password he had created for the file, and the scroll's photographs came into view. Translation would help him tonight more than sleep or meditation. The intense concentration necessary would slough away everything else. At the moment, that sounded extremely appealing.

> *I left my parents and started on my mission. Soon after, my mother and brothers tried to seize me and stop me from preaching. They thought that I had gone mad. It hurt me that my own family did not believe in me. My brother James and I argued all the time. He was always my parents' favorite. During the last month, we have reconciled our differences and now share most of the same views. If I die when I go to Jerusalem, I've told James to take over my mission.*
>
> *I went into the countryside, to the small towns*

and villages. My own town rejected me, as did the people living in the surrounding areas. Most of my teaching went unheeded. This frustrated and angered me, so much so that I cursed the towns of Chorzin and Bethsaida to eternal damnation. I regret doing this. Controlling my anger and frustration has been a struggle for most of my life.

Only a small group of pious Jews have believed in me. I have avoided the cities of the Gentiles, for my message is meant for my own people, the tribe of Israel, who are suffering both spiritually and politically.

Here in Galilee we are not governed directly by the Romans, but by their puppet Herod. I am surrounded by Galileans who are prideful, nationalistic, and militaristic. Judas the Galilean has started a group known as the Zealots and they plan to overthrow the Romans by force. This is in keeping with the messianic prophecy: our land must be free of the Roman invaders and never again will man fight man. Most of our people believe that the Messiah, or the anointed one, is a military leader who will lead us to victory and become the King of the Jews.

I look forward to a day when the world belongs to one community, the human nation. Yet my own family is fractured. The hostility between the Sadducees, the Pharisees, the Baptists, the Zealots, and the Community disturbs me. We are all Jews. The sects may take different paths, but they all lead to our God. A few of my closest companions wish me to help lead a military battle against our conquerors. If we are successful, they believe that I will become the promised messianic King of the Jews. However, my people are too divided in their ways for this to happen. Therefore, I choose a different path, a more spiritual one. Many Jews believed the world was about to end as the Baptist had preached. I believed that too. Now I believe differently. Many thousands of moons will pass before the end of time.

Many thousands of moons. Josh pondered the last sentence even as fatigue took hold of him.

Chapter 26

AT THE END OF ETHAN'S SECURITY SHIFT, THE BODY-GUARD checked on the sleeping Danielle and then turned duties over to his relief person. He left the premises and headed down the street. Concealed inside his light brown jacket was a special issue micro Uzi.

Ethan walked two blocks to the bus stop. It was a dark, moonless night and the streets were unusually quiet. The air was rarely this still.

He heard the sound of a car engine and turned toward it. A black Mercedes pulled up beside him.

"Do you want a ride home?" a voice said from inside the car.

Ethan saw that the driver's face was familiar; it was one of the archaeologists who worked with him at the IAA. He was tired after a long shift, and happy to take the man up on his offer. "Thanks for the ride" he said as he climbed into the passenger seat. "The bus doesn't come very often at this time of night."

"Think nothing of it."

Ethan realized that they weren't alone in the car. He turned around and saw two huge men dressed in black. Their faces were expressionless. A thread of uneasiness ran down his spine.

"How are things going at the hideaway?" the driver asked. Ethan turned toward the front of the car, though something told him he should keep an eye on the men in the back.

"Fine. No problems."

"No further threats?"

"No. Nothing."

"That's good. We certainly don't want anything terrible to happen. By the way, you didn't tell anyone that you gave me the location of the safe house, did you?"

Why would he ask that? Ethan didn't remember giving the archaeologist this information. He was certain that the man already knew.

"No, of course not."

"Good work, Ethan. You have served your purpose well."

Ethan now knew he was right to be afraid. He also knew that he had done the opposite of "good work." By unwittingly revealing their location, he'd put Danielle and Josh in danger.

He needed to save those he was charged to protect. He needed to save himself. Ethan reached for his Uzi, but before he had a chance to act, he felt cold steel across his throat.

Then sudden, blinding pain.

Chapter 27

Monday morning, Josh arrived at the museum accompanied by two security guards, and walked into the conference room. Seated at the oval table were Moshe, Reverend Barnaby, Alon, Jonathan, Michael, and Father Andre.

"You look beat," Jonathan said.

"It's been a tough weekend. I didn't sleep well last night," Josh told them, leaving out the part about having spent most of the past ten hours translating the scroll. He noticed that none of the others seemed as affected by yesterday's explosion as he was. Was that what happened after you lived here a long time?

"Gentlemen," Moshe said, "before we begin, we need to discuss some legal issues regarding the scroll. We won't know until later in the week if the scroll is authentic. If it is, though, we must maintain complete secrecy. I want all of you to give me your word that you will not discuss our findings with anyone until we get clearance from the government to release them."

The others around the table nodded. Josh stared at his associates and then turned to Moshe with a troubled expression, "Why is the government so concerned about secrecy? What are they afraid of?"

Moshe seemed to find Josh's question ludicrous, "If the scroll is authentic, it will affect every corner of the world."

"Of course," Josh said, "I've understood that from the moment I read the opening words. But isn't it too early to worry about the impact of the scroll? It hasn't been authenticated yet, and even if it was there is no way to verify that the author was Jesus."

Reverend Barnaby addressed him in a calm and soothing voice. "Josh, you do understand that there has never been any historical evidence of Jesus' life. If the age of the scroll is authenticated, and if it contains the essence and the words that are similar to the New Testament, many people will believe it is real even if we don't have definitive proof."

"I understand why the government wants to keep it a secret," Michael said. "Jerusalem is the capitol of faith. Look around and you'll find thousands of people visiting supposed holy places—yet not a single site can be proven to be linked to Jesus or any other biblical figure."

Father Andre was obviously irritated. "Faith is not in the head but in the heart. Everyone who visits the holy sites here comes away with a deeply religious experience and is spiritually uplifted."

Moshe held out a hand. "You know how much I appreciate lively debate, but we need to get back to business. We must follow the government's orders of secrecy. Agreed?"

Josh still didn't see the point, but he agreed with the rest.

Moshe reached into his briefcase and pulled out a stack of confidentiality agreements. "Then I'm sure you won't have any problems signing one of these." He handed a copy of the contract to each of the archaeologists.

"You don't trust us?" Father Andre said, clearly hurt.

Moshe shook his head. "I've worked with many of you for years. You know that I trust you. The government insists on this."

Grudgingly, they all signed.

Barnaby handed Moshe his paper. "Will we still get the initial inscription tests tomorrow?"

"Yes," Moshe answered.

"Do you have the preliminary pottery tests?"

"I received them when I arrived this morning. Our experts matched the scroll's jar with some artifacts from the museum's collection. The tests showed that it matched the storage pottery used in the first century C.E. The jar's color and composition was a perfect match, but the initial patina testing was inconclusive. There were no coins found with the jar, or any inscriptions that would help us get a more precise date. They plan to continue further testing."

As if on cue, Steven Fishman, head of C14 testing, strolled into the conference room and handed Moshe a note. His results on the radiocarbon testing weren't expected until later in the week.

"I've been caught off-guard," Moshe said. "The testing is proceeding more quickly than we had expected based on earlier indications. Therefore, I have a surprise for you. The first test of radiocarbon dating is complete. Steven, please tell us your findings."

Fishman had the appearance of a distinguished scientist, resembling Einstein with a better haircut. This morning he was obviously excited and enthusiastic. "Gentlemen, I received permission to test the scroll using accelerator mass spectrometry. As you're all aware, AMS testing requires only a fraction of the sample size of older, more conventional b-counting tests, yet costs two to three times more. We were extremely lucky to have been granted approval.

"When I arrived this morning," Fishman continued, "I performed the AMS test. But I had enough of the scroll's sample remaining to use the surplus for the b-counting method. As you know, this method takes days to get final results. I plan to use the findings from that test to validate the first. The AMS dating results show that the scroll's parchment was from the Second Temple period, between 50 B.C.E. and 50 C.E. And because the sample was free from any contamination, I consider the results both accurate and reliable."

This didn't surprise Josh. He knew in his heart that the scroll's dating was authentic. He sat quietly and observed the reactions of his colleagues. Moshe, Michael, Jonathan, and Barnaby were obviously overjoyed. Father Andre and Alon, on the other hand, were unemotional. Did they always react this way to dramatic news?

"I wish I could give you an exact date, gentlemen," Steven said, only mildly apologetic, "but the C14 testing is conclusive within plus or minus fifty years of the artifact's actual age."

"So it's authentic," Barnaby said gleefully.

Steven nodded. "Based on the AMS testing it is."

There was excited murmuring among the group, but Alon cut it short. "Just because the scroll dates to the first century C.E. doesn't mean that the author was who he claimed to be. Literary impersonation was common in antiquity."

"Alon has an excellent point," Josh said. "Once we have final verification of the scroll's authenticity and we have translated it, we can try to determine whether Jesus could really have been the author. At least then we can make an educated guess."

The tenor in the room calmed.

Father Andre looked at Moshe. "Where is the scroll now?"

"We have kept the scroll in a special safe and have instituted heavy security measures. We are in the process of safely photocopying it, and starting tomorrow you will be broken up into teams of two. Each team will receive one of the scroll's sections. When you are finished translating it, you will present it to me and I'll give you another part of the scroll to translate."

"Will we be able to see all of the translations?" Father Andre asked.

Moshe nodded.

"And will we see the original scroll again?"

"Yes," Moshe told them, "but only under the proper circumstances."

"You seem so secretive. First with the confidentiality agreements and now this. Moshe, what's going on?"

"I can't tell you, Andre. I'd like to, but I can't."

"They just don't trust us," Alon said.

"I can't believe they wouldn't trust us," Reverend Barnaby said, his mouth set in a grimace and his eyes darting around the room as though looking for support. "As long as I've been here this has never happened."

"I assure you all that there's a good reason for secrecy at this level," Moshe said calmly. "A very good reason."

With the exception of Moshe, all of the research team went to the museum's restaurant for lunch.

"I've never seen so many security people here," Reverend Barnaby said when they sat down. "They're all over the place. There are people here I've never seen before."

"Tightened security and confidentiality agreements." Father Andre turned to Josh. "Your discovery seems to have changed our culture."

Alon and Michael nodded.

"It might change everyone's culture if we can verify the author," said Jonathan enthusiastically.

Josh chose not to respond to Father Andre in any way other than meeting his eyes. He still wasn't sure how to feel around these men—and never forgot for an instant that one of them was involved in killing his friend Avner, attacking Dov, kidnapping Danielle, and threatening to harm him and steal the jar for who knew what sinister purpose.

Josh realized that he hardly knew the three Israeli archaeologists, Jonathan, Alon, and Michael. It didn't seem likely that any of them could be involved in a secret society, especially one with some sort of Christian connection, but he'd already faced bigger surprises in Israel.

Josh decided that it was time to get to know these men a bit better, and knew that a friendly, casual approach was his best bet if he wanted to figure out which one of them was the traitor. He turned to Michael. "I heard you've been at the IAA for only a short time."

Michael nodded. "Yes. Just a few months."

"Do you like it?"

"What's not to like? The work is always fascinating. Not always as fascinating as what we're doing right now, but fascinating nevertheless."

"What made you want to be an archaeologist?"

Michael's eyes moved away from Josh as he considered the question. "My happiest memories of childhood were when my dad took me to some of the holy places in Israel and explained their histories. When I was eleven, he took me to a mound made up of the remains of a succession of previous settlements and let me dig. He took me all over the country, always exploring, always having a good time. He loved history and I think it rubbed off on me."

There was genuine warmth in Michael's voice when he spoke about his father, and this touched Josh. "He sounds like a good man."

"He was." A veil seemed to come over Michael's face when he said this, and his eyes dropped to the table. "Then two years ago, he got on the wrong bus."

By now, Josh knew all too well what this meant. "I'm

sorry," he said, though the words seemed painfully inadequate.

"Thank you for saying so. This city takes its toll on everyone."

In the past week, Josh had come to understand that on a very personal level. Surprising himself, he reached out and patted Michael on the arm.

Josh noticed Alon watching them. When he turned to look directly at the man, Alon quickly glanced away. Josh thought of engaging Alon in conversation, but decided better of it. He figured he'd learn more by watching Alon's actions than listening to his words. Josh had noticed that Alon tended to seem distant much of the time, as though he were in another world. Their only real conversation had been the confrontation after yesterday's explosion. Josh had known people like him before, people who lived in their own minds. Did that mind hold brilliant ideas—or did it hold secrets?

Josh next turned his attention to Jonathan. With his long red hair and walrus mustache, he looked more like a '60s rock star than an archaeologist.

"Jonathan, how are you enjoying our little project so far?"

"It's awesome," Jonathan enthused.

Josh laughed unguardedly for the first time that day. The phrase sounded funny coming from Jonathan, with his heavy Israeli accent. He must be a fan of American movies.

"Interesting choice of words. Have you ever been to America?"

"A few times. I visited some relatives in New York and California. The surfing was better there than it is here. Are you single?"

"Excuse me?" Josh said, caught off guard and unsure how to answer him honestly.

"Are you single? We should go out some time. I'd be more than happy to escort you to Tel Aviv. It has some of the hottest clubs—and Israeli women sure know how to have a good time."

Josh thought immediately of Danielle. He'd never been one to go out searching for a "good time" anyway, and it was the last thing he'd consider now. "I think my plate is pretty full right now…."

"Work hard, play harder is my attitude; always has been. Don't let me give you the wrong impression, though. I finished third in my class at Hebrew University and I'd rather be on an archaeological dig than anywhere else. Our little project is the most exciting thing I've encountered in years— and that includes a weekend a few months ago that I can't quite remember but will never forget."

Josh chuckled again. Had he ever been as loose as Jonathan? How many people ever were?

An alarm cut through his thoughts, and a voice came across the loudspeaker: "Please stay where you are."

Father Andre ducked under the table, and several of the other archaeologists followed his lead.

Josh remained in his seat, ready to help in whichever way he could if that became necessary. As security men moved through the restaurant and in the hallway beyond, it occurred to Josh that this attack—if that's what it was— might be a diversion intended to create chaos in the building and make it easier to steal the scroll. If this was the case, though, Josh couldn't do anything about it. The thought filled him with anxiety.

Then the alarm stopped abruptly and an eerie quiet pervaded the room. A minute later the voice once again crackled through the loudspeaker. "Thank you for your cooperation as we conducted this test of our security systems."

Father Andre and the others rose from under the table, and all around the room diners returned to their conversations and meals.

If I lived here a million years, I'd never get used to this, Josh thought even as he realized that in some ways he'd already begun to get used to it.

Chapter 28

JOSH ARRIVED BACK AT THE CONDO WITH THE TWO SHIN Bet agents assigned to flank him. When he entered the apartment and saw Danielle reading in the living room, his body relaxed. How much better would his life be if he could just bask in her glow all the time?

Her eyes brightened when she saw him. She bounded from her seat, dropping her book on the floor and came up to kiss him lightly on the lips.

"How are you feeling?" Josh asked.

"Stir crazy. The *muscles* here won't let me go anywhere. I'm sure I can sweet-talk Ethan into it, but he hasn't shown up yet."

"Isn't the idea that you're supposed to spend a few days recuperating in a safe environment?"

Danielle waved a hand in the air. "Sitting in a stuffy room all day does nothing to aid in my recuperation."

Josh chuckled. The Israeli people were an incredibly resilient lot, but most of them paled in this regard next to Danielle. "If you want to get out of here, you're going to have to take it up with the authorities. When was the last time you spoke with your father?"

"He called this morning. He's coming over tonight."

"I'm sure you'll find a way to persuade him."

Danielle got a gleam in her eyes that made it clear that she'd spent a lifetime successfully persuading her father. Josh wasn't so sure he wanted her to succeed now, though. He didn't want Danielle to feel cloistered, but he liked knowing she was in a place where no one could find her.

"You're going to have to play with me until then."

"Who said I had time to play with you?"

Danielle leaned closer. "Are you saying you don't want to play with me?"

Josh actually felt his body get warmer. "I definitely didn't say that." He looked around at the four agents stationed in various places in the room. "What did you have in mind? We're not exactly alone."

"Come with me to my bedroom."

Josh's spine tingled. "Your bedroom? Did you miss the part about our not being alone?"

Danielle smiled hypnotically. "Just come with me to my bedroom."

Josh wasn't sure he was ready for this—especially considering the muscle hired by Danielle's father—but he took Danielle's hand and followed her into the next room, where a chessboard was set up on a table.

"You want to play chess?" Josh said, abashed.

"What did *you* think I meant by 'play'?"

Josh thought about the way it had felt to kiss and hold her and his knees nearly buckled. "I took you for a checkers girl."

"Checkers is for children. Sit down and prepare to be beaten."

Shaking his head in wonder, Josh took a seat across from Danielle. The guards remained outside. What the Shin Bet agents *thought* was going on here was anyone's guess. For all he knew, Danielle had already tried to drag one of them in here to play with her.

Josh hadn't played chess since graduate school. That turned out to be a problem in the early moves when Danielle presented him with an opening he'd never seen before. He got his bearings about ten moves in and held his own through the endgame. Then his rustiness showed through again. It was obvious that Danielle had a plan and he didn't. He guessed she would checkmate him four moves before it happened.

Danielle smiled brightly as she toppled his king. "You play pretty decently."

"Really? How would you know?"

She patted him on the hand. "I was the chess champion of my college. I beat everyone, including a boy who is currently ranked as one of the best ten players in the world. You gave me a better fight than a lot of people."

Josh didn't feel particularly comforted. "I'm going to want a rematch, you know. I haven't played in a while. I'll be much better next time."

Danielle rose from her seat and moved over to Josh's side of the table. Caressing his neck, she sat on his lap. "Speaking of rematches, I've been looking for one with you for the past couple of days." She nuzzled close and kissed him on the ear. "If you're much better at that the next time as well, I don't know how I'm going to control myself."

Josh shifted her body and kissed her with all of the passion he felt for her. Her body melted into his and he felt a surge of energy unlike anything he'd ever felt before. He explored the muscles of her back, feeling her breasts press against him. When Danielle reached down to pull his shirt out of his pants, he lifted her from their chair and carried her to the bed. As he placed her down gently, he saw the hunger in her eyes and he realized he needed this woman desperately.

"I can't tell you how much I've wanted this," he whispered.

As he lay next to her, he heard a phone ring in some

distant corner of his mind. He paid it no heed as he began to loosen the buttons of Danielle's blouse.

He could not, however, ignore the hard knock on the door.

"Do you think you can take a message?" Danielle said anxiously.

"It's your father. I told him you were busy, but he said he needed to speak with you."

Josh buried his head in the bed. Danielle kissed the back of his neck and said, "I'll make this quick. Don't go any-where."

"I *can't* go anywhere," Josh said in frustration.

Danielle opened the door and took the phone from the guard. "Hi, Dad."

"Shalom." It was her father's voice, but his greeting lacked its usual warmth.

"Dad, are you okay?"

"Something has come up and I can't see you tonight. I'm sorry."

"You sound upset; are you all right?"

"Don't worry about me, I'll be fine. How are you feel-ing?"

"I'm fine. I'm more than fine, actually."

"That's very good. I'm so glad to hear it."

The abruptness in her father's tone jarred Danielle. "Dad, are you sure you're okay?"

"Yes, I'm totally fine. I'm sorry I interrupted you, but I didn't want to leave a message when I was canceling. I'll see you tomorrow, all right?"

"All right," she said weakly. "Shalom. I love you."

"I love you too, darling."

Danielle broke the connection and stared at the phone. She never had conversations like this with her father. They knew each other too well not to be honest with one another. Why wouldn't he tell her what was wrong?

She sat on the edge of the bed. Josh was still lying down, but now he was on his side with his head propped on his arm.

"My father's not coming today," she said.

"Is everything all right?"

"I don't think so. He sounded strained."

"It's probably just a complication at the IAA. They seem to have quite a few of those."

"Yeah, probably," Danielle said quietly, knowing absolutely that it was something more. "Josh, would you hate me if I asked you just to hold me?"

Josh sat up instantly, took her in his arms, and pulled her back down to the bed. "I'll hold you whenever you want."

He wrapped his arms around her tighter. Danielle loved the feel of this man next to her. But it wasn't enough to minimize her sense that something was terribly wrong.

Chapter 29

THE TWELVE CHOSEN ONES ROSE AND BOWED AS THE Master appeared in the chamber. "Greetings, my brothers," he said, his voice anything but warm. "We have learned through our resources that the first tests have authenticated the scroll. It has been proved to have been written when our Lord walked this land. I believe more strongly than ever that it is the sacred scroll of the prophecy. If this is true, it will validate all of our beliefs and we can begin to execute our plans.

"There is, however, the possibility that the scroll contains a different message. If it does, we must destroy it—and all of those who know about it—before the heretical contents are released to the public.

"Whether the scroll supports our beliefs or not, we must obtain it at all costs."

The Master eyed his followers. He felt his power, his total control over them, which gave him enormous satisfaction.

"I will allow nothing to stand in our way. The time is now; the world has reached the pinnacle of corruption, and it is our destiny to destroy those who are to blame. We must convert the non-believers into believers, or else deliver them to the same fate as those cleansed by our brothers during the Inquisition. We must clear the path for the return of the Spirit of God. Nineteen hundred years have passed since

Marcion, may he be exalted, broke from the heathens and became our first great Master. Our brothers have remained strong of faith and deed since that time, persevering against great opposition and under the cloak of secrecy. All of their sacrifice has been to bring us to this moment."

The Chosen Twelve nodded in unison, as if rehearsed.

"Many of our allies hold high governmental positions throughout the world, and are awaiting my signal. That hour of judgment is near. We will triumph. There is no power in this world that can stop us.

"You have been chosen because of your faith, your intelligence, and your physical strength. You will need all of these to fulfill the divine plan."

The Master gazed beyond the men, beyond the walls, and into a future only he could clearly see.

"My brothers, we are witnessing the dawn of a new world, and we, ourselves, are the light."

Chapter 30

THE JERUSALEM SUN SHONE BRIGHTLY IN THE MORNING sky, casting a light of hope and dreams on the city below.

Josh turned on the television to catch the morning news. The first story he heard caused his heart to sink.

"Twelve people, including two suicide bombers and two small children, were killed in an attack on a Jerusalem shopping center."

Josh turned the TV off in disgust. He tried to control his anger, but tears flooded his eyes. When would the violence end?

An hour later, Josh sat in the Rockefeller Museum with the other members of the archaeological team, waiting for Moshe to appear with their assignments. Josh hadn't heard from Moshe since he called Danielle—and that call had left her uneasy the rest of the day. She was convinced that something was troubling her father, and one look at the man as he walked into the room confirmed it for Josh. Moshe looked downtrodden, as though the weight of the world was much too heavy for him.

Moshe stood at the front of the room, his head tipped downward. "Before we start our work today, I must share some dreadful news. Yesterday afternoon, the police discovered the body of a museum security guard. It was Ethan Benjamin, who had been previously reported missing. Most of you knew him. He worked here for five years."

Josh startled at the news. Ethan was one of Danielle's personal bodyguards. She had told Josh that Ethan was late for his next shift, but Josh hadn't given it another thought. He should have been more curious about an Israeli security person being late for an assignment—that kind of thing just didn't happen. Here was yet another reminder that he needed to pay attention to everything now. His old approach to dealing with the world was no longer valid.

The other archeologists were obviously shocked and saddened, but Moshe seemed virtually incapable of standing. Was this all because of Ethan's death, or was there another reason?

"His body was found on a deserted street in East Jerusalem," Moshe said.

"Was he killed by a terrorist?" asked Father Andre.

"No, we believe it was a cult murder. His body was burned and his throat slashed. We identified him from the wedding ring he was wearing on his burnt left hand."

Another ritual killing, just like Avner—two people with only a fleeting connection to the scroll. For the thousandth time, Josh wondered what he had brought into the world.

"Do we have any idea who killed him?" asked Reverend Barnaby in a shaky voice.

"No. The murderers left no clues. Our investigators assumed that since he had just left his security shift, his abduction occurred before he boarded his bus home. It appears he was killed and then taken to another place where his body was burned."

Josh sat quietly, observing the others. There was no question in his mind that someone responsible for Ethan's death sat in this room right now. Every moment that man was allowed to continue his treachery was a moment when innocent lives were put to risk. Josh had to learn the identity of this traitor before anyone else died.

Moshe spoke up again. "It is time to get on with our business, as difficult as it might be after this news. Later today, or tomorrow, the head of the IAA fraud department will be coming here to speak to all of you about this project."

"Is that necessary?" Alon protested.

Moshe's expression grew darker. "At this point, everything is necessary."

No one said a word.

"Meanwhile, we will get to work on the translation. We will break up into teams of two. Alon, you're with the Reverend Barnaby. Jonathan and Michael, you two work together and I'll work with Father Andre. As we all previously agreed, Josh will be an observer."

Moshe gave a signal and lab assistants brought in three large photographic sheets, placing one on each team's table.

"These are excellent photographs of the first three sections of the scroll. I realize that you are all fluent in Aramaic, but please be sure to take your time. If you have any problems or need assistance of any kind from your colleagues, please don't hesitate to ask. We want this translation to be as accurate as possible."

The men began to review the sheets when Isaac, head of the inscription department, walked into the room. "Moshe, the inscription dating is complete."

"And the results?"

Isaac turned to address the entire group. "We matched the scroll's writing with that of the Dead Sea scrolls for comparison purposes. We found the lettering and the style of writing similar. As you know, most of the Dead Sea scrolls were written in Hebrew, not in Aramaic, like this scroll. Hebrew and Aramaic are closely related, however. We found similarities in the shape of the letters and the writing slant of the inscriptions. Our conclusion is that the document was written sometime between 50 B.C.E. and 50 C.E."

"The tests are validating each other," Barnaby said. "The chances are increasing that the scroll is authentic."

Moshe raised a finger. "Don't jump to any conclusions. There are still other tests that need to be completed."

The archaeologists began to work translating pages that Josh had already read. How would they react to the words in these pages? Would they believe, as Josh already did, that they were written by the hand of Jesus of Nazareth?

Josh envied their discovery. At the same time, though, two bigger questions loomed in his mind: How many more people would die because of the scroll? And who among the people working in this room would be responsible for those deaths?

Chapter 31

DANIELLE WAS GETTING CABIN FEVER, AND JOSH NEEDED to get out from under the weight of his thoughts. It was time for them to have a real date.

Since her bodyguard had been slain, Moshe had become uncharacteristically—yet understandably—inflexible about Danielle venturing into the city under any circumstance. "I hold you responsible," he had told Josh, and Josh didn't know whether it was meant as a show of trust or as an accusation. Either way, their night out together would have to wait.

For the present, Josh would have to get creative if he wanted to take Danielle on a romantic date within the confines of the safe house. After some careful deliberation, he decided to order in from Chakra, one of the city's best restaurants. Their menu was first rate—especially the lamb-meat dumplings—and Josh was pretty sure that he and Danielle could handle the mood part on their own. For the final touch, he sent the Israeli guards to pick up their order from the restaurant, ensuring at least a short period of actual privacy.

"I'm so glad to finally be alone with you," Josh said as he opened a bottle of Jerusalem Heights Winery Cabernet. He poured two glasses and carried them over to the couch, where he handed one to Danielle and then cuddled up beside her. "I doubt that your father would be pleased about this, though."

"I think my father knows that there are limits to how

far he can go to protect me," she said. "Besides, whatever it is you have planned for tonight, I assure you that I'll be a willing accomplice."

Danielle raised her glass and they drank to the evening ahead of them, but it still didn't sit right with Josh. He was no match for her powers of seduction, yet he couldn't help but worry about her safety.

"Moshe's really changed since Ethan's death," Josh said. "It's like he's keeping me at arm's distance. Is he just worried, or do you think there's something else going on?"

"I think he feels a little responsible," Danielle told him. "If he hadn't assigned Ethan to guard me, this probably wouldn't have happened."

Josh knew a little something about feeling responsible for the misfortune of others. "He can't be sure of that, though. There's no doubt in my mind that Ethan was killed because of the scroll, but it could have been completely unrelated to his protecting you."

"I suppose. I think my father really liked Ethan. He used to talk to him about his kids all the time."

Once again, Josh felt the burden of his discovery. Already, a number of innocent people had suffered as a result of his finding the scroll. Would it be worth it? It was unlikely that Ethan's family would ever think so.

Josh made a conscious effort to move his thoughts elsewhere. He couldn't give Ethan's kids their father back any more than he could return Avner his life. He would continue to mourn both of these things, but he also knew that there was another precious life sitting beside him and he needed to do what he could to make that one better.

"Okay, so yesterday I learned—much to my surprise—that you are an unmerciful chess player. What other secrets do I need to know?"

Danielle took a sip of her wine and smiled coyly. "If I told you, they wouldn't be secrets anymore, would they?"

"Are you saying I need to uncover them by myself?"

"Isn't *uncovering* half the fun?"

The sexual overtones of that line were impossible to miss. Josh immediately remembered the feel of their bodies pressed together on the bed—before the phone had interrupted their passion for the rest of the day. He shuddered with the sensation.

"Yes, I'm quite fond of uncovering," Josh said suggestively. "Maybe you can give me some clues, though."

Danielle shrugged. "I'm just a humble woman from a humble home."

"Why do I find it difficult to believe either of those things?"

Danielle laughed. "Why am I the one being interviewed here? I know nothing about you other than the fact that you have an oversized brain and you're a great kisser."

"You think I'm a great kisser?"

"Maybe your brain isn't so oversized after all."

"No, this is really interesting to me. You know, I never really thought about whether I was a good kisser or not."

Danielle leaned closer to him and fixed him with her eyes. "You're a magnificent kisser, Josh. World class. Can we move on now?"

"Do you know a lot about how guys kiss?"

Danielle's expression got steely. "You're kidding, right?"

Josh threw up his hands. "I withdraw the question." He looked sheepishly into his wine. "Sorry, latent adolescence just creeps up on you sometimes."

"And it is especially useful when trying to avoid certain subjects."

Josh shook his head. "I'm not avoiding the subject. There just isn't that much to tell that you don't already know.

It takes a lot to feed an oversized brain, you know."

"Does that mean your intellect has consumed your baser instincts?"

"No, not at all. Trust me; I still have plenty of base instincts. I just don't let them out to play very often."

"Why?"

"Because they don't give me the same charge."

"Oh."

Danielle went suddenly rigid and she pulled away from him a bit. It took Josh a few seconds to realize that he'd said the wrong thing. When he did, he reached for her again and took Danielle's hand. "I should have said that they *didn't* give me the same charge until I met you. If I didn't admit that my base instincts go off the charts when we're together, I'd be lying through my teeth."

Danielle squeezed his hand and then raised it to her lips and kissed it. "Thank you."

"Except it doesn't feel base at all when we're together. It feels, I don't know, elevated."

"Many philosophies hold that a powerful romantic connection borders on the spiritual."

"I've read that. But I never felt it before."

"Here's a secret for you, Josh: neither have I. But I'm feeling it now."

Josh kissed Danielle as deeply as he could, knocking over her wineglass as he pulled her up from the couch. "I seem to have lost my appetite," he said slyly. "What do you say we move into the bedroom so that the guys can have a nice, quiet dinner when they return?"

Making love with Danielle was everything Josh expected it to be. She was obviously a more experienced lover than he was, and in a tiny corner of his mind he wondered where she had learned how to give so much pleasure. The rest of his mind, however—conscious, unconscious, spiritual, all of it—was completely overwhelmed with sensation and the most intense outpouring of emotion that Josh had ever known.

Josh literally could not get enough of Danielle's body. The smoothness of her skin, the roundness of her contours, and sculpted beauty of her figure entranced him. Even now, when their passion was at least temporarily sated, he couldn't stop touching her. His fingertips ran dreamily along her side as their heads pressed together for tender kisses.

"You realize that I'm going to have to keep you in this bed for the rest of our lives," he said softly.

Danielle purred gently. "I wish that were possible."

"I'm never letting you go, Danielle."

"Mmm, that sounds exactly right." She kissed him again and then shifted her body to rest her head against his chest.

I'm never letting you go, Danielle, Josh repeated. This time, he said it only to himself. Yet somehow, he was certain she could hear him.

Chapter 32

JOSH AWOKE EARLY THE NEXT MORNING. LYING THERE with Danielle in his arms he had experienced the most restful sleep he could remember; but even under the best circumstances he never slept for more than four hours a night. As the pale sun stretched through the venetian blinds, Josh felt a deep peace. The smell of Danielle's hair, the warm weight of her draped across his chest...this was right, this was exactly how it was supposed to be. The absolute last thing he wanted to do was disturb her, so he decided to meditate instead.

Josh closed his eyes and breathed deeply, beginning the induction process he had discovered when he was in college. He visualized walking down a flight of stairs, and as he descended each step, he went deeper and deeper into his mind.

He meditated in different ways for different purposes. If he was searching for an answer to a vexing question, he would ask the question repeatedly in this state. If he was looking for a deeper understanding of an intellectual puzzle, he would take that down to his unconscious with him. If he felt the need for relaxation, he would attempt to do nothing other than empty his mind.

Josh didn't need relaxation today. After his night with Danielle, his body felt more relaxed than it had since before he arrived in Israel. Therefore, he decided to drift, to see what his mind wanted to tell him.

Somewhere in the depth of his meditative state, Josh encountered a series of images, almost as though they were being shown on a movie screen inside his mind: The faces of his adopted parents, Miriam and Emmanuel, appeared and disappeared before him. He saw himself running and laughing with them, playing in the backyard at age four, maybe months before they died in a plane crash. This scene faded and he saw a woman walking alone. She was statuesque and dark-haired, and although he'd never seen her before, she seemed incredibly familiar to him. It was as if she knew him completely and was only waiting for him to remember, to follow her. But then the scene shifted again and Josh saw a man driving alone on a highway, without another car in sight. Now it was the man who he seemed to know. As quickly as it had appeared, though, this image faded into another, that of a little boy walking toward him. There was no background; the boy seemed to be walking on air. Josh tried to get a fix on the boy's face, but for some reason he couldn't see him clearly.

Out of a mist, the shadows of four men materialized and then vanished into thin air, replaced by a man dressed in blue jeans and a white shirt. The faceless wraith attacked Josh and they began to wrestle. Time seemed suspended as they locked in a seemingly eternal struggle. Neither Josh nor his opponent could subdue the other until, suddenly, Josh stared into the phantom's face and saw his own image.

At the instant of recognition, Josh began to rise out of his trance. He felt his head against his pillow and Danielle's arm around his chest. He also heard a faint knocking on the bedroom door. Delicately moving Danielle's arm to keep her from waking, Josh moved from the bed, put on his pants, and answered the door. Boaz was standing on the other side.

"I know it's early, and I'm sorry to interrupt you, but I think you should see this. A minute ago, I went onto the balcony for a smoke and I found a rock with this message attached."

Boaz handed Josh the note.

We can kill you at anytime, and that time is near. Enjoy every breath, Josh. You never know when it might be your last."

"We will need to move you both," said the bodyguard.

"I don't want to do that."

"You really don't have any choice. They know where you are."

"And if we move, they'll just find us again." Josh wasn't trying to be heroic; he knew deep inside that they wouldn't be able to run from this. Whatever confrontation lay ahead, it was something that he would have to face head on when the time came.

"Doing nothing is a mistake," Boaz protested.

"Doing *anything* could be a mistake." Josh looked back toward the bed and saw Danielle sleeping peacefully. "Move Danielle if you insist. The most important thing is that she remains safe."

Chapter 33

Josh climbed back into bed and pulled Danielle close to him. With every moment he spent with her, she became more precious to him; and now, once again, their happiness would have to be cut short. He would convince her to go somewhere else, even if that meant that they needed to be separated. If anything happened to her, it would be worse than if he himself had died.

Danielle opened her eyes and looked directly into his. "Have you been watching me sleep?" she asked with a dreamy smile.

"Guilty as charged."

She snuggled closer. "What do I look like when I'm sleeping?"

"Eternity," Josh said simply. The word had flashed into his head and was out of his mouth before he even considered what it meant.

Danielle's eyes sparkled and, without another word, she laid him on his back and began anointing the entire length of his body with kisses. Time and space melted as they explored each other with all of the passion they had shared the night before.

By 10:30, Josh had joined the other archaeologists in the Lab, where they awaited Moshe's arrival. When the head of the project finally showed up fifteen minutes late, he was not alone.

"This is Goner Goldman," Moshe said. "He's the director of the IAA fraud and theft investigation unit."

The tall, husky man stepped forward. "My department is aware of your project; in fact, it's become quite a hot topic among my people. Fraud and artifact theft are serious problems here in Israel. So many people want a connection to their religion that they're desperate for a relic or keepsake. For this reason they are easy victims for unscrupulous dealers. Too many people wind up with bogus 'artifacts.'"

"What does this have to do with us?" Father Andre said. "We will hardly be selling the scroll to an antiques dealer."

Goner nodded. "You're right, of course. However, one could say that it is infinitely more important to prevent fraudulent or illegal activity in this case. Wouldn't you agree, Father Andre?"

The older man nodded in silent affirmation.

"Because of the potential importance of your project, we will be monitoring the situation closely. We will be here from time to time to ask you questions. We hope you'll be cooperative."

Jonathan raised his hand. "What kind of questions?"

"We will be talking to each of you privately to discuss your progress on the scroll's translation and any personal thoughts you may have concerning the scroll."

"I still don't understand the purpose of this? What does either fraud or theft have to do with us?"

"Our interest is purely in securing the progress of your findings. Thank you for your time and cooperation."

Once Goner had left the room, the photocopies and translated passages from the day before were handed out again and the archaeological team began their work.

"I wish they would leave us alone," Michael said.

Alon agreed. "These interruptions are only wasting time."

Moshe cleared his throat to get their attention. "The government and antiquities authority just want to ensure that this project is handled properly. They are not only protecting themselves but also protecting us."

Father Andre wore a worried look. "I'm beginning to think that this entire thing is a waste of time. If the bit we've translated so far is any indication, this looks to me like an elaborate, ancient fraud. These cannot be the words of Jesus..."

"We just started," reassured Reverend Barnaby. "It will be fine."

Andre seemed unconvinced. "Nothing can challenge my faith in our Lord," he said softly, nearly to himself.

"Faith is not based on logic," Josh said. "It's based on how you feel. It gives hope in darker times, it helps you deal with your fears and, under the best circumstances, it helps make you a better person."

"I assume you are suggesting that fanaticism is not one of those 'best circumstances,'" Moshe ventured.

Josh thought about this for a moment. "Anything taken to an extreme can be dangerous. One man looks at his holy book—be it the Bible, the Koran, the Baghavad Gita—and he sees love and the proper way to act toward others. Another, who is driven by hate, looks for passages that justify his hatred and bigotry."

"Mine is a Lord of peace and love," Reverend Barnaby said emphatically. "'Love your enemies, bless those who curse you, and do good to those who hate you.' Jesus said this on the Sermon on the Mount."

Josh nodded. "That's a wonderful expression of love and tolerance, but those who hate would rather read, 'He who does not abide in me is thrown away like a withered branch. Such withered branches are gathered together, cast into the fire and burned.' The Catholic Church used that passage for hundreds of years to justify the killing of non-believers at the stake."

Barnaby glared at Josh. Certainly he'd read that passage himself hundreds of times. Why did it make him so uncomfortable now?

Chapter 34

E<small>VEN FROM TWO BLOCKS AWAY</small>, A<small>LU COULD SEE THE</small> condo in the distance. It had taken a great deal of effort and careful investigation to learn this location, and he had to be careful to avoid being spotted by the security men posted outside the building...or by his own brothers. He was in a precarious position: he couldn't risk falling out of the Master's good graces, and yet he was tormented by thoughts of Danielle. He knew that she really cared for him. He had disobeyed the Master by not killing her, and paid a price for that. But it was nothing compared to keeping Danielle alive; nothing compared to the possibility of being with her.

Orphaned and disfigured after the accident that killed his mother, Alu had become a pariah. Utterly alone, he had wandered the back alleys of Jerusalem numbed by a bitter, abiding rage. But the Master took him in and taught him the holy truths, and Alu began to see that sacrifice was the only path to God. As he learned to accept the blessings of his own suffering, he came to worship the man who had helped him find his destiny. And although he had never seen the face behind the serpent mask, Alu knew that the Master's love had finally made him whole.

When his Master ordered him to kill for the first time, he was stunned. He wasn't sure that God condoned murder, though Alu realized that the Master understood God at a much higher level than he ever could. He had been assigned to kill a member of their group who was suspected of leaking information to non-members. Alu was hesitant at first, but when the moment of truth was upon him, he was surprised by the intensity of the pleasure he took at driving his knife into the fallen brother's gut. From that point onward, killing had become a sacred act.

The Master was always generous with his praises whenever Alu made a kill. After proving himself as a competent assassin and a true follower, Alu was elevated to become one of the twelve Chosen Ones. On that day, the Master spoke words to Alu alone that gave him a deeper sense of their mission. "We must bring the Church back to its roots, Alu, back to the fundamentals written by Paul and only partially accepted by the Bishops in 325 at Nicea. We will put on our armor, destroy the non-believers, and make the world one, united in Christ."

Even after all this time, Alu could hear the portentous words that the Master had spoken on that day. His heart surged with the power of their meaning, and with pride in the role that he could play in assisting that mission. The Master was an extraordinary man, a sacrosanct servant of God.

Yet as Alu stood here observing Danielle's temporary home, he knew that he had a more vital mission. The memory of Danielle's face caused an even greater surge in his soul. If he could be with her, his life would be complete. Today, he would only watch. But soon he would see Danielle again—and the next time, he would possess her forever.

Chapter 35

THE DEAD SEA SCROLLS HAD BEEN WRITTEN BY THE Essenes, a Jewish monastic desert sect of the first century B.C.E. through the first century C.E. When the scrolls were discovered in 1947, a team of archaeologists was assembled comprised of scholars who were Catholic priests, Protestant clergy, and one layman. No Jewish archaeologists were included in the group. Worse, most of the clerical archaeologists were considered to be anti-Semitic and anti-Zionists—a conflict of interests that was simply standard practice at that time.

In response to that legacy of exclusion, Israel made a conscious effort to regularly include scientists of different religions and different nationalities in their archaeological programs. The IAA's selection process in pulling together a team for the scroll was no exception. Though the team was led and made up primarily of Jews, once again Christians played an important role. One of those Christians, Father Andre, now approached the other, concern creasing his face.

"Barnaby, I'd like you to come with me into the hallway. We need to discuss the first part of the translation."

Barnaby nodded.

The other archaeologists were immersed in their work and paid little attention to the men leaving the lab.

Andre and Barnaby moved to a quiet corner in the corridor.

Father Andre appeared dazed. "I have serious concerns about what the scroll may say. Don't you think that..."

"Relax, Andre," interrupted the American. "We've just begun the translation."

"You know that I'm a conservative Catholic."

Barnaby nodded. "Yes, and?"

"I'm worried that the scroll will invalidate Jesus' divinity and messianic mission."

"Why be concerned? We don't even know if Jesus wrote the document."

"Yes, but I have the feeling that's it's not going to turn out right."

"Don't be so pessimistic, Andre. I've spent my whole life searching for the historic Jesus. If he's the scroll's author, we'll finally have historic proof of his existence."

"That may be enough for you as a liberal, but I don't want my beliefs challenged."

"Think about what you're saying. If you truly believe, nothing can challenge your faith. Besides, it's nearly impossible to authenticate that the scroll was written by Jesus."

Andre took a deep breath. "You're right."

"But I hope it was. The part I read brought me closer to him. I loved his humanness. The Scroll's author is a great man and teacher—a true prophet."

"You would think that way. You even sympathize with those Christians who try to invalidate some of the teachings and stories in the New Testament."

"I love Jesus as much as you do. If the scroll allows me to know him better and contains some surprises, I will be happy."

Andre's expression made it obvious he didn't share this sentiment.

"Have you informed the Vatican of the scroll's existence?" Barnaby asked him.

"No, I'm waiting for more of the translation. But no

matter what the scroll contains, I will not allow it to shake my beliefs."

Barnaby put his arm around Father Andre's shoulder. "That's as it should be."

The day passed quickly, and the archaeological team began wrapping up their research for the day. Jonathan was the first to leave, begging an early parole so that he could prepare for a hot date later that night. Michael offered a ride to Alon, who lived on the outskirts of Jerusalem, and shortly thereafter, Father Andre and Barnaby left the building together, parting at the street where they walked in opposite directions toward their respective homes.

It was nearly a mile from the museum to his apartment, and Father Andre was glad to have the fresh air—and the solitude—as he pondered the words he had translated that day. He had only walked a few blocks, however, when he was approached by two tall men in priestly garb.

"Hello, my brother," said one of them

The voice took Andre out of his reflection. He looked at the priest, but at first didn't recognize him. Then he realized he'd seen him before, but couldn't recall where.

"Hello," Andre said. "Can I help you?"

The large man stopped walking, and Father Andre temporarily lost sight of the other. "In fact you can."

Andre was about to ask how he could be of service when a foul-smelling cloth was forced against his face. Realizing only now that he was in danger, he struggled fiercely, but futilely.

Just before he went unconscious, Andre noticed a black car slowing to a stop only a few yards away.

Jonathan had been driving a little more than a mile when he noticed the car that was tailing him. He tensed and looked in his rearview mirror, and then relaxed when he eyed the fatherly figure of a Catholic priest behind the wheel.

Jonathan left Jerusalem and headed to Tel Aviv on Route 1. The black car was still behind him. Something told him that this wasn't right. Certainly, there were other cars on the road, and certainly, the priest was as likely to be headed to Tel Aviv as Jonathan was. But when Jonathan changed lanes, the other car changed lanes as well. When Jonathan accelerated, the car kept speed with him.

Then, suddenly, the black car was gone. Jonathan turned to look over his shoulder, but couldn't find the vehicle anywhere. How had it disappeared so quickly? Was his mind playing tricks on him?

He took a deep breath, relaxed, and thought about the woman he'd be seeing in less than an hour. In the bar the other night she'd made it clear that she was a lot more fun in private than she was in public. Jonathan invited her to dinner at his place, though he was pretty sure they wouldn't be eating any time soon.

Suddenly his attention was drawn back to the road by a glaring set of headlights reflecting in his rearview mirror. He slowed down to verify his worst fear—the black car had reappeared and was right on his heels. Halfway to Tel Aviv with adrenaline pumping through his body, Jonathan gunned his engine. Weaving between cars at high speed, he raced to elude his pursuers. He didn't know what these people wanted with him, but he wasn't about to slow down to find out.

Just outside the city limits, Jonathan swerved too close to a woman in a Mercedes. He could see the fear in her eyes as he turned his wheel hard in the opposite direction, barely maintaining control of the car. As he spun across an empty lane, he was certain that his pursuers were trying to drive him to his death...but when he managed to right his vehicle, the black car was nowhere in sight.

"How do you think the project is going?" Michael asked as he drove.

"Fine so far," muttered Alon.

Michael laughed disdainfully. "You are the least talkative person I've ever met. We're working on the biggest discovery of our careers and all you can say is 'fine'?"

"Talking can get you into trouble. The less said the better. Silence is golden."

"Well, that was three whole sentences. Thanks for opening up."

They were driving on one of the back roads of Jerusalem when Michael noticed that a black car seemed to be making every turn with him. As he slowed for a red light, the dark vehicle stopped less than two feet behind his car. Michael turned around and in the light of the intersection could see that the driver was a priest. That's strange, he thought, and decided that he'd better try to lose him, holy man or not. When the light changed and Michael sped off, though, the priest remained on his tail.

"I think we're being followed by a priest," Michael said, his voice wavering.

Alon turned his head to look.

"I think you're being paranoid. What's unusual about a priest driving a car? There are hundreds of them in this city."

"They don't usually tailgate. This guy is right on top of me."

"Do you think priests have some divine driving ability? They're as likely to be lousy drivers as anyone else."

Alon was probably right. Michael was probably just being paranoid. The scroll project and the ugly events of the past few days had him more on edge than he realized.

As they came to another stoplight, Michael closed his eyes and told himself to relax. He never saw the black car pull next to his. Or the semi-automatic that blew off the top of his head.

The sound of heavy footsteps got Reverend Barnaby's attention. He turned his head and saw two men in priestly attire walking quickly in his direction. They were gaining on him with every long stride.

Something told Barnaby to get away, and fast. He looked around for someplace he could go to avoid these men, and was relieved to see an Arab couple approaching from the other direction. Barnaby ran to them and greeted them warmly. The Arabs seemed surprised, but returned his greeting in kind. This was just what he needed. There was a coffee shop not far away. Maybe they would walk that far with him.

Remarkably, though, the priests continued their approach. Sidling up next to him, they looked at the Arabs with obvious disgust, and—to Barnaby's horror—pulled out their guns.

As the priests dragged him away, Barnaby watched the Arabs' blood pooling in the cracks of the sidewalk and he knew that he had unwittingly brought death upon the friendly strangers. He prayed to God for forgiveness.

Chapter 36

JOSH FOUND IT AMAZING THAT HE COULD WALK INTO the condo with his head full of thoughts and release all of them within seconds of seeing Danielle. He had squandered several romances over the years because he had been too distracted to maintain them. Now he was nearly incapable of anything other than a laser-like focus on this dynamic woman.

"Did you make any progress today?" she asked after kissing him lightly on the lips.

Josh still wasn't sure what the guards made of these displays of affection, but he was able to push that question out of his mind as well.

"Progress isn't particularly easy to define here. They translated more of the scroll and we got a lecture on security. Is that progress?"

"I guess we'll know soon enough. I wish I could be there with you."

Josh kissed Danielle again and took her hand. The guards wouldn't follow them into his bedroom and they could have more privacy there. "I wish you were working on this as well. It isn't safe, of course, especially since we assume that someone on the team is responsible for putting you in danger."

Danielle closed the door behind them, then kissed his neck and unzipped his jacket. "I'll bet I could figure that out as well."

He kissed her passionately. "On second thought, I'm not sure how much either of us would get done if we were together at the IAA."

He enfolded her in his arms and they slowly made their way to the bed, falling onto the covers. Josh thought of nothing for the next hour other than the smoothness of her skin, the depth of her eyes, and the fire of her touch.

Later, as they lay languidly together, Josh realized that these moments of afterglow were like his meditation time—impossible to quantify and extremely refreshing. But as he floated in this space, Danielle's body molded into his, a knock came on the door.

"Josh, can I come in?"

It was Moshe. "Give me a minute, Moshe. I'll be right out." He turned to Danielle and kissed her hair. "I guess this is when your father finds out about us."

"He probably knows already. He's the one who hired the guards, after all."

Josh dressed quickly and walked out into the living room. Danielle followed close behind. Moshe glanced from Josh to Danielle, but didn't share his thoughts.

"Hi," Josh said tentatively. "I wasn't expecting you."

"Josh, we've got big problems, and I do mean big."

"What are you talking about?"

"Danielle, please leave the room," Moshe said sharply.

"She can stay. She's an unofficial member of our team, isn't she?"

"We no longer have a team. Father Andre, Reverend Barnaby, and Alon have been kidnapped."

"No!" Danielle said, gasping. She grabbed Josh's arm.

Josh wasn't nearly as surprised. "We should have had guards on all of them. We should have known something like this would happen, especially after the attacks on Danielle and Ethan."

"It gets worse," Moshe said, his voice a low moan of defeat.

"How much worse can it get?" Danielle said.

"They killed Michael."

"Oh my God," Danielle said, sobbing. She looked like she had lost a close friend, and tears began to trickle down her face. Josh hugged her tightly as Moshe continued.

"Only Jonathan managed to escape before his kidnappers got him."

Josh tried to make sense of all of this. If all of the archaeologists were assailed, which of them was the traitor? He stared at Moshe and then rejected the notion. "Would Jonathan be able to identify his attackers?"

"They were priests, or men dressed as priests."

"Real priests? I doubt it. Is that all he has?"

"That's all I learned. The only other piece of hard information we have is that when the abductors took Reverend Barnaby, they killed two Israeli Arab bystanders."

Josh shook his head. "Just to make things a little worse."

"Our own security people and Shin Bet are already searching for more clues. It's quite possible the Mossad will join them as well."

Danielle tugged on Josh's arm and tried to sound hopeful. "With that level of firepower, you'll catch these fanatics in the next twenty-four hours."

"I'd like to believe that," Moshe said, "but I'm not sure. These people are very good. They obviously have spies everywhere. They're not an official terrorist group, but they act like one."

"How do you know so much about them?" Josh asked, suddenly angry. "Is there more you haven't told us?"

"It's part of my job to know about these things. And no, there is nothing more of substance to tell you at this point. Everything else is speculation and leads."

Danielle took a step toward her father. "What can I do to help?"

Moshe put up a hand. "Nothing, Danielle. You are to stay out of this, do you understand?" He pointed to the guards. "And make sure that these people always have you in their sights."

Chapter 37

THE GUARDIANS SAT BEFORE THEIR MASTER IN THE ancient, subterranean hideout.

"My brothers, I am so proud of you," he told them. "Our mission was a complete success. We have three prisoners who will be interrogated and then offered in exchange for the scroll.

"Now we must go even deeper undercover. We must be more cautious than ever, or we risk the destruction of our brotherhood and ultimate failure in the eyes of God. Our recent actions have called more attention to us, but they were absolutely necessary. We must make sacrifices, like our brothers before us. Our mission is clear and nothing can stop us.

"For years, we have operated like monks and maintained a low profile, as we waited for the prophecy to come true. We dared to hope that the scroll that was recently discovered would be the document foretold by prophecy, the divine words of our Lord and the harbinger of his return. But it is, sadly, a fraud, written by an imposter claiming to be our savior. Now we must destroy the scroll before it can cause irrevocable damage."

The room buzzed at this news until the Master raised a hand to silence the group. He turned to a guard. "Bring in the first prisoner."

The guard returned with Father Andre.

"Welcome," the Master said, taunting the priest sarcastically. "I trust that you have enjoyed our hospitality so far. No?"

Father Andre remained silent, but the nervous twitching of his eye betrayed his resolve.

"Well, you haven't even begun to suffer yet." The Master's voice grew cold and hard. "Of course, if you cooperate then we may be willing to trade your life for the scroll. Is there anything you'd like to say on your own behalf?"

The twitch on the priest's face quickened. "I'm just a simple priest who lives a modest life of prayer, study, and the advancement of archaeology. I do not believe in violence or killing. They lead only to the fires of Hell."

"Father, you have no need to fear for our souls. We have killed many before you, but we will not suffer the torments of Hell, for we are the Guardians of the true church and we protect its teachings. Killing in the name of God is not a sin."

"You should be ashamed to use religion as a way to justify your actions. I pity you."

One of the Guardians took out a thin black whip and struck the old priest across the back.

Father Andre winced in pain, but didn't make a sound.

"Stop," the Master said sharply. "Don't hit him again; I'm enjoying our discussion. You are a Catholic Priest, are you not?"

"Yes," Father Andre said through gritted teeth.

"Of course you are. I know all about you. You are a traditionalist. In fact, we share many similar beliefs."

"I'm sure that we do not," Andre said, gaining strength from his morals. "I most certainly do not subscribe to the killing of innocent people."

"Why not?" the Master asked, his voice dripping with sugar and bile. "Our Lord condoned the deaths of nonbelievers."

"That's a lie."

"Perhaps you aren't as astute a student of the Bible as I believed." The Master grabbed an unlit torch from the stone wall. He shoved it into Father Andre's face. "This very torch was used to burn people alive during the Inquisition. It's one of our many heirlooms."

Father Andre looked at the torch as though it was going to ignite spontaneously and set him ablaze. The Master took special pleasure in the priest's discomfort.

"One of our ancestral brothers wrote a little tome called *The Protocols of the Elders of Zion*," the Master said. "It's one of the great anti-Semitic works of the last hundred and twenty-five years. Perhaps you've read it, Andre? I know you share my beliefs about the Jews."

"You're wrong," protested the priest. "I may be biased in some ways, but I don't hate anyone."

"Really? You've seen the scroll. Don't you agree that it's the work of an imposter?"

"I haven't translated enough of the document to reach any conclusions."

"But our Lord is depicted with a strong Jewish identity."

"He was Jewish."

"Blasphemy! Jesus said, when he faced the Jews, 'You snakes, you generation of vipers, how can you escape the damnation of Hell?'"

"Jesus may have been upset with some of his people," retorted Andre, "but he loved his religion and his fellow Jews. His mother and father were both Jewish, and so were all of his disciples. He even told his disciples when they went out to preach that they should only preach to the Jews. 'Do not take the road to gentile lands,' he said 'and do not enter any Samaritan city. Go only to the lost sheep of Israel.'"

"Not true! Don't you know your own enemies? Most everyone else in the world does. When we take power, we will kill all non-believers: Muslims, Jews, and Christians who have deserted their religion. Even the Buddhists, Hindus, and the atheists shall feel our wrath." The Master's voice got louder. "You don't know the truth...only I and my followers know the true essence of Jesus."

"Do you believe in the Second Coming?" Father Andre asked.

"Of course. We wait for it. That is when we will have our final victory."

"So you believe that Jesus will return."

"We know that he will, and in our very lifetime."

"Then when he returns," said Andre, filled with righteous indignation, "you'll kill him...because Jesus is a Jew."

Behind his mask the Master's eyes narrowed in a mixture of shock and disgust as his voice boiled with rage. "Get him out of here."

Chapter 38

RELUCTANTLY, JOSH AGREED WITH MOSHE'S DECISION to suspend the official translation of the scroll while investigators searched for the abducted members of the team. With Jonathan taking a few days to recuperate and Moshe himself the only one officially still on the project, there was really no alternative. What no one, not even Danielle, knew, however, was that Josh had a copy of the document on his laptop. Now, with Danielle off on a shopping expedition with one of the Shin Bet guards, Josh opened the file and picked up where he had left off.

Josh had arrived at the portion of the Scroll where the inscriptions were faint. This was the section of the scroll that would prove the most arduous to translate. Some of the letters were invisible and others had parts of the Aramaic missing altogether. The translation was difficult and time consuming, but slowly the words emerged.

Most of the people wait for the promised Messiah.
There have been many who have claimed to be him.
Yet none fulfilled Isaiah's prophesy that Israel will be
free of foreign domination and all wars will cease.
Here in Galilee, John the Baptist was killed by
Herod, who feared that the prophet's growing crowd
of followers would ultimately lead a revolt. John was
harmless, only preaching repentance. Yet, like so

many others who had attracted a following, he was killed.

My way is about more than repentance. I have hoped to help build a righteous kingdom here on earth to end the suffering, heal the sick in spirit, and prepare humanity for its ultimate reunion with its creator. I preached to a few, and then the few became many. I chose a few pious Jewish men who were close to me and they became my disciples. I preached to the uneducated and the poor, for their plight was the worst. They addressed me as Rabbi, and sometimes as "my Lord." But they meant this title as one of respect only, just as when the people in Galilee and Judea call me the son of God, as they occasionally refer to one another to signify that we are all children of God.

I began to worry, however, when some of my followers took to calling me the Messiah. I have yet to fulfill the prophecy. The Romans have killed many men who have called themselves prophets and messiahs. Most of them were men of peace, yet they all died horrible deaths.

Josh read the translation multiple times, trying to glean some new sense of meaning from it—meaning he might even be able to use in his current situation. He knew about the common use of the title "Lord," but he'd been unaware of this usage of the term "son of God." Certainly, the man emerging from these pages was similar yet different than the Jesus of faith promoted by the Church. Yet he seemed entirely real. If they could somehow prove that Jesus himself wrote the scroll, it would change many perceptions. In some ways, it would change the world.

At that moment, it dawned on Josh for the first time

that this could be the reason why someone was willing to kill to get the scroll. What if someone wanted it not for the riches such a discovery would bring, but for a different reason entirely—to destroy it in order to keep people forever in the dark about who Jesus really was?

Again, Josh reminded himself to be aware of every sign and signal. This new notion might be meaningless. Still, he couldn't afford to reject anything.

Danielle had returned some hours ago, while Josh was still working, yet she had not disturbed him. He was grateful for her gracious understanding and support, but now that he was finished translating for the night, he longed to be in her presence again. Josh headed for Danielle's room. As he opened the door, he saw that she was fast asleep. As tempted as he was to crawl into bed with her, he knew the translation had taken a lot out of him. While he would no doubt revive as soon as he was in her arms, he'd be a wreck in the morning. For the first time since they became lovers, Josh allowed himself to be sensible.

He went back to his room and, before he could sit down on the bed, the phone rang.

"Josh, it's Moshe. The kidnappers called the IAA and offered to exchange Barnaby, Alon, and Father Andre for the scroll."

"How are you going to deal with that?" Josh asked, suddenly alert whether he wanted to be or not.

"I think that their lives are more important than the document."

Josh was stunned by this response. "You plan to give the kidnappers the scroll?"

"That's my recommendation, but the government and security officials will make the final decision."

Josh could barely believe what he was hearing. "So the

fanatics will wind up with the scroll and we'll wind up with three dead bodies."

"Why do you say that?"

"I think the fanatics want the scroll because they want to suppress what it contains."

"That's quite a deductive leap."

"Not as much of one as you might think." He hesitated and then realized that he had no choice but to plunge ahead. "I translated more of the scroll than I told you I did."

Moshe was quiet for several seconds. "How much have you read?"

"Not as much as I would like."

"And you think there's something in there that a radical group would try to prevent from getting out."

How much did Josh really believe this? How far out on the line was he willing to go with three lives in the balance? "I think it's a possibility. If I'm right, the kidnappers will kill Barnaby, Alon, and Andre because they won't know how much of the scroll they've read."

"I can't trade the lives of three good people based on a possibility."

"I know you can't. But you know better than I do that there's a very good chance they'll kill the hostages after they get their ransom. It happens all the time."

"I've already recommended that we turn over the scroll. Nothing you've said just now convinces me otherwise."

Josh realized there was no point in further trying to dissuade Moshe. Not yet, anyway.

"Did the kidnappers give a deadline?"

"They want the scroll in forty-eight hours or one of the hostages dies."

"Give me as much of that time as you possibly can."

"Why? What can you do to help with this?"

"Promise me you'll give me the time."

Moshe was once again quiet for several seconds. "Make the most of it," he said, "but know that I cannot wait around for you. There's too much at stake." With that, he hung up.

As tired as Josh was, he couldn't sleep. He had to continue to translate the scroll before it was too late, and devise a plan that would either rescue the hostages or—at the very least—buy more time.

Chapter 39

Underneath the Old City, the Master paced the stone floor of his secret hideaway, waiting for two of the remaining Guardians to bring in the prisoner. Most of his followers had already relocated as a precautionary measure. After the recent kidnappings and killings, the hunt for his sect had intensified, so most of the members scattered and took refuge.

As he waited, the Master donned the serpent mask and adjusted the small harmonic device that allowed him to change his voice. It wouldn't do for the prisoner to recognize him. Not yet.

A door opened, and the Guardians brought in the Reverend Barnaby. He was shackled in chains; but unlike Father Andre, Barnaby wasn't wearing a blindfold.

"So, you're the leader of this evil group," Barnaby said derisively. The Master was glad that the holy man still had some fire in him. It was always more interesting that way.

"Clearly you are mistaken, my friend," the Master said sweetly. "We are not evil at all. We are the Guardians."

"Call yourself what you want. You're kidnappers and murderers."

"Soldiers, maybe. But murderers? Why would you say that?"

"When you kidnapped me, one of your thugs killed two innocent Arabs."

"Oh, that. That wasn't murder. That was a public service."

Barnaby's face contorted. "An Arab life is just as precious as yours—more so, actually."

The Master's hackles rose. "Keep talking like that and you'll join them," He snarled. He motioned to the wall behind him. "Behold my sword. It dates back to the twelfth century, when it was wielded by my Crusader brethren. In the years since, this sword has spilled the blood of many non-believers."

Barnaby's chin thrust forward. "I'm not afraid to die. When it happens, I will be near my Lord and Savior. He alone shall judge me on my righteousness and treatment of my fellow man."

"What a lovely little speech," the Master said with a laugh.

Barnaby's face reddened. "Unlike you, I care for people. Whether they are fellow Christians or Muslims or Jews, they are all my brothers."

The Master stepped closer and saw the reverend's eyes widen. There was fear there, regardless of the holy man's protests otherwise. "You should have stopped at Christians. You will be judged, indeed, you ignorant man, for your sympathies toward the Moslems and those Christ-killers, the Jews."

"The Jews didn't kill Christ. He chose to die to save mankind. If anyone is to blame, it's humanity."

The Master whirled on his heel. "Do *not* test my patience. If you continue to talk this way I will be forced to kill you."

"No one is forcing you to do anything. Are your so-called Guardians recognized by the Catholic Church?"

The Master found no reason to lie. "We are considered too radical for the Vatican. However, the day will come when they will recognize us, or we'll take control of Rome and destroy those who stand in our way."

"I doubt the Catholic Church would ever recognize a group as contemptible as yours."

"What do you know of evil? Evil is the bastion of the non-believers of this world who do not accept the teachings of Paul."

"Do you believe in Christ?"

"That's an absurd question."

"He was a Jew."

The Master laughed again. "I see you have been duped by the Jewish conspiracy."

"How could it be a conspiracy when millions of Jews have been killed in Christ's name over the last two thousand years by maniacs like you?"

Millions, the Master thought. *If only that were true.* "That's just another Jewish exaggeration," he said, spitting the words, "like the Holocaust."

Barnaby's face reddened. "I've been to the concentration camps of Auschwitz, Buchenwald, and Dachau. I've witnessed the horrors of the ovens and gas chambers and have seen the pictures of innocent victims."

The Master waved a hand at his captive. He was well aware of the commonly spread fiction that six million had been killed during the Holocaust. That was nothing but a ludicrous attempt to gain sympathy. "So maybe a million were killed. When I come to power we will kill the rest."

"And the Christians who don't believe the way you do?" Barnaby asked, horrified.

"They will be given a chance to see the light. Those who do not will join the other non-believers in Hell."

Barnaby's face was deep crimson now. "It is you who will rot in eternal Hell with the devil. You two belong together."

This exercise had lost its entertainment value. The Master was open to a lively debate on occasion, but he expected his inferiors to be more creative with their end of the conversation. As Barnaby's words reverberated around the small chamber, the Master reached for the wall, pulled the eight hundred-year-old sword from its sheath, and removed his mask.

"Oh my God—not you! How could you?" Reverend Barnaby gasped disbelief.

Without answering Barnaby's pointless question, the Master swung the sword with the ferocity of an experienced executioner, cleanly severing the holy man's head from his body in a single blow.

Chapter 40

THE SECURITY GUARDS DREW THEIR WEAPONS AS SOON as they heard the knock on the front door of the condo. When they looked through the peephole, however, they immediately opened up.

Josh recognized one of the men as Goner Goldman, head of the IAA Fraud and Theft Department, but he had never seen the two men who joined him.

"Hello, Goner. Who are your two associates?"

Goner gestured toward the men. "This is Aaron Brodsky and Giuseppe Kaplan."

The two could not have been more opposite. Though they both appeared to be in their forties, Aaron was gawky, with eyes that bulged and a face that had seen better days, while Giuseppe had a regal quality to him that was offset only by his piercing, hazel eyes that seemed to observe everything.

Josh shook hands with them. "Giuseppe—that's an unusual name for an Israeli."

"Giuseppe is Italian for Yoseph. My parents are from Italy. Giuseppe means 'God will multiply.'"

"I see," said Josh, duly edified. "So what can we do for you?"

Giuseppe held up a hand. "Is there anyone else here?"

"Yes. Danielle is in the other room."

Upon hearing her name, Danielle strolled out into the living room, dressed in jeans and a tee shirt. "Hi, guys,"

Danielle said. It seemed obvious to Josh that she recognized all three men.

"Shalom," they said in response.

Danielle joined the group near the door. "Can I help you with anything?"

"We must speak with Josh in private," Giuseppe said.

Goner turned to Danielle. "It would be a good idea for you to take one of the security guards and go shopping."

Danielle smirked at him. "I'm not in the mood to shop, but I get the message loud and clear. I'll make myself scarce for a little while."

"Danielle, don't inform anyone that we're talking to Josh—and that includes your father," Aaron said sharply.

Danielle nodded in agreement, though with a little glint in her eye that Josh interpreted as her indication that she thought Aaron should lighten up. She put a hand lightly on Josh's arm. "I'll see you later. You'll be around?"

"I'll be here."

"Good," she said with a smile that spoke volumes, then she left the condo, escorted by Gideon.

Josh watched the door until it was closed, and then turned back to the men. "What's going on?"

Aaron walked deeper into the living room. "We're here to ask you a few questions relating to the hostage situation and the scroll."

"Before I answer any questions, I'm going to need to know who I'm answering. The only person I know here is Goner."

Aaron's eyes narrowed. "I'm with Israeli security."

"Shin Bet?"

"Shin Bet agents never acknowledge who they are. Just think of me as security."

"I'm the security head of the IAA," said Giuseppe casually as he scrutinized the place.

"Where's Moshe? Doesn't he work with you guys?"

Giuseppe nodded. "Occasionally, but he's not an official part of security. All of your archaeological team is under surveillance, and so are other IAA personnel. We believe the leader of this fanatical group works at the IAA. We suspect that he has at least one or possibly two of his cohorts working there as well."

"Do you have any ideas about who they are?"

"We have our suspicions," Aaron said as he circled the room. "But in Israel, as in America, you have to possess sufficient evidence before you can arrest someone."

"Can you tell me who you suspect?"

Aaron shook his head. "That wouldn't be wise at the moment."

Josh wasn't sure how to interpret that. Clearly, these security men wanted information from him, but they weren't willing to be forthcoming themselves. "Are you planning to accede to the kidnappers and give them the scroll?"

"We haven't made a decision," Giuseppe said. "We're still debating the proper course of action."

More empty answers. This could get old quickly. "I maintain that the proper action is not to give in to the kidnappers' demands. They'll kill the hostages regardless. And if the fanatics get the scroll, they will destroy it."

"Why would they do that?"

"I can't tell you why yet, exactly. I have a very strong sense that this is true, though. Listen, I've been thinking about this nonstop since I last spoke to Moshe. I need your cooperation. I have a plan to trap the kidnappers. It requires access to the research lab tonight. Also, I want you to have extra security there and make sure the scroll is heavily guarded."

"It is already under maximum security," Goner said. "What is your plan?"

"I think everything these fanatics have done up to now

is for the purposes of diversion. I believe their real plan is to try to steal the scroll. We need to do something to make sure that doesn't happen."

Chapter 41

DANIELLE AND HER BODYGUARD STROLLED THROUGH the narrow passageways of the Christian Quarter of the Old City Markets. The street was filled with shoppers and pilgrims—but it was also filled with danger.

Alu gazed at Danielle and his heart raced. He knew the risk he was taking. But he knew that she could care for him, and if she did, it wouldn't matter whether the Guardians found out. She was worth losing everything.

Alu waited for his opportunity to get near her. He spotted a known pickpocket surveying the crowds, like a marksman aiming for his target. He moved quickly and decisively, grabbing the petty thief and forcing him against a sheltered stone wall. Alu held him just off the ground, suffocating the flow of blood to the young man's arms, and stared through the fear in his eyes.

"I have a job for you," he said gravely, setting the man back on his feet. He pointed toward the crowd. "See the woman over there?"

The pickpocket stammered as he spoke. "You mean the one in jeans and a tee shirt?"

"That's the one. I want you to steal her purse and run off with it."

The man's eyes darted, but he didn't move.

"Now!" Alu said, his voice menacing. "Do it!"

The thief took one last cautious glance at his attacker, and then he sprung into action.

The pickpocket moved through the crowded street and came in close to Danielle, swiping her purse as she turned her head. As Alu expected, Danielle's bodyguard chased after the thief. Security guards operated on instinct, and this time it was the guard's very instinct that betrayed him. He'd foolishly left Danielle alone in the middle of the crowd. Alu would make sure that she was never that vulnerable again.

He came out of the throng, clapped a large, chloroformed mitt over Danielle's mouth, and swept her off her feet. He was as gentle as he could be, carrying her with her head nestled in his arms. The crowd might have assumed that they were a couple and that she'd become ill. Alu carried Danielle across the street into a near-empty souvenir store on the Via Dolorosa. He brought her to the back of the store, and then down a flight of stairs into a cold, dark room.

He laid her down and knelt beside her, waiting a moment for Danielle to regain consciousness.

"Danielle, I don't want to hurt you. I only want to talk to you."

He eyes were wide with terror. "Why are you doing this? You released me."

"Haven't you been thinking about me?" he asked, confused. "I felt something between us."

"What are you talking about?"

"I…I love you."

Danielle's face darkened as she shook her head from side to side. Alu hadn't expected her to react this way. She was supposed to be glad to see him again, and to tell him that she loved him, too.

"I know you're shocked," he stammered, his confusion turning quickly to humiliation, "but…"

Alu didn't get the chance to finish his thoughts, however, because suddenly, somehow, the Master was towering over him.

"Why did you bring this woman here?" the Master bellowed. "I warned you never to disobey my orders. Now you have signed your death warrant!"

The Master lunged and Alu tried to fend him off, but he suddenly felt a sharp, overwhelming pain. All the fight drained out of him and he collapsed to the floor. Alu looked over at Danielle, aching to caress her just one more time. He couldn't seem to make his hulking body respond, though, no matter how hard he thought the thoughts. *Reach out your hand. Just touch her face.* So instead he simply stared, imploring silently until the sight left his eyes.

Chapter 42

Josh's meeting with Goner, Aaron, and Giuseppe continued into the early afternoon. "What do you know about these fanatics?" Josh asked, as he poured them each a glass of strong Turkish coffee.

Aaron took a sip of the brew and nodded approvingly. "Most of our information is confidential and can only be divulged through security clearance."

"What information can you share?"

The three security officers glanced at each other before Giuseppe answered. "There were twelve unsolved murders last year in Jerusalem that were not committed by any known terrorist groups. We suspect that this organization committed at least a few of them. The group has kept a low profile. It's only been in the last week that we feel we can connect these murders to this sect."

"Does the group have a name?"

"We found hate material written against Arabs and Jews that bore the name 'the Guardians.' They hate the Arabs with a passion, but that's mild compared to their feelings for the Jews. They refer to them as 'the Christ-killers.'"

"We know that Jews didn't kill Christ," Josh said. "Crucifixion was a Roman form of execution. The Jews' form of execution at that time was stoning."

Giuseppe and Aaron nodded.

Josh continued, "Pontius Pilate was one of the cruelest

of the Roman Prefects. He crucified thousands of Jews. The Emperor even called him back to Rome to explain his excessive cruelty. Pilate hated the Jews, especially the ones he thought might threaten Roman rule. He ruthlessly crucified them without an ounce of mercy. In fact, of the thousands of Jews killed, there has been only one skeleton ever found. The Romans never allowed a Jewish burial for their crucified victims. They left the bodies of the dead on the cross to be eaten, first by birds of prey and then by wild dogs. They intended not only to humiliate the Jews, but also to give them a warning: that this is what would happen to those who disobeyed the authority of Rome."

"You know your history," Giuseppe said.

"I know a lot more about hatred and bigotry."

Giuseppe laughed humorlessly. "Well, you're certainly in the right place. This is the historical epicenter of hatred." Josh gestured with a pointed finger. "But it is also the center of faith. Some day that contradiction will be rectified."

Aaron put down his coffee cup and poured himself a refill. "But which way?"

Josh hated the sound of cynicism in the agent's voice. He stared into his coffee, seeing beyond the brown liquid into his own past. "I used to be a pessimist. I thought humanity was a lost cause. I would read the newspaper and get sick to my stomach from all of the negative headlines. I would turn on the television and despise the cruelty I witnessed. I was like most people; I didn't think I could do anything about it, so I tried to become immune to it all. I focused on my own problems. Now I realize that I was wrong. I intend to make a difference—somehow, in some way."

None of the men spoke in response. Josh hadn't meant to sermonize, but the words had just tumbled out. It was almost as though someone else had spoken them instead. Josh knew that it was time to change the subject. "What's your plan to protect the scroll and rescue the hostages?"

Giuseppe answered, clearly grateful for the change of tone. "We haven't yet decided what to do about the hostages, but the scroll is in a high security safe at the museum."

"How will you protect it if the Guardians have already infiltrated the IAA?"

"No one is allowed access to the scroll. Only my closest associate and I have the safe's combination."

"I hope your closest associate can be trusted."

"I would trust him with my life."

"Do you have any plans about exchanging the scroll for the hostages?"

"We agree with you that organizing an exchange is useless," Aaron said. "Unless we rescue the hostages, they'll be killed."

Josh was glad to hear they were on the same page. "I have a plan that may rescue the hostages without giving their captors the scroll. It would be a test of the fanatics' true intentions."

"Let's hear it."

"Do you have any ancient jars that are similar to the one that contained the scroll?"

Giuseppe nodded. "The jar itself was fairly common."

"Well, then, do you have one you can afford to lose?"

"I think we can use one of them."

"As I said before, I'll need access to the museum tonight. No one can know that I'll be there. I'll need a couple of items: some sheepskin and a writing instrument, one that was used approximately two thousand years ago."

Giuseppe's brow furrowed. "Exactly what's the point of your plan?"

"The point is to get the hostages back and discover the identity of the Guardians' leader at the same time."

Chapter 43

DANIELLE STILL HADN'T RETURNED BY THE TIME THE security men departed. That seemed a little strange, since she couldn't have anticipated that Goner and the others would be here as long as they were. Still, she had been cooped up for so long since her abduction that Josh figured she was probably cherishing the time outside.

He went back to his room and opened the file containing the copy of the scroll. He was still guessing about the motivations of the Guardians—if they were indeed the kidnappers in the first place. He needed to go as far as he could into the document; only once he understood its secrets would he be able to understand why someone would resort to such extremes in order to control it.

Right away, Josh noticed that there was something different about these new passages. As always, they were written in Aramaic and, as always, translation was slow and laborious. But this was further complicated by missing letters. As Josh stared at the page on the screen, the spaces where letters were missing jumped out at him. Was there an image here? No, there didn't seem to be. But maybe there was a message of some sort. The first omission came fifty letters into the passage, where only one letter was invisible. The next came at one hundred letters, where five letters were missing. The pattern continued at the 156th letter, where five more letters were missing. Then, at the 211th letter, there were seven missing characters. Josh was perplexed, and his confusion increased when he saw that seven more letters were missing at the 268th letter. The final omission came at the 325th letter, where this time there were eight missing letters. After that, the text proceeded without interruption.

Josh looked at the pattern of missing letters and wrote 1-5-5-7-7-8. It didn't seem to signify anything. He wrote the letters in a variety of combinations and directions, trying to see a pattern or a code. If there was a message here, it was one he couldn't understand. .

None of this is random, he thought, though it seemed as though the words came from outside of him. He shook his head in an effort to clear it. He was having trouble thinking objectively about everything. Was he concentrating too hard, or was he not concentrating enough?

Josh got up for a minute to see if Danielle had returned, but the only other people in the condo were his bodyguards. Where had she gone? And why did he suddenly feel so nervous about her.

Knowing he would drive himself crazy if he started imagining scenarios about where she may be, he went back to his room and focused on the translation. As always, he sank into the process, oblivious to the time passing.

> *I originally believed the teachings of the Pharisees that one day the dead will rise up physically. Now I share the beliefs of a group in the desert known as the community, that the resurrection will be spiritual rather than physical. I do not fear death, for I believe that my spirit is eternal.*
>
> *I live in an occupied land. My flock suffers in a world of inequality and injustice. My desire is to bathe them in the light of hope and a better tomorrow. We are all equals before God.*
>
> *Where does God exist? He lives in the heart*

*and in the mind. A part of each of us goes back to the
beginning of creation. It is the divine spark. Open
yourself up and you can feel it.*

*I heal by faith alone. I give life to those who are
spiritually dead. I have seen demons with faces of
guilt, unclean spirit, frustration, misdeeds, and lack
of faith. I have cast them out of people and replaced
them with a feeling of faith, a clean spirit, and well
being. We as humans have a choice between good and
evil actions, for they both reside in us. If you rob,
rape, or commit murder you will suffer the consequences of your actions. Small things can be forgiv-
en, but forgiveness must be earned.*

*Faith is not an excuse to kill or do harm to your
fellow man or woman. Anyone who uses our scriptures or other religions' teachings to justify harmful
actions against others will suffer the direst consequences—the eternal loss of their soul.*

As Josh read the translation, he thought immediately of
the Guardians. He was more convinced than ever that this
fanatical group—whoever they were—didn't want the public
to see the words in this scroll. Right behind that thought
came another—that they would do anything to prevent the
scroll from seeing the light of day.

Josh glanced out the window. It was getting dark. Again,
he got up to see Danielle. She still wasn't home. And he
knew with absolute certainty that she was in grave trouble.

Josh was unsure how to act. Why did that always seem
to be the case when it came to Danielle? Should he go out to
look for her? Where would he look if he did? Jerusalem was
too big, and he had no idea where to start.

He looked at his watch and saw that it was approaching
7:00 p.m. He was supposed to leave for the museum shortly.

How could he do that when the woman he loved was in danger? On the other hand, he was certain that it had been the Guardians who abducted her before; if they had her again, then his plan at the museum could help save her. In fact, it might be the only chance they had.

Just then, the phone rang and Josh reached for it quickly, hoping to hear Danielle's voice on the other end of the line.

"Hello?" he said, his voice cracking with hope.

There was a moment of silence, and then a familiar voice. "We have the hostages and we want the scroll."

Josh's blood ran cold. "What are the names of the hostages?"

"You know who they are."

"Don't play games with me. Just tell me what you want."

Again, the voice hesitated for a moment. "Bring the jar and the scroll to the front of the Church of the Holy Sepulcher tomorrow at 4:00 p.m. No tricks or the hostages will be killed. I want you—and you alone—to hand over the jar and its contents. Only then will we release the hostages. If we observe any police or other security, however, the hostages will die...and so will you. It will be a long and torturous death, I assure you."

Josh knew what he'd told Moshe and the security people about a hostage exchange. Faced with the situation himself, though, he wasn't sure how to react. Could he maintain his resolve that an exchange was futile if it meant there was some chance Danielle could be saved?

"Is Danielle Ben Daniel one of your hostages?" Josh said, failing to mask the trepidation in his voice.

But the line had already gone dead.

Chapter 44

DANIELLE LAY BOUND, GAGGED, AND BLINDFOLDED IN the trunk of a car trunk or van. She could hear the sound of the engine, and the vibrations and occasional bumps of the road, which told her that she was being transported—but to where? It was impossible for her to know, and she wasn't sure she wanted to think about it. Instead, she struggled futilely against her bonds. It was almost inconceivable that this was happening again.

The car jolted and Danielle felt a spear of pain rise from her left leg. The ropes were too tight. Whoever did this to her didn't care whether she lived or died. The darkness became invasive and time seemed to stretch infinitely. They'd been driving a very long time.

She thought about the man in the serpent mask, the man who had killed Alu. She'd heard his voice before. But where?

Would Josh come after her? *Could* he? When she came back the last time, he talked about how frustrated he was trying to find a way to get to her. Would this time be any different?

To say that their romance had been a whirlwind was an understatement. Danielle had never fallen for a man like this. She knew all about infatuation—she'd been through her share of tempestuous flings—but this was something else entirely. As strange as it seemed, something deep inside of her told her that she had known Josh before.

Still, since she met him, her life had been in constant peril. Maybe this was a sign to get out before it was too late—if it wasn't too late already. Maybe being with Josh was too dangerous.

The car hit another bump in the road, and Danielle forced those thoughts from her mind.

Chapter 45

Staring out the passenger side window of one of the IAA's unmarked security cars, Josh fixed his gaze on the fiery orange sphere, the remnants of the descending Jerusalem sun.

They arrived at the museum just before 8:00 p.m. Josh didn't notice any guards outside the building, but when he went inside, he immediately spotted Giuseppe and several other members of the security staff. Three more security men were positioned in the research lab, and at the rear of the building, posted just outside the safe containing the scroll, were two more. Yet Josh didn't feel very secure. The Guardians were resourceful, and had proven themselves more than capable of pulling off the unexpected.

Resting on a table in the research lab was a replica of the jar. Josh was relieved to see that it looked identical to the genuine article. Lying next to it were sheepskin and a writing instrument from the first century. By the time he had made his final preparations, the sun had set and an eerie twilight spilled in through the windows. It was as if Josh had entered another world, another time.

Josh pulled out the first sheet of sheepskin and began writing in Aramaic—the precise words he had translated from the scroll. He had studied the words so closely that they had been seared into his mind. There was something more going on here, though. The scroll activated some previously

200

dormant part of his brain, a part that registered critical events with utter clarity.

It took more than an hour to complete the first sheet, and only slightly less time to do the second. Then, as he was beginning work on the third, the roar of an explosion rocked the room. It came from the rear of the building, and Josh knew immediately what had been hit: the safe.

Josh ran into the hallway, where he was joined by four security men headed in the same direction. But before they reached the back of the builder, gunshots rang out, echoing through the long corridor. When they rounded the corner and arrived at the site of the blast, two security guards were lying lifeless on the floor, blood and body parts everywhere. The front door of the safe had been blown open and Josh stared in shock into a large hole in the back wall. He looked for the jar, but knew that it was nowhere to be found.

More shots were fired somewhere outside the building, so Josh scrambled through the hole in the wall out into the back grounds of the museum. There he found two more bodies; only this time, the men were dressed in the traditional garments of medieval Arab assassins. Only their dead eyes were visible behind their veils. The air stank of explosives and excrement.

Giuseppe jumped over the wall, followed by Goner. "There were three assailants. We killed them all."

"I thought you had the place totally secure," Josh said accusingly.

"We deliberately ordered our men indoors so as not to attract attention," Giuseppe said. "This should have enabled us to capture any intruders inside. We certainly didn't expect them to come over the back wall and use explosives."

"There are only two dead bodies here. Where's the third?"

Giuseppe looked toward the street. "We shot and killed

him as he was fleeing in the getaway car. It was an unlicensed taxi, probably one owned by a local Arab."

"I thought the Guardians weren't Arabs."

"They're not. These men were professionals, mercenaries."

Josh moaned at this new bit of information. He was reminded once again how ill equipped he was to be a player in this game. "Please tell me you recovered the scroll?"

"We didn't have to."

"What do you mean?" he asked, incredulous.

"It wasn't there. We take precautions very seriously here."

Chapter 46

JOSH RETURNED TO THE CONDOMINIUM HOPING AGAINST hope that Danielle would be there when he arrived. It was nearly 2:00 a.m. Boaz, the bodyguard, was snoring on the couch. Josh shook him until he woke up.

"I'm glad to know you were here taking care of business."

Boaz yawned. "I just fell asleep. What time is it?"

Josh pointed at the clock on the wall.

"Two o'clock, I can't believe it!" Boaz said in what seemed like genuine surprise. "The last time I checked it was only 12:30."

"Is Danielle here?"

"I haven't seen her."

Josh hated the feeling he got in the pit of his stomach. The death and destruction he saw at the museum had been just another reminder of how serious his enemies were. He knew that they had taken Danielle again. What he didn't know was whether or not she was still alive.

Josh went to Danielle's room to confirm for himself that she wasn't there, and then headed toward his own bedroom. He certainly wouldn't be sleeping; maybe he could make some further progress on the scroll. When he got there, though, he saw the computer case open on his bed. Someone had broken the lock and stolen the laptop.

Josh stormed back to the living room.

"Boaz, your job when neither Danielle or I are here is to watch the condo and not let anyone in."

"I didn't."

"Well, someone broke into my room and stole my laptop."

"That's impossible. I've been here the whole time."

"You were asleep for at least an hour. Why weren't there any other security people here?"

"Amos is the outside guard. He's supposed to be on duty from eleven to seven."

Josh looked toward the door, catching the eye of his own bodyguard. "We didn't see him when we came in."

"How could that be?" Boaz said, bounding up from the couch. He looked outside the door for Amos, and then headed down the hallway. Josh followed closely behind.

Amos was nowhere to be seen, and Boaz started for the elevator.

Josh called to stop him. "Let's use the stairs."

As they descended the staircase at breakneck speed, Josh nearly stumbled over a body lying on the first landing.

"I think we found Amos."

Josh felt the man's pulse. Amos' heart was still beating. He had a small lump on his head. Someone had obviously knocked him unconscious. Josh tried to wake Amos, and after a moment, he succeeded.

"Where am I?" Amos asked in a groggy slur.

Josh and Boaz grabbed Amos' arms and walked him upstairs to the condo. After they had laid Amos on the couch, Josh went back into his bedroom to check the windows. They were shut and locked. He went into Danielle's bedroom and did the same thing, but they, too, were secured.

"What happened?" Boaz asked.

"Whoever stole the laptop must have surprised Amos and knocked him unconscious. They must have had a key, or they would have awakened you. When I got close to you, I noticed a faint smell, like chloroform. They saw that you were sleeping and wanted to make sure you stayed that way."

Boaz nodded gravely.

"Why don't you take Amos home? When he feels better I want to talk with him."

Boaz looked at Josh's guard. "There shouldn't only be one man on duty."

Josh was in no mood to be polite. "Not much difference, is there?"

Boaz tried to argue, but quickly acquiesced. *He knows he screwed up*, thought Josh. *He just doesn't realize how badly.* Before he left with Amos, though, Boaz insisted that Josh take his 9mm handgun for his own protection.

"Two armed people are better than one," he said.

But would two armed people have any impact against the resources of the Guardians?

Chapter 47

EXHAUSTED, JOSH LAY IN BED, TRYING IN VAIN TO FALL asleep. His heart was racing; he could hear and even feel it pounding in his ears. He closed his eyes again, but he began tossing and turning—it was futile.

He got up and dragged himself to the corner of the room, assuming a half lotus position. Maybe if he meditated, he'd relax enough to sleep. He needed any help he could get now, because he was sure that the next day would be one of the hardest of his life.

Josh closed his eyes and began breathing deeply. It didn't help. Images of Danielle ran through his mind. Her touch, the feel of their bodies together, the look in her eyes that he'd never seen with another woman. He wondered if he would ever see it again.

He wondered the same thing about the scroll. The original was gone. So was the copy on his laptop. He couldn't access the one he had uploaded to his office server, and even if he did, no one would believe that it was real. Unless he somehow recovered the original, the world would never read the words that he translated—words that he'd committed to memory.

Josh tried deep breathing again. He visualized cross-fading red, blue, yellow, green, and purple colors, but still couldn't relax. Finally, he went to his staircase induction. This seemed to have some impact. With every step he took, he felt himself going deeper and deeper into his unconscious. He counted each step as he descended: 199, 198.... He went deeper and deeper until he was fully relaxed and in touch with his unconscious.

Nothing presented itself to him for several minutes. Then the four shadows appeared again, turning into faceless phantoms. Then, they were joined by a fifth faceless phantom that moved to the middle of the formation, as if taking a place of honor. Then, the apparition in the middle took a step forward and his blank features morphed into those of a man with dark brown eyes and a prominent nose. He was quite ordinary looking, but had the most intense eyes that Josh had ever seen. Josh hadn't met the man—or ghost—before, but there was something strangely familiar about him.

The wraith spoke in a deep, resonant voice, as if reading Josh's mind, "I am who I am."

"What do you want of me?" Josh asked.

"You have the power, the intellect, and most importantly the courage to make a difference in this world."

"So does everyone else."

"Not like you. The world has not seen the likes of you in many, many years. Look at the five of us. We are all a part of you."

Josh had no idea what this meant.

"You needn't be confused. All you ever were and will be lives inside of you already. Go deep into your genetic memory, for we are there, in your unconscious.

"You will need all the power you have, and even that may not be enough. The world is far more complicated today and the problems more severe; but you must walk the path that is your own."

The spirit smiled. "I wish you success this time. If you need me, just listen to the voice of your intuition."

As the last word left its mouth, the wraith disappeared.

For several long moments, Josh's mind remained still. No new images emerged. Then his thoughts began to descend. What was going on here? Was there a larger point to the events that had overtaken his life? When he discovered the scroll and translated its opening words, he anticipated a transcendent experience, a truly life-changing evolution inspired by its message, maybe even the proof he'd been searching for his entire life. Instead, Josh was reminded why he'd always questioned the value of true faith. Faith divided. Faith consistently led to violence. And, all too often, faith was left unrewarded.

His dark mood grew darker. He had meditated hoping for answers, not confirmation of his skepticism. He tried going deeper again, descending the stairs of his mind. He counted backward dozens of steps and stopped. Waiting on the dimly lit stairway was a sheet of paper—a page from the scroll. He stared at it intently, trying to determine why it was here.

He noticed words he'd skipped over when he translated the page—words he couldn't identify in Aramaic.

Ribbono shel Olam.

Looking at them now, he understood what he'd missed before. The words were Hebrew, not Aramaic. Why would the author do that?

And what did they mean?

Ribbono shel Olam.

He'd heard this phrase before, though he couldn't recall where. They certainly weren't common parlance. Josh searched his mind for a translation and found it. *Master of the Universe.* Josh looked at the sentences around the phrase and found no connection. Why was it here?

Josh focused on the words and began to repeat the phrase:

Ribbono shel Olam.
Ribbono shel Olam.
Ribbono shel Olam.

He felt his trance deepen, as though he'd entered a new part of his mind. After a few moments, he heard a voice that was familiar but decidedly not his own.

"There is tremendous power in these words. I repeat them over and over and it connects me to the divine spark. That divine spark is in you. It's in all of us, but few have known its presence and fewer still have ever used it. All the answers you seek, you will find."

The voice disappeared, and Josh suddenly felt the room around him. He heard sounds he'd blocked while meditating, then opened his eyes and noticed that his body was covered with sweat.

Had his transcendence just begun?

Chapter 48

Josh slept for nearly four hours, awakening at around 8:00 a.m. on Saturday morning. He dressed quickly, and then shoved the 9mm handgun in an inner pocket of his light khaki pants. Josh wasn't comfortable carrying a gun, but under the circumstances, he didn't feel he had a choice. Boaz was right about that.

With his bodyguard beside him, Josh walked to the Old City. Every few steps, he glanced around for anyone who looked suspicious. He observed every vehicle and every person within a hundred yards. At this point, anyone could be an enemy.

Josh entered the Old City through the Jaffa Gate. Each time he came to this place he felt like he'd stepped back in time. He loved the narrow stone streets and the architecture from both ancient and medieval times; but Josh's destination was somewhat more modern—an Internet café located in the heart of the Jewish Quarter. As Josh ambled along, he observed old Arabs, Orthodox Jews, priests, pilgrims, and tourists. It was the priests who concerned him. Every time he encountered someone dressed in priestly attire, he feared that they were members of the Guardians. None who passed by, however, presented any threat.

Josh arrived at the Internet café, but it was closed. He'd somehow managed to forget that it was the Jewish Sabbath and that none of the businesses and restaurants in the Jewish Quarter would be open.

He headed to the Christian Quarter, hoping to find another place to link up. Unlike the Jewish Quarter, the Christian Quarter was jammed with tourists and pilgrims. He walked down several streets, and when he finally found a café where he could get online, he chose a computer near the back, away from the other users. Josh connected to the Internet and typed the password that allowed him to enter into the Archaeology Department at the University of Pennsylvania. Josh was relieved that the password system at Penn, created by some of the brightest minds at the school, was nearly impossible for even the most sophisticated hacker to break into.

Once he had entered his department's network, he typed in another six-digit password, which took him to yet another window, where he typed in a third password of eight digits. He now was able to communicate with his office desktop. He logged the password for the scroll's file and the pictures of the document appeared.

Now would come the tough part. Josh knew that he had an extraordinary memory. This had been the case for as long as he could remember. He had incredible recall for even the tiniest of details. But could he possibly memorize five pages of Aramaic against the background noise of a busy coffee shop? If he was going to translate the remainder of the scroll and decipher its secrets, he had no choice.

Using some of the techniques he had mastered in mediation, Josh focused deeply on the pages. In less than an hour, he had the entire remainder of the scroll memorized, forever etched in his mind.

"What were you doing back there?" his guard asked as they began their walk back through the Christian Quarter.

"I needed to study something."

"You seemed to be studying pretty hard."

Josh eyed the guard closely. "It was important."

They continued through the Christian Quarter, Josh still looking behind to see if anyone was following. He had a bad feeling about someone, but continued walking. After another hundred yards, though, Josh saw that the stranger was still there. The man was dressed like a tourist, wearing a New York Yankees baseball hat and a white t-shirt with the words "Jerusalem City of God" imprinted on the front. He was clean-shaven, with no real distinguishing characteristics. Except for the fact that he was well over six feet tall, the man was quite ordinary.

Josh and his guard stepped into a souvenir shop and pretended to browse; but Josh's eyes never left the stranger, who stood in front of the store, presumably admiring the Old City sites.

"What do you make of that guy," Josh asked his guard.

"I've been wondering the same thing. Let's be careful here."

A few minutes later, they left the souvenir shop and headed in the direction of the Jaffa Gate. The stranger still lurked in the background, so Josh changed direction and made for the Church of the Holy Sepulcher. When they reached the entrance, the stranger had vanished.

Josh studied the long line of tourists and pilgrims that wound through the rotunda, where Christ's tomb was located. He didn't recognize anything out of the ordinary—at least, not now. But the exchange was supposed to take place here at 4:00 p.m., and Josh had no idea whether the Guardians knew that he didn't have the original scroll. Would their plans have changed? Was Danielle one of their hostages? What was his next move?

Josh turned to the guard. "We can go," he said. The guard didn't ask where they were headed, which was good, because Josh wasn't sure how he would have answered if he did.

Chapter 49

Hoping that a change of scenery would give him a new perspective, Josh sat at the terrace bar of the legendary King David Hotel, the address of visiting celebrities and heads of state. In spite of everything on his mind, he couldn't help but admire the stunning views of the Old City, a place where myth and reality co-existed. While he reflected upon the events of the past several days, the loud ringing of his cell phone shook Josh from his reverie.

"Where have you been? We've been trying to contact you for the past hour." It was Giuseppe Kaplan.

"I had my cell phone turned off for a while. What's the matter?"

"Early this morning another incident occurred outside the museum building."

Josh felt as if the wind had been knocked out of him. "What's happened?"

"I'd rather not discuss it over the phone. I'm sending a car to pick you up in fifteen minutes."

"I'm at the King David Hotel."

"We'll get you at the main entrance."

Josh stepped out of the vehicle and took a couple of deep breaths before striding toward the entrance of the museum. The head of IAA security stood in the foyer, waiting to greet him.

213

"Please follow me to my office," Giuseppe said grimly.

"What's this all about?" Josh dreaded the answer, knowing in his heart that he was about to learn something awful.

"Let's go to my office. I'd rather discuss this matter in private."

Once there, Josh positioned himself in the stiff, uncomfortable chair directly across from Giuseppe's desk.

Giuseppe held out a pack of cigarettes and asked, "Do you smoke?"

"No, but don't let me stop you."

Josh waited in agonizing silence as Giuseppe took out a lighter and lit a cigarette, an Israeli brand Josh did not recognize.

Giuseppe took a couple of drags and then spoke. "This morning at 6:37, large suitcases containing the remains of two dead bodies were discovered near the facade of the building."

Josh held his breath as Giuseppe continued, "The bodies were both dismembered and beheaded. One was that of Reverend Barnaby Smith, and the other was Gideon Shapiro, one of our security guards."

Josh stared at Giuseppe, stunned. Gideon was the man who'd left the condo with Danielle. Repeated attempts to contact him had failed. Now they knew why. "What about Danielle?"

Giuseppe took one last puff from his cigarette before extinguishing it in the ashtray. "I was hesitant to show you this, but it's important that I do. There was a picture attached to Gideon's torso. It was a photo of Danielle."

Giuseppe handed him the picture and Josh experienced a sudden, intense pain in his chest and stomach. In the photo, Danielle lay on an altar with her hands bound and her eyes closed. Tears sprang instantly to Josh's eyes. Sadness and hatred overwhelmed him.

"Is she..."

"Danielle may not be dead. The photo is not conclusive. My team is investigating any possible clues to the location of the picture. We've commenced searching some religious sites—especially ancient ones—for a match to the altar in the picture."

If she's alive, I need to rescue her, Josh thought, his mind burning with white-hot dread. *If she's not, I need to make every single Guardian pay for her death.*

Josh placed a hand on Giuseppe's shoulder. "I no longer want the protection of your security guards. I can take care of myself. I need the freedom to operate alone."

"That's crazy. You're still in grave danger and require around-the-clock security."

"I can do what I need to do," Josh told him in no uncertain terms.

"I can't authorize you to act alone."

"You don't have to authorize me to do anything. You just need to stay out of my way."

Giuseppe was silent for several seconds. Josh knew that he wouldn't accept any interference from the man.

At last, Giuseppe reached for another cigarette. "You must keep us abreast of all of your activities."

"I will. Of course, I doubt that will be necessary, since you'll almost certainly be monitoring my every move."

Giuseppe sighed and nodded. "Of course."

"So where's the scroll?"

Before Giuseppe could answer, a security agent hurried into the office. "There is someone on the phone who insists on speaking with you. He claims to possess information pertaining to the Barnaby and Gideon murders."

"Buzz him through and make sure you put a tap on the line."

"Can you put him on the speakerphone?" Josh said. "I'd like to hear this."

Giuseppe hit the speakerphone button. "This is Giuseppe Kaplan."

"I take it you've had the opportunity to admire our handiwork?" the familiar voice taunted from the other end of the line. "The girl is receiving special treatment, too. We intend to have more fun with her yet."

Josh couldn't contain himself. "You are sick bastards." The voice in the speaker laughed. "I hear you have company. I presume it to be Mr. Cohan? I want him to know that we have great plans for him as well."

Still seething from within, Josh regained his composure, sat silently, and listened.

Giuseppe leaned toward the phone. "What do you want?"

"I still hold hostages. I didn't think I would have to exchange them for the scroll, but after last night's debacle, I'm willing to be generous and make a trade. I will call you later with my instructions."

The line disconnected.

Josh felt a level of rage he'd never experienced before. He wanted to reach into the phone and choke the life out of the caller with his bare hands. "What are you going to do about this?" he demanded, turning his anger in the only constructive direction he could.

Giuseppe nodded slowly, clearly shaken by recent events. Josh guessed that one never became inured to this kind of thing. "I'm not sure. Did you finish last night's project?"

"No, I was interrupted by the explosion."

"I want you to complete it."

"Do you plan to use it?"

"Only if we have to."

Josh didn't want to be delayed, but he understood that the charade could still have value. "I'll finish it before I leave the museum. Then I'm going to track down the Guardians."

"How do you intend to do that?"

"I don't know," Josh admitted. "I'm going to let my instincts guide me."

"You're going to need superhuman instincts, then. Are you sure you don't want protection?"

Josh stared directly into Giuseppe's eyes. "Admit it, Giuseppe. You can't protect me any more than you protected Danielle. I don't need the extra baggage."

Chapter 50

JOSH LEFT THE MUSEUM AND GRABBED A TAXI TO THE corner of St. Mark's Road and Khabad Street, where the Christian, Jewish, and Muslim Quarters overlapped. There, he climbed a steep staircase up onto the rooftops of the Old City. It was a perfect vantage point, offering a panoramic view of the crowds below.

You're going to need superhuman instincts. Giuseppe's admonition rang in Josh's ears. Instinct was all he had to work with—that and a loose smattering of details about a possibly mythical sect. He was going to need more than superhuman instincts to find Danielle. He'd need the hand of God himself.

Josh scaled higher until he saw the magnificent, four-teen-carat gold Dome of the Rock—the third holiest place in the Moslem world, behind Mecca and Medina. From there, Josh spotted his next destination. Dodging satellite dishes and hurdling over dividing walls, he came upon a majestic view of the Church of the Holy Sepulcher with its two imposing domes. The larger of the two domes was especially impressive, as it guarded the tomb of Christ directly beneath it. As he looked down from the rooftop, Josh saw hundreds of people moving in and out of the church's entrance. He had found the perfect vantage point for monitoring the teeming crowd below.

After an hour, Josh was beginning to second-guess his

plan. Either nothing suspicious was going on around the church, or else his instincts had failed him after all. Just as he was on the verge of giving up, though, he noticed an unusually tall man towering over the tourists and pilgrims below. Two things attracted Josh's attention: the Yankees baseball hat, and the large black crucifix around the man's neck.

When the man entered the church, Josh ran down the nearest staircase and across the street, doing his best to blend into the throngs outside the church entrance. From inside the crowd, his sight line was largely restricted. Still, Josh trusted the feeling in his gut that told him to just be patient. About twenty minutes later, the man in the baseball cap reappeared, heading out along the Via Dolorosa. Josh followed closely behind him, maneuvering through the masses of people that jammed the old stone streets. After about a quarter of a mile, the man ducked into a shabby storefront with a hand-painted sign emblazoned with the words "Sword of God."

Josh moved casually through the aisles of so-called relics and other, mostly Christian bric-a-brac, keeping a cautious eye on the supposed tourist. But when he reached the back of the store, the man seemed to have suddenly vanished. All Josh found were heavy drapes hanging from the ceiling to the floor, moving ever so slightly. He realized that he must have been spotted. For a moment, Josh considered ducking behind the drapes himself; if there was a back exit, then he may still be able to catch up with the suspicious stranger. But then he noticed that in and amongst the usual souvenirs were other items not normally found in other shops in the quarter —like an exact replica of a crusader's sword. *The Sword of God*, Josh thought, and the whole thing began to make sense. He must be close to the Guardians' secret hideout. Were they trying to trap him? If so, he didn't intend to take the bait.

When Josh returned to the condo, he found Aaron, another of Giuseppe's security men, waiting for him.

"What do you want?" Josh asked, making no attempt to hide his irritation. He wished the IAA would leave him alone to do what he needed to do.

"There's been some buzz around the museum, and I wanted to clue you in. Apparently, some more tests have come back, the ones that were supposed to be dating the scroll, and the results were inconclusive."

"Inconclusive?" Josh said, exasperated. He didn't have time for this right now. "All the initial tests showed the scroll to be authentic."

"The last C14 test raised some questions."

"Questions? What questions could it have raised that they sent a security guard to deliver the message? And why are you telling me this now?" Josh was running out of patience. Danielle was still out there somewhere, and the longer he was held up with "inconclusive" small talk, the greater his chance of losing her forever.

"I just thought you'd want to know," said Aaron pointedly, "given everything that's going on."

What was Aaron's point? Was he suggesting that Josh might have led several men to their deaths and put Danielle at risk for the sake of a fraud? Josh had asked himself many times over the past few days what he had brought into the world when he discovered the scroll. The consequences had already been more horrible than he could have imagined. But there was no doubt in Josh's mind that the scroll was real.

Still, the insinuation hit home and he was suddenly aware of the overwhelming guilt and fear he'd been feeling—or, rather, not feeling, but working hard to bury beneath the distraction of constant activity. Josh couldn't afford to let his emotions get the best of him; if he did, he'd be no use to Danielle at all. But could avoiding them be somehow impeding his progress? He was going to have to find a way to sit with the fear, whether he liked it or not. He sat down on the couch, took a deep breath, and concentrated for a moment on releasing his clenched muscles. "Where's the scroll now?" he asked.

"We have it," said Aaron, taking a seat. "The scroll was removed from the museum's safe a full twenty-four hours before the attempted theft. It is in a secure location."

"Have you told anyone where you've hidden it?"

"Even I don't know. Only two people do, and their identities are secret."

Josh leaned in. "What do you know about the group calling themselves the Guardians?"

"The Guardians, huh?" said Aaron, raising an eyebrow. "That's a name that doesn't come up very often. They're a religious cult. They claim to have been around forever."

"How long is forever?"

"According to our intelligence, nearly two thousand years. They believe that they're the only true Christians."

Josh grunted. "It's amazing how every group claims to be the only one with 'The Answer.' When did you learn about them?"

"They've been here since before we started our operations in the Old City in 1967."

Josh leaned back and shifted his focus beyond Aaron, out the window, to the view of the city beyond. "When Mark Twain visited Jerusalem in 1869, he wrote about meeting a radical Christian cult that sounded very similar to the Guardians of today."

"That I didn't know," Aaron confessed.

"Those who lead the Crusades belonged to a secret cult."

"Yes, the Knights Templar."

Josh nodded. "Exactly. The Templars started out with

only nine members, whose primary job was to protect pilgrims visiting the holy sites in Jerusalem. I highly doubt that they were Guardians. But there were others, some of those involved in the fighting itself, who specialized in the killing of non-believers. These knights belonged to an unknown secret society—possibly the Guardians."

"What does that have to do with today?"

Josh shrugged. "Maybe nothing; but it may have a connection. In any case, the Guardians have lived under your watchful eyes for forty years. Why haven't you arrested them?"

Aaron played with a pencil on the coffee table. It was obvious to Josh that the question embarrassed him. "They've only recently become engaged in undisputed criminal activity. Until now, we were never able to link them directly to any crimes. We pride ourselves on religious tolerance. Even if a group is extreme in their views, as long as they stay within the law we don't bother them. Since your discovery, though," Aaron paused for a moment, "things have changed. The Guardians have turned violent. Or maybe they've just got bolder. Either way, we're planning to take them out."

"That's old information," said Josh. "Tell me something I don't know."

"Like what?"

"Something new about their beliefs?"

Aaron put down the pencil. "Admittedly, we know very little. We have discovered some hate literature that we believe is attributable to them. They also have a secret, which they claim has been handed down to them through the ages."

"And do you know what that is?"

"We never found out. All we know is that it pertains to the beginnings of Christianity."

Josh got up again and walked to the window, gathering

his thoughts as he watched the everyday bustle in the street below. It looked like any other city, filled with regular people living their regular lives. But Josh knew that looks could be deceiving. He thought back to the discovery he had made earlier that afternoon. Should he share the new information with Aaron? Would working with him be a help or a hindrance? Josh wasn't sure, but he also knew that there were enormous risks involved in trying to go it alone.

"I think I've learned something," he said cautiously. He told Aaron about his surveillance of the Church of the Holy Sepulcher, about the man in the Yankees cap, and about his discovery at the Sword of God.

Aaron sat transfixed while Josh told his story. At the end of it, he nodded appreciatively. "You're better at this detective business than I gave you credit for."

"So what do we do now?"

Aaron stood. "We have to go in after them. Don't go anywhere until you hear from me. I'll organize a raid for tonight."

Chapter 51

BELOW AN OLD ABANDONED CHURCH NEAR THE SEA OF Galilee, some 70 miles north of Jerusalem, the Master awaited one of his agents. He did not like to be kept waiting. The Master paced the ancient floor, pressing his temple to control his growing ire. But when he heard his man approaching, he quickly donned his mask, concealing his emotion beneath the serpent's head.

The agent finally arrived in the dark catacomb. He bowed and the Master motioned for him to sit on one of the stone benches, set against a cavern wall.

"Give me your report."

The agent squirmed to sit comfortably on the cold, unyielding surface. "Nothing is happening at the IAA. I think they've moved the scroll to another location."

"Do you have any idea where?"

"No one I've talked to seems to know."

The Master thought for a moment, pacing again. "Does anyone there suspect that you are working for us?"

The agent shook his head. "I don't think anyone has the slightest idea."

"Good. You have done well."

The agent seemed pleased with the compliment. Then his eyes dropped to the floor. "Master, may I ask you why you want the scroll."

The Master paused, toying with the idea. "There is

much that you don't know about our group. If I tell you," he said, "it would be...shall we say, against your best interest to share the information with anyone."

"Master, I swear that I will tell no one."

"Our lineage goes back almost 2,000 years. During that time, there has been a long succession of Masters. It is my honor to hold this position now, and to foster its tradition. We hold a sacred secret, a spiritual key that I alone understand. The day will come when I will share that secret with the next Master, who will take my place as the keeper of the truth."

The agent interrupted enthusiastically, "What does the secret have to do with the scroll?"

"Don't ever interrupt me," the Master said darkly.

The agent shrank back against the wet stone wall. "Forgive me Master. I'm your humble servant. I would never offend you, nor jeopardize my chance at becoming a Guardian."

"You shall be rewarded for your services very soon." The Master nodded and continued. "It pleases me to share this with you now. Part of our doctrine, our own sacred text, alludes to a document written by Our Lord and Savior, Jesus Christ. According to the prophesy, when this document is found it will validate our teachings and the secret entrusted to me. On that day, the balance of power will begin to shift and the mission we have waited hundreds of years to fulfill will be set in motion."

"Then why were you upset when I reported the details of the scroll's inscriptions?"

"Because," the Master hissed, "the words of your scroll are blasphemous. It is not the sacred document of prophesy, but a vile sham."

"Then why do you still pursue it?"

The Master scowled. His agent was asking too many questions. Still, the Master prided himself on the integrity of his convictions, and no harm could come from telling the truth. "If it were ever published, the message of the false scroll could irrevocably damage our cause. It contradicts our beliefs and invalidates our sacred scriptures. Even if it is revealed to be the fraud that it is and published for mere curiosity's sake, it could still plant the seed of doubt in some of our weaker members. We pursue the scroll to destroy it."

The agent nodded. "I understand. Thank you, Master, for taking me into your confidence. But now that I have kept my end of the bargain, can you tell me when I will become a Guardian?"

The Master slowly reached inside his long robe, as if scratching an itch. He wanted to relish the moment. "You can never be a Guardian," he said, his voice filled with disdain. "As useful as you have been, you are nevertheless a Jew, defiled by your own heathen blood."

The agent rose to his feet. "But Master, have I not served you well and done all that you asked of me?"

"You have," said the Master. "And you have been well paid for your services."

"My loyalty is not for sale," the agent said, wounded by the insinuation. "I hate the Jews as much as you do. Were it not for them, my father would not have been killed during the Lebanese invasion. I have served you out of respect and devotion to our cause."

"It was *never* your cause," the Master spat. "Your birth parents determined your fate."

"But Master, I've been a loyal servant. I've sacrificed everything for you, even willingly betrayed my friends and colleagues."

"So you have," the Master said with a sinister smile, "and so you will have your final reward. You loved your late father deeply, yes? As your services are no longer required, I am sending you to join him."

With a deft economy of effort, as if waving away an irritating fly, the Master pulled his sword from under his cloak and decapitated the informer, Jonathan.

"Guards," he called, and two of his followers appeared in the doorway of the Master's chamber. He glared at the body and then at his men. "Take this carcass and incinerate it."

Chapter 52

THE PEEPHOLE OF THE STEEL DOOR SWUNG SHUT AND Danielle was finally alone—at least for now. Exhausted, she went to lie on the low cot that had been pushed up against the stone wall of her cell. *A bed of rocks is more comfortable than this*, she thought. She considered lying on the floor, thinking that it might be more comfortable. But the floor was filthy; with what, she didn't want to know.

She had to get out of there, but didn't even know how many kidnappers there were, much less where she was being held. She needed a plan.

She gazed at the ceiling, racking her mind for a way out of this. One thing was for certain—she would have to rely on her own resources, and right now all she had to work with were her brains and her body. She had long known how to use her powers of seduction to get what she needed, but now the thought gave her pause. Still, it just might be her only chance to escape with her life.

Danielle already knew that her captors were sexually inhibited. *There's no shower here in the cell*, she thought, *but I'll bet they have one somewhere*. Perhaps they would take her there if they thought there'd be something in it for them.

This was a dangerous plan. Alu had been clearly wounded, and therefore easy to manipulate. But she had only played on his emotions, and even he had come close to raping her, she was certain of it. If she intentionally aroused these men, it could have devastating consequences. The one small hope she had lay in something she had overheard one of her captors saying to another—that no harm could come to her before The Master saw her. While she hardly welcomed that meeting, it probably bought her some time.

Soon enough, Danielle heard the sound of the peephole opening. She ran to the door and pressed her face against the tiny hole, pleading with the two guards who stood on the other side.

"Please," she said, doing her best damsel in distress, "it's so dirty in here. Can I at least take a shower?"

But it didn't seem to work, and the peephole swung shut, cutting off Danielle's only view to the world outside.

After about an hour, the steel door opened again. This time, two men dressed in black gestured for her to follow. Only their eyes were visible behind the veils that covered their faces. Out in the corridor waited two more men who were dressed the same way.

Obviously they didn't think they needed this much manpower to contain her. The guards were here for another function. Danielle felt her flesh crawl, but she had to remind herself why she was doing this. Besides, she might be able to stir up some dissention in the ranks.

Danielle followed the four men through the narrow hallway, past what she could only guess were more locked cells on either side. Eventually, they came to a large open door. The guards pointed for Danielle to enter the room. It was a large shower room with six showerheads.

Danielle suddenly panicked, remembering the gruesome accounts she had heard of the Holocaust. But she had come this far and had to keep her wits about her if she was to have any chance at all. She dropped her robe, allowing herself to be on full display for the leering guards. Breathing deeply, trying to maintain her composure, she began to lather herself. She tried to convince herself that this was all part of her plan, that she actually had the upper hand here. But when she looked back toward the door, Danielle saw that the four men had been joined by six more. Although her back was turned to her abductors, she could feel the menacing heat of their stares.

The soap slipped out of her hands and landed by her feet. By habit Danielle bent over to retrieve it, not realizing at first what she had done. Danielle had tried hard not to be provocative, but the accidental dropping of her soap was all the men needed to see. A quick glance confirmed her worst fear. At least six of the men were trying to hide erections under their robes. The violent lust in their eyes made her recoil, but again she managed to compose herself, this time by grabbing the towel provided for her and busying herself with drying off.

"May I have my robe now?" she asked, her voice trembling with just the right combination of helplessness and suggestion to keep the charade going.

Three of her captors rushed to grasp the flimsy garment. She thanked them and donned it quickly, wishing the material wasn't quite so sheer. The next few minutes would be the riskiest.

As Danielle entered the hallway, the tension suddenly erupted and her fears were realized. Before she knew what was happening, several of the men were upon her—seizing her, tearing at her robe. The putative holy men began groping her in the most intimate places, in carnal defiance of their orders.

Danielle had taken a chance and lost. And for what? What had she accomplished? What had she done? She had no more leverage now than she had before.

Just then, a booming voice tore through the hallway. "What are you doing?"

The guards released her instantly, cowering on the floor like small children. Danielle also fell to her knees.

"You have dared to defy me, and now you shall be punished!"

Danielle's eyes darted around the dimly lit corridor, searching for the man behind the voice; but he remained invisible.

"Take her back to her cell at once," he bellowed, and his lackeys scrambled to their feet to comply.

Safe from harm—at least for the moment—Danielle realized that although her scheme hadn't worked according to plan, she had gained some valuable information. She knew the type of place where she was held, and also knew that there were at least eleven kidnappers in the hideout.

Ironically, the chief kidnapper himself had been the one to rescue her. That meant one of two things: either he meant to do her no harm...or else he had other, even more sadistic plans. But her strategy had actually worked better than she had even hoped. They may have gotten in a few illicit jollies, but at least eight of her captors were about to suffer far more than she had.

Danielle allowed herself a brief moment of satisfaction. It was fleeting, though, for she realized her next encounter would almost certainly be with the Master himself.

Chapter 53

JOSH AND AARON STOOD TOGETHER ON THE ROOFTOP that overlooked the Church of the Holy Sepulcher. *Man has such a capacity for majesty and reverence,* Josh thought as he gazed upon the magnificent structure. *Why must it so often be perverted?*

"It's a beautiful night for a raid," Aaron said softly, bringing Josh back to the moment.

"Have you done many of these?"

"Too many—but usually the targets are Islamic terrorists, not Christian ones. We're treading on new ground here. That is, if your deductions are correct."

Josh wasn't sure how to respond, so he didn't. Were his deductions correct? They had been based almost entirely on instinct and speculation—what his gut had told him about the man in the Yankees cap and what he'd seen inside the Sword of God. How much of this speculation was driven by his desperate desire to save Danielle? And how much did he trust that what he hoped was instinct wasn't just the workings of his own anxious mind?

"We knew about the old religious store on the Via Dolorosa," Aaron continued, giving Josh a moment's reprieve. "It's been a fixture of the Christian Quarter for as long as we've been tracking the area. We've observed many priests going in and then taking a considerable amount of time coming out. At first, we assumed they were just buying religious icons. Later, we determined that it was a meeting place for some harmless organization of priests. They never broke the law. It wasn't until you called and our surveillance team verified your information that we felt reasonably certain that this was their hideout. With a little luck, tonight should put an end to the problems they've caused."

"When will the raid begin?" Josh asked.

"When it is dark enough."

"Don't you think that it's already dark enough? The streets are practically deserted."

Aaron looked at the sky as if determining whether it was the right shade. Then he took out his walkie-talkie. "Are we ready?"

"We're waiting for our man outside the store to give us the signal," crackled the voice on the other end.

Aaron tipped his head to Josh in empathy. "Waiting is always the hardest part."

Josh just wanted to get on with things. Was the woman he loved in some terrible danger just dozens of feet away? And what if they didn't get there in time?

At last, Aaron gave the signal. Like a conductor leading a symphony orchestra, he waved his men into motion with a sweeping gesture and they commenced their attack. Heavily armed police and security men broke down the store's front door, and Josh followed when the debris had been cleared. They quickly moved to the back of the shop and tore open the drapes. Four feet behind was a stone wall. Could it really be a dead end? Josh knew what he had seen. He knew that there was something more back here.

After close inspection, the police found the lever that opened the wall, and they descended a spiraling masonry staircase. By the time they reached the bottom, they were in total darkness. Once the police switched on their flashlights,

Josh saw that they were in a large room with stone benches. It was as silent as a cemetery at midnight.

They walked cautiously to the end of the room and opened an old wooden door, which opened onto a long corridor. There, Josh saw several more doors, each leading to what looked like a prison cell.

They searched every inch of the space, but found nothing. Finally, one of the policemen shouted from the end of the corridor. "Over here. There's another door."

The rest of the strike force moved in. They lifted the latch and flung the door open. Up ahead, through the murky air, was a large tunnel that broke off into a network of smaller ones. There seemed no end to the myriad secret tunnels and passages that lay beneath the Old City.

"It looks like we've missed them," Aaron said, his voice a mixture of disappointment and frustration.

Josh's own disappointment was exponentially greater. "They knew we were coming."

"The man you followed probably tipped them off," Aaron said. "Let's take a look anyway. They were in a hurry, and may have been careless."

He and Josh walked through the doorway and into the tunnel. It was impossible to know which way the Guardians had gone.

Aaron shook his head slowly. "We've been observing them since you called. We saw two suspects go into the hideout, but they never came out. Now I know why. They used the tunnel to escape our attack."

"They left hours ago. I was here around 3:30 this afternoon, when the fanatics tried to lure me into a trap. When I didn't follow them into their hideaway, they must have realized that I knew the location of their hideout and figured I'd be back. From the look of things, though, it seems that most of them left before this afternoon. I'd like your men to check the rooms, particularly the ones that looked like prison cells, for any sign of recent occupants."

"We're doing a lot more than that. We're questioning all the store employees. We're also bringing in a generator to light up every inch of this place. I'm sure our investigators will turn up some important clues."

The police spread out and started searching the tunnels. Aaron and Josh walked down the main artery, stopping at the entrance to one of the many smaller passages.

"I've got a hunch, Aaron. Let's follow this and see where it leads."

Aaron regarded Josh with a puzzled expression, but followed him for about two hundred yards until they came to an abrupt halt. Here, an enormous stone slab had been rolled into place in front of what appeared to be another doorway. But there seemed to be no fresh marks aside from their own footprints in the dust. Whoever had blocked this tunnel had done so a very long time ago.

Chapter 54

FROM THE EXTERIOR, THE OFFICE BUILDING LOOKED no different from any other in Nazareth. It was plain and indistinguishable, with a modest storefront at the street level that turned a reasonable profit selling pamphlets and maps to the steady stream of tourists that came to visit the basilica and the Sea of Galilee only a short distance away. It was, however, far from ordinary.

The building had been a Guardian sanctuary for more than fifty years. It had more than 30,000 square feet of space above ground, where a respectable enterprise not only funded their operations, but also served as a front for the Guardians' international headquarters. But below...that was where things got really interesting. The underground bunker—equipped to withstand a nuclear war—ran the length of the structure, consisting of twelve rooms; the largest of these, the assembly room, was more than 2,500 square feet and could seat seventy-five people. In contrast to the Jerusalem hideout, with its ancient stone benches, it had all the comforts of a modern theatre, complete with stadium seating and an elaborate lighting system that lent even more drama to the true focal point of the room: the elevated altar, elaborately carved and inlaid with pure gold.

It was here that the Master presided over his flock, here that the most sacred rituals were performed. But now the assembly room was empty, except for the Master himself. He sat on the dais, illuminated by the crimson glow of a single lamp, awaiting the evening's entertainment. It amused him to think that if that fool Alu had not captured her again, the woman wouldn't be here at all. Of course, she had served some purpose as a hostage; but now that the archaeologist had stumbled onto their Jerusalem location and upset their plans, that function was now useless. At this point, the Master simply looked forward to a bit of fun before he killed her.

The hostage was escorted into the assembly hall, draped in a light robe that exposed her every contour.

"Remove the garment and lay her on the altar," the Master commanded. "But bind her loosely," he said, his words dripping with rancor. "I'll enjoy watching her fight a little."

When they had carried out the Master's orders, his followers bowed and left the chamber. This was to be a private interrogation.

The Master, in his serpent's mask and robes, watched his subordinates go and then turned to the woman. He had never paid her much attention, but now, laid out before him, his passion began to rise. "You are as beautiful as they say," he told her. "I see now what Alu found so appealing."

"Alu was psychotic," Danielle laughed, her voice surprisingly arrogant considering her situation.

The Master leaned close to her and she recoiled. "You are to speak only when I tell you to. Do you understand?"

Danielle was silent.

The Master inspected her body from head to toe like a slave trader. The Jewess aroused him. "You *are* seductive," he taunted. "The Guardians, of course, are all celibate. Only one may make love to a woman. Fortunately, that is I."

The Master studied Danielle's face, caressing it as she stared defiantly into his mask. Her eyes, her hair, the angle of her cheekbones, and even her voice reminded him of someone he'd known a very long time ago. Someone equally alluring. How could he have missed it before? This was going to be even more pleasurable than he had imagined.

He moved down her body, cupping his hand around her right breast and lightly grazing the small birthmark beneath her nipple. Suddenly he tensed. *It couldn't be.*

"When were you born?" he demanded, pulling back.

"On May 28th. I'm twenty-seven years old."

The Master's blood ran cold. "Where is your mother?"

"She died when I was five," Danielle answered, her voice betraying more confusion than fear.

"Were you adopted?"

"I don't think so. If I was, my parents never told me."

The Master regarded Danielle, deciding what to do with her. His mind reeled. He searched for a sign.

Finally, he went to a phone and barked orders to his waiting minions, "Take her back to her cell and give her real food, not just bread and water. And dress her in something less revealing."

The Guardians came quickly to retrieve Danielle. When they had unbound her and led her away, the Master stood alone in his assembly room, mystified.

Why had fate dealt him such a cruel hand?

Chapter 55

DEEP INSIDE THE NETWORK OF TUNNELS THAT RAN beneath the Old City, Josh and Aaron puzzled over the large stone slab that blocked their path. Josh noticed a small opening to the right of the rock, where the ground met the stone, but it appeared too small for anyone to crawl through.

"The Guardians can't possibly have escaped through here," Aaron said. "This rock hasn't been moved in decades, maybe centuries."

Josh pressed his hands to the stone, trying futilely to make it budge. But an odd feeling crept over him, a kind of knowing in his cells that told him there was something very special on the other side. A voice deep inside him whispered, *This is the place.* What did that mean? Did it have something to do with the Guardians? Josh searched his soul for an answer. No. The message meant something else.

"Aaron," Josh said softly, "let's not waste our time here. We need to concentrate on finding the Guardians' escape route. This isn't it."

Aaron looked quizzically at Josh for a moment, and then nodded. Halfway down the tunnel they were met by three security men carrying pickaxes and crowbars.

Josh held up a hand to stop them. "You can turn back. We've changed our plans. Have you had any luck finding the escape route?"

"No," one of the men said, "but we found this." He

handed Aaron what appeared to be a prayer book, probably left behind by accident in the Guardians' haste to evacuate.

"Let me see that," Josh said. He flipped open the worn leather cover and saw that it was a Bible—only the entire Old Testament and most of the New were missing. The book contained only the works of Paul and a small portion of Luke.

"Over here," called an excited policeman from somewhere deeper inside. "It's another way out."

Josh, Aaron, and the others headed back into the main tunnel, then followed the voices until they came to another narrow passageway that veered off to the left toward a second staircase. At the top of the stairs was yet another thick wooden door, which this time opened not onto a dead end, but into a small, familiar chapel. They were in the Church of the Holy Sepulcher.

"It's easy to see why the Guardians didn't attract attention here," Aaron said, alluding to the fanatics' priestly garments. "But how would they get the hostages out without being noticed?"

"Maybe the hostages weren't kept in this hideout," Josh offered.

"Or maybe they had already been killed." As soon as he had spoken Aaron realized what his words would mean to Josh.

"I know that Danielle is important to you," he said, putting a hand on Josh's shoulder. "And I hate to give you bad news…but I would be surprised if she was still alive."

Josh's heart told him Aaron was wrong.

One of the security men walked up to them and reported that they had a few of the store's employees upstairs, ready to be interviewed. Aaron and Josh retraced their steps to the store, where they found three frightened women being detained by two security officers.

Aaron addressed all three women, taking no time for pleasantries. "What do you know about the priests who convened in the rooms downstairs?"

"I don't know anything," said one of the women, her voice shaky. "I saw the holy men come and go—they own the store, so I figured they were supposed to be here. They disappeared behind the drapes and I didn't ask questions. Sometimes I saw them come out and other times I didn't. They never spoke to any of us."

"Have any of you ever been downstairs?" Aaron asked.

"We are forbidden to go behind the curtains," the oldest woman said. "We were told that only the priests were allowed."

"Did you notice if anyone accompanied the priests recently?"

The youngest woman raised her head. "I was working earlier in the week and I recall them bringing in someone who looked ill. He may have been another priest. I wasn't sure, but I thought that the holy men were going to help him."

Josh stepped into the interrogation. "Have you seen them bring in anyone else, a woman perhaps?"

"We have many young women who come in here, but they're all shoppers."

The others nodded in agreement.

Aaron asked a few more questions, but it was clear that the women knew nothing about what went on beneath them. After a while, he sent them on their way.

The police continued their routine, gathering evidence and questioning the owners of the neighboring shops. When the phone rang, Josh picked it up, expecting to hear Giuseppe on the other end of the line.

"I want the scroll," demanded a deep voice. "No tricks, no fakes, and no ambush. We see every move you make, as you now know, but I am offering you one last chance. We still have the hostages. On Monday, we will make an exchange. You give us the scroll and we'll hand over one of your friends. In twenty-four hours, if we're satisfied with what we've received, we will give you another hostage. As for the third, go to the Church of St. Mary Magdalene on the Mount of Olives. I've left you a little consolation prize beneath the thirteenth pew. Do as you are told and you will hear from us tomorrow with the location for our trade."

The line went dead.

Chapter 56

THERE WAS MUCH TO BE DONE, BUT JOSH KNEW THAT his body would betray him if he didn't get at least a little bit of sleep. He lay down planning only to nap and instead fell into a deep, dreamless sleep. A few hours later, he was awakened by the sound of the doorbell.

Aaron entered the room quickly, not bothering with the formality of being invited in. "Our men retrieved the package from the church."

"What was there?" Josh asked, still groggy.

Aaron held up a small zip-lock bag filled with ashes.

"Whose..."

"It's nearly impossible to know," Aaron said soberly.

Josh's heart sank. Another person had been killed because of the scroll—but he refused to believe that it was Danielle. That was little consolation for him now, though, since he knew that the ashes had to belong to either Father Andre or Alon.

"It came with a note attached," Aaron said, handing the letter to Josh.

Ashes to ashes and dirt to dirt...I've done you the courtesy of delivering a tidier package this time. Next time, however, I may not be so kind.

The time for games has passed. Follow my instructions to the letter or the other hostages will die far less pleasant deaths. The scroll will be mine, one way or the other; the conditions are up to you.

243

Josh looked up at Aaron, disgusted. "We can't trust a word that this guy says."

"I know we can't. Unfortunately, we don't have any leverage if we want any chance of getting the hostages back alive. He's holding all the cards."

Josh felt more frustrated than ever before. The fanatics kept raising the stakes and Josh felt powerless to counter their actions.

"There's more," Aaron said. "We received another phone call. It had to do with the rules he refers to in the note. They want you to deliver the scroll. They made it clear that they wouldn't accept anyone else."

"It sounds like a death sentence."

"At this point, I have no idea what to tell you. All I know is that there are still two lives at stake. We once traded four hundred terrorists for the bodies of three of our slain soldiers. Even the remains of our dead are important to us. We must find a way to rescue those hostages."

Josh's mind whirred. One of the hostages was Danielle. He was certain of this. Aaron was right—they needed to find a way to rescue whoever was left. "Are there any archaeologists at the IAA who you trust?"

"*Most* of them are trustworthy."

"Choose two who are the most competent at detecting fake artifacts and get them over to the IAA as quickly as possible. Don't tell them that the fake jar and scroll are imitations. Ask them to give their opinions regarding authenticity. If it passes with them, there's a good chance we can fool the Guardians. That's step one."

"What's step two?"

"I need a laptop computer, since mine was stolen. I also want background data—as much as you can get—on the scroll's research team, including parental background information. Can that be done before 8:00 tonight?"

"What are you thinking about doing?"

"It's not worth telling you unless it pans out. Otherwise, it's just more speculation—and we've all had more than enough of that.

In less than an hour, Aaron's people had delivered a new laptop to the condo. Josh familiarized himself with the machine, logged into the Internet, and went to work. He began by typing the word "hate" into a search engine, and got a staggering 13,000,000 hits. He'd have to narrow the search. Next, he typed in "hate groups," but there were still over 2,500,000 listings. He searched for "Guardians" and narrowed it down to 200,000 sites. Then, finally, when he typed in "Jewish hate groups" and "Guardians" together, the number dropped dramatically. He slogged through these links for about an hour and a half, finding nothing but dead ends. But when he came across an icon of a serpent wrapped around a cross, Josh knew that he had found what he was looking for. He clicked the link and was brought to a low-budget site for a group called the "Guardians of the Truth."

The homepage alone was a temple of hate, filled with stereotypical lies and bigoted propaganda, some of it so vile that it validated the Christian doctrine of sin and evil. If Satan existed, Josh thought, he would have been a regular visitor to the site. He may even have written some of the articles himself.

THE GUARDIANS

THE ONLY TRUE CHRISTIANS

Do you want to know the real Secrets of Christianity? We are in posession of never revealed information and future prophecies and events that will happen. We have members all over the world, but to join you must fill out a questionnaire. After filling out the questionnaire and we have verified your information, if we think you're qualified, we will contact you by e-mail. Our members are male and must be willing to be celibate.

We invite you while you're visiting our site to browse some of our favorite books and articles. Click on the links for excerpts.

Books:
The Protocols of the Elders of Zion (written by one of our members more than 120 years ago)
Mein Kampf

Articles:
The Moslem plague
Buddhism's Enlightenment is the path to Hell.
Who the real chosen people are (they're not the Jews)
Who Killed Kennedy and why?
Why traditional Christian orthodox groups misinterpret the Bible and will never reach heaven
Why Hate is the most important part of love
Holocaust, an important solution to world population control
The Jews and Moslems are the offspring of Satan.
Iraq—a good start
The Inquisition didn't go far enough
How Hindus missed the boat and when they die, their pyre won't be their only fire.
5 Popes we loved

5 Popes who burn in Hell
The one hundred who control the world and
lead us on the path of moral destruction
Why Hitler failed.
The real Paul
Why atheists are destroying the world
Why Jesus wasn't kosher.

Links:
None—ours is the only site where the truth is told.

Chat:
Click here to communicate with us or others that share our views.

Josh scrutinized the site, looking for clues. He scanned some of the articles, but most were just the typical junk found on hate sites, filled with lunatic rants and littered with typos and philosophical holes. It just didn't add up. They'd been dealing with a powerful group of highly intelligent, highly organized fanatics, but this site made them look like raving buffoons.

Josh was about to give up. He had read as much as he could take and could feel the blood hammering in his head. As his rage swelled, Josh felt himself slipping into the very emotion that the Guardian thrived on—hatred. He wouldn't let himself contribute to their mission.

But then he spotted something that captured his curiosity. There were several articles written by someone who called himself the Master. Josh opened the first article, a diatribe, and quickly found that The Master was a non-partisan hater. He hated Jews, Muslims, Protestants, and even liberal Catholics. But he was also calculating and articulate...which sounded familiar. Josh looked for clues in the article, but all he could find were venomous words and bigoted ideology. The man clearly had cancer of the soul, but what really frightened Josh was his obvious charisma and power of persuasion. Josh couldn't help thinking of Hitler, and for the first time he realized what he was really up against. This was bigger than the handful of people who had already suffered so much since his discovery of the scroll. It was even bigger than the love he felt for Danielle—something he wouldn't have believed possible but now he was even willing to sacrifice his life for. Josh realized that if they weren't stopped, the Guardians would unleash their perversion onto the world, leaving nothing but ashes in their wake. He couldn't let that happen.

Josh closed his eyes and tried to relax. He wouldn't be able to intellectualize his way through this, and knew that meditation was his best option for accessing the higher wisdom he needed. He tried to envision the staircase, to count the descending steps as he had so many times before. But his mind's eye was blank. He saw nothing but blackness and one faint, intermittent flash of light. Josh took a long, deep breath, concentrating on the sensation of the air as it passed in through his nostrils and back out again. He kept breathing in this way for several more minutes, and soon the vision became clearer: it wasn't a light at all, but an ordinary blinking cursor. With a flash of insight, Josh was suddenly pulled up and out of his meditative state. When his eyes opened, they were pointed directly to the "chat" link at the bottom of the computer screen.

It felt silly, but Josh clicked on the button and the page began to load. It was a regular message board, with hundreds of threads. Josh looked at one of the most recent ones, from someone who called himself "Bones."

We're close to getting the item. I'm still @ home
and look forward to hearing from u.

Beneath that message was a response of sorts, but it was
nothing but a series of numbers.

24 12 14 22 7 12 19 22 26 23 10 6 26 9 7 22 9 8

As he continued to read, Josh saw other messages in
numeric codes. The Guardians were using their web site to
communicate. If he could break the code, Josh might discover their plans or even their new hideout.

It was yet another puzzle to solve, and fast.

Chapter 57

DANIELLE SAT IN THE SMALL, WINDOWLESS ROOM THAT served as her prison. Her conditions had improved, but one thing was absolutely the same: she was locked in, with no way to get out. Danielle did the only thing that seemed to help her get through these hours—she thought about Josh. They'd shared so little time together, yet Danielle felt a connection with him she had never felt before. She replayed the moments in her mind, recreating every detail of their conversations, their walks, and their lovemaking. The one thing she avoided thinking about was the obvious reality that their time together was likely over.

Her new captor was not like the old ones. Danielle knew that she wouldn't be able to trick the Master into setting her free. As desperately as she longed to be with Josh again, she understood her situation all too well: she was going to die here.

Danielle heard the rattling of a key in the lock and a guard entered her cell, interrupting her thoughts.

"You must have pleased the Master," the masked man said. "Your dinner tonight is more than bread and water."

Danielle stared at the large man. Her gaze seemed to upset him.

"What's your name?" she asked, reaching blindly for any chance she could get.

"You are not supposed to speak," the man said, his voice filled with scorn. "I could beat you for that."

"The Master would kill you for touching me," she said,

not sure where her bravado had come from or where it was headed.

The guard slapped Danielle hard across the face. She was stunned both by the force of the blow and the fact that he had hit her at all. She held a hand to her cheek.

"Don't think you're special, whore. The Master likes to play with his victims. If you think he's going to be nice to you, you're a fool."

The guard approached her menacingly and pinched her face between the fingers of his huge hand. "Maybe he'll even let me have a little fun with you before you die."

Something snapped in Danielle at that moment. She couldn't take the humiliation or the domination any longer. She turned her head quickly and bit the man's hand. He howled and pulled back.

"You'll pay for that, bitch!" the man shouted, striking her with a blow much harder than the first one. He hit her again and then again.

After that, Danielle stopped feeling the punches.

"Stop at once!" the Master roared when he entered the room to find the guard beating Danielle.

The man turned and shrank back immediately. "She provoked me, Master."

The Master threw the guard against the wall. "If that is the case, then you are far too easily provoked. Perhaps this job is ill-suited to you. Perhaps you need something that requires less...thinking. Let me make one thing clear to you right now. If you ever again touch her, you will experience Hell well before I actually deliver you there."

The Master gazed down at Danielle, who lay bloody on the floor.

"Leave us alone and get a medic in here."

The guard left as quickly, and the Master knelt, taking

the unconscious Danielle in his arms. He checked for a pulse. When he felt one, he sighed and just held her.

When the medic arrived with a gurney, the Master laid her gently down, brushing the hair away from the gash on her forehead. The Master pointed at Danielle. "If she dies, you will too. Do you understand?"

The medic nodded, the blood draining from his face.

Chapter 58

Aaron returned to Josh's place later that evening with a large black briefcase.

"I've brought you the background material you requested," he announced as he set it down on the kitchen table and opened the clasps. It was filled with file folders and documents.

"That was fast," Josh said. "I'm impressed. Did you look at this stuff?"

Aaron shook his head. "I didn't, I just received it."

"Can you stay here a while so we can go through this together?"

"As long as you have coffee, I'm with you."

"I just made a pot," Josh told him, grateful for the company. "I have a feeling I'm going to be up all night."

Josh poured cups for both of them and handed one to Aaron.

For the next hour, they reviewed the files Aaron had brought with him. After going through countless pages, Josh's intuition spiked again. "There's some interesting info in here," he said, rubbing his eyes. *Investigate everyone*, he thought. "I still need to check the backgrounds of a few more people, though. I want the genealogy records of Father Andre, Alon, his mother and father, Moshe, his deceased wife, and Danielle." Josh had a hunch about Moshe's relationship to Danielle—something that could have profound implications on everything that was happening. "How quickly can you get it?"

"How about right now," Aaron said, opening his cell phone and calling his office. He asked them to contact museum Bet Hatfutzot Genealogy's research center in Tel Aviv, which had data on over 3,000 Jewish communities worldwide. Then Aaron called another agency that had records of every adoption made in Israel since 1948.

"I'm also trying to get information on the Christian souvenir shop in the Old City," he told Josh. "My source has records that go back before 1948. Meanwhile, Jonathan's mother called and said she hasn't seen him since he left their home early yesterday morning. She said he always calls her to check in. Before I came over here, my agency checked with local police and hospitals, but they had no knowledge of his whereabouts."

"I forgot to add Jonathan to the list I gave you earlier," Josh said.

"Don't worry, I've already included him."

Josh looked down at the files again. "Aaron, I don't think we should do the hostage exchange; it's a guaranteed failure. We need to come up with another plan."

"I'm beginning to feel the same way."

"When I received the laptop you sent over, I searched the Web trying to find some clues or information about the Guardians. I think I found their actual Web page. They're using their message board to share information in the form of numerical code. If I can break it, it might lead us somewhere."

"Do you know anything about code breaking?" Aaron asked, clearly in doubt.

Josh reassured him. "To some degree what I do for a living is code breaking."

"All the same, my agency has some of the best code breakers in the world."

For a reason that wasn't clear to him, Josh still felt some reluctance about sharing everything with Aaron. "If I can't break it by 8:00 tomorrow morning, then you can give it to them."

Aaron stood. "I'll see you tomorrow morning at eight, then."

Thanks for the vote of confidence, Josh thought as he watched Aaron leave. He turned back to the files. The information here could be helpful. Something told him that the information in the code might net more, though.

It was time to get back to work.

Josh worked late into the night to decipher the Guardian's message to "Bones." He scrutinized the series of numbers, attempting to relate them with each other by starting with a simple alphabetical code: A=1, B=2, C=3, and so forth. As expected, this approach led nowhere.

Could the numbers relate to a foreign language? Could the message be in Hebrew? That alphabet had only twenty-two letters. Classical Latin was another possibility with its twenty-three letters. What if the letters were reversed, where A=26 and Z=1? He tried that and, stunningly, it worked.

24 12 14 22 7 12 19 22 26 23 10 6 26 9 7 22 9 8
C O M E T O H E A D Q U A R T E R S

That was much too easy. Was it possible that the Guardians' idea of a code was this simple-minded? Certainly, he'd cracked this message. But was it here for a reason he didn't understand?

He looked at other messages, hoping they would lead to more clues. *Come to headquarters* didn't mean much by itself, especially since he had no idea where headquarters was. None of the other messages translated the same way, though. Their codes were much more complex, and two more hours of attempted decryption brought him nothing.

Josh hit the back button and returned to the site's home page. What else could he learn here? He moused over to the History tab in the navigation bar. Josh could have sworn that it hadn't been there before; but the phone rang before he could follow the link.

"Josh, this is Aaron."

"Any new information?"

"We have a new incident. Do you remember Steve Fishman?"

"Yeah, of course. He's the head of Artifacts Dating at the IAA."

"He's dead. We found his body around 11 p.m. in a ditch near the Old City walls. His corpse was in pieces. Only his head was intact. There was a message in his mouth that read 'traitor.'

Josh felt his body go slack. Another death directly attributable to his discovery. "Why would they want to kill Fishman?" he asked.

"I don't know," said Aaron, who seemed as confused as Josh was. "He was a quiet guy, the kind people never notice. I'm going to check his background and get as much data as I can. My guess is that we're going to find some connection between Steve Fishman and the Guardians."

"Wait," Josh said. "Steve reported that the scroll was authentic, based on his C14 testing. Later, he reported that a second test using a different type of radiocarbon process was inconclusive. Do you think there's a connection?"

"Anything is possible. If we had a better sense of what the Guardians really wanted, we might be able to understand what they're doing here."

"I'm working on that," Josh assured him.

"So are we."

They hung up and Josh went back to the laptop. He had no time to mourn for Steve Fishman. The only way to honor his life was to prevent his killers from accomplishing their goals. Right now, that meant going back to the laptop. He clicked the History link on the Guardian's site.

We are the only true Christians. Our brotherhood traces directly back to Paul, and knows Christianity's most closely guarded secrets, revealed to us by Paul, our first Master, declared so twenty years after his death. Since Paul, our sect has had many great Masters who have led us for nearly 2,000 years. During that time our brotherhood has been the keepers of the great secret. Some of our Masters were well-known men like Marcion, Innocent IV, and Torquemada. Others expressed their greatness more quietly.

At the council of Nicea in A.D. 325, our eighth Master was one of the attending bishops. It was Emperor Constantine who called the bishops together in Nicea, and it was there that Christian doctrines were canonized.

Members of our organization were originally part of the Catholic Church, but broke away from it. For more than a thousand years our members pretended to be Catholics while practicing our own beliefs in secret. Most of the time we were in good standing, particularly at times when they did the right thing: suppression of non-believers.

More than four hundred years ago, the Church discovered our existence and declared us heretics and we were excommunicated. Our members went underground to avoid being burned at the stake. We changed the name of our group to the Guardians, protectors of the true faith.

The day will come when we will take over the Church and cleanse the earth of all evil. The only survivors will be the true believers.

Our organization has members all over the world. Some of the world's most powerful and influential men are our Brothers. They maintain their secrecy so that the Elders of Zion do not kill them. The center of our faith is not Rome, but the true center of Christianity, the Holy Land. There our Master rules with the Chosen Twelve.

Our members take vows of secrecy. If they betray their vows they are punished or killed. We must protect our brotherhood. Read our articles, and if you share our beliefs, contact us through e-mail and when our revolution begins, you'll be part of it.

This copy was a good deal more literate than the rest of the site—a fact that only reinforced Josh's hunch that the page had only recently been uploaded. But why? His eyes dropped to the left-hand corner of the page, where he saw the image of a black crucifix with a snake wrapped around it. He had definitely seen the image before but, now that he could study it more closely, he was able to interpret its more subtle details. The snake was a symbol of rebirth and the icon of several pagan religions. This particular snake was an Israeli Saw-Scale Viper, one of the most aggressive and deadly serpents in the Middle East, and most likely the one mentioned in the Bible as the Fiery Flying Serpent. What did this all mean?

Josh read through the Guardians' self-proclaimed history again. If this was a secret organization, why would they reveal so much information to the casual observer? There had to be a reason and, on some level, Josh felt that it directly related to him.

The only question was how.

Chapter 59

THE CHOSEN TWELVE HAD CONGREGATED IN THE candle-lit basement, along with 20 other influential members of the sect. Excitement and anxiety filled the air as they mingled and spoke amongst themselves, eagerly awaiting the arrival of their leader. But as the Master entered the theater and strode to the altar, the room went suddenly still.

"Welcome my brothers," said the man in the serpent's head mask.

The Guardians bowed deeply and then took their seats.

"I have important matters to discuss with you. It has been brought to my attention that a few among you have questioned some of our recent actions. Let it be known that I do not condone indiscreet acts of violence. Those who were killed stood in the way of our holy path and had to be destroyed. Nothing can be allowed to prevent us from fulfilling our mission. The word of God must come before our individual feelings or desires. This is the duty with which you have been charged.

"To kill the non-believer is to reaffirm our faith, and to reap a spiritual reward. One day soon the world will be united in our beliefs, and the survivors will bask in the glory of the light and the One who returns to make it shine eternally."

The Master stepped forward on the dais, raising his clenched fists into the air. "For most of our history we've sat quietly and watched as the violence and evil surrounded us. Did we partake?"

"No," the members shouted in unison.

"Passivity didn't work and so we decided to take action. Some of our actions are indeed violent, but they are essential to the attainment of our goals. Our brothers before us engaged in savage deeds, which some people deplored. But the results were glorious—the deaths of thousands of non-believers. Our adversaries are convinced that we are consumed with hatred. They are ignorant and know not the greatness of our sacred truth: we are filled with love. It is our love that inspires us to change the world. They are unaware that it all began with our first Master, the blessed Paul, whose secrets we guard and cherish."

At that the crowd rose and broke into a thunderous cheer.

"As you know," shouted the Master, calling the meeting back to order, "part of my responsibility is to assure the succession of our future leaders. One day my own son will become the seventy-eighth Master of our line. But even now we must prepare for the greater vision. A privileged few among you will be selected to witness the coming ritual of sexual union, which will ensure future purity of our line.

"But now," shouted the Master, charging to the front of the stage, "we are threatened like never before. Recent events have led to a confrontation with powerful forces of evil. We must prepare for the great battle that lies ahead, one in which some of you will sacrifice your lives. Remember that there is no greater honor than to die on God's battlefield. The true martyr is guaranteed a place in Heaven."

The Master leapt up onto the altar. "We beseech, oh Lord, send back the Spirit of your Son...."

His followers dropped to their knees, weeping in ecstasy as they joined him in prayer:

Let us cleanse the Earth with blood and fire,
Let us make ready for the hour of His return.

Chapter 60

In many ways, Josh felt as if he was back at the beginning. He had more clues, some of them provided by the Guardians themselves; but he knew no more about their location than he ever had. He also had no idea whether Danielle was still alive. The only thing keeping him from going mad with worry was an inexplicable faith that he would see her again.

Back in his room at the condominium, Josh sought answers in the scroll. Though almost nothing else seemed clear at the moment, he felt certain that there was something in the text that would help him understand what was going on around him—if only he could translate the rest of it and dig deeper.

The first step was to enter a light meditative state. This had worked for Josh in the past when he needed to recall huge chunks of information that he'd "photographed" in his mind. He closed his eyes and started down the stairway to his subconscious; but he found the descent slow, as though he was heading in the wrong direction on an escalator.

Too many thoughts crowded his mind. This was a time for action, not repose. Yet Josh knew in his heart that he *couldn't* act—not until he had some sense of direction. His surveillance in the Old City might have given him the broadest sense of where the Guardians hid, but unless he got extremely lucky, he'd never find the actual place in time.

Ribbono shel Olam.

The words sprang to his mind as though someone else had put them there. The words had extraordinary power. They had led him once to a sense of connection with the divine he'd never experienced before. Yet in the time since Danielle had gone missing, he'd lost track of them.

Where would they lead him now?

Using the Hebrew words as a mantra, Josh focused all attention on the sound:

Ribbono shel Olam.
Ribbono shel Olam.
Ribbono shel Olam.

Remarkably, all distractions slipped away. Josh felt himself pulled toward something. He had no idea where he was going, but he allowed himself to be carried without question.

Abruptly, his journey stopped and a page from the scroll appeared before him. He read the Aramaic words, but unlike before, the translation came to him almost instantaneously, as though understanding the language was not an act of scholarship, but the expression of his mother tongue.

I fear that there are those who will misinterpret my message and attempt to use it for their own gain. These forces have corrupted my teachings. Be wary of them for they will try to destroy all those who oppose them. Tell my story and the truths that it reveals. There is unfinished work that must be completed.

Forces will attempt to destroy the new messenger. Beware for these forces may have the face of righteousness. This face is only a disguise. It is a mask even unto the demon himself.

He who is unclean of spirit will pervert my teachings, yet seek refuge in my home. He is not welcome there and must be cast out.

The words faded and Josh found himself fully awake. *There are those who will misinterpret my message and attempt to use it for their own gain.* This had to be a prophetic vision of the rise of the Guardians. Jesus had known instinctively what the world learned many times over the next two millennia—that great evil could be done in the name of religion.

But what did he mean when he said, "He will pervert my teachings, yet seek refuge in my home"? Those words had been written before the establishment of the Church, before the Christians came to think of the sanctuary as God's house. What did that tell Josh that he didn't already know? Jesus lived in Nazareth. Was that a clue? Even if it were, he needed a more precise location.

Where was Jesus' home in Nazareth? No one seemed to know. Few of the actual locations of Jesus' life were marked in any way. Josh searched his memory. He'd studied this area so carefully. What had he learned that he could use now?

Another image emerged in his mind: the dome of the Basilica of the Annunciation. It was a church in the middle of Nazareth, erected on the spot where legend held that the Angel Gabriel appeared to Mary and revealed to her that she would bear God's child.

Could this be what Jesus meant by his home?

Could this be where Josh needed to go?

Chapter 61

JOSH TRIED TO EAT, BUT HE HAD NO APPETITE AT ALL. Earlier, he'd tried to sleep, but that hadn't worked either. Every time he closed his eyes, the image of the Basilica of the Annunciation flamed into his head. This was more than just a hunch. It sounded crazy, but Josh sensed that the scroll—maybe even the scroll's author—was speaking to him directly. A few weeks ago, he would have scoffed at such a thing. Now, though, the evidence was all too compelling.

Aaron wasn't answering his cell phone or the office line at the IAA. Intellectually, Josh knew that it was early morning, and that Aaron had the right to a night's rest. But Josh's instincts protested loudly; every minute they stood still was a minute they gave over to the Guardians—a minute that could cost Danielle her life.

Josh considered going to the basilica on his own to begin the search, but he was rational enough to realize how foolish that would be. Recent circumstances notwithstanding, he wasn't a detective. So Josh did the only thing he could—he waited.

Josh paced the living room of the condominium, too restless to relax. Simply making it to 8:00 a.m. was difficult; but each of the twenty minutes that followed was excruciating. Finally, the doorbell rang.

"I apologize for running late," Aaron said. "But it was worth it. I have some important information to tell you. Do you have any of that good, strong coffee?"

Josh pointed the way. "It's in the kitchen. I made a pot, but I'm not having any. The last thing I need this morning is caffeine."

They both headed for the kitchen.

"What do you know about the Basilica of the Annunciation?" Josh asked, getting to the point.

Aaron looked at him, confused, while he poured his coffee. "It's built on a sacred site in Nazareth. Why do you ask?"

"It's where the Guardians are hiding."

Aaron stopped dead, holding the coffee pot aloft. "How do you know that?"

"I got a tip."

"From who?" Aaron asked, unnerved.

"A very reliable source."

Aaron nodded slowly and put down the coffee pot. "That makes some sense."

"I think so," said Josh. It seemed odd that Aaron didn't prod him further for details about his source, but he appreciated not needing to argue his case.

Aaron took a sip of coffee and closed his eyes for a moment, as though willing the stimulant into his bloodstream. "It makes sense because early this morning Jonathan's car was found on the outskirts of Nazareth. Our investigators believe that Jonathan passed information to the Guardians concerning the IAA and the scroll."

"How did they reach that conclusion?" asked Josh, disappointed. He had grown to like Jonathan...or, at least, he thought he had.

"He's been under surveillance recently. He was observed on numerous occasions in the Old City's Christian Quarter, engaging in long conversations with priests."

If that was true, Josh wondered, *then why had it taken them so long to become suspicious?* Sometimes the process seemed intentionally obtuse. "What else?" he pressed.

"Last week a large sum of money was deposited into his checking account. There were also at least three instances in which he told people that he was going clubbing in Tel Aviv, but didn't. We suspect that in actuality he attended Guardian meetings on those nights."

Josh called up the image of Jonathan's flaming red hair and walrus mustache. It was hard to believe that someone who looked so jovial could be so evil. Still, Josh knew by now that appearances meant nothing. "That's one leak," he said. "Now we need to find the other."

"We'll find it."

"Have you started your investigations in the area where you found Jonathan's car?"

Aaron looked at his watch. "Yes," he said, "they began a little over an hour ago."

"I want to go to the Basilica of the Annunciation."

"We will. You need to see this first. We went to the museum early this morning and investigated Steven Fishman's office. We found a letter in his desk."

Aaron handed the handwritten sheet to Josh

If you are reading this, then I am already dead. Know that my death was not an accident or suicide, regardless of how things may seem. The truth is that, for reasons that now seem foolish, I made the mistake of accepting $25,000 to invalidate the scroll's early dating tests. At the time I didn't believe that my actions would have any real impact. It was only later, when the fanatics revealed their true agenda that I realized what I had done. I am tormented by the knowledge that I have contributed to their evil scheme. Only two things matter now: First, I am sorrier than you can know for having lied. Every test I conducted proved beyond any doubt

that the scroll is from the Second Temple Period.
Second, the Guardians must be stopped. I only hope
that you have found this note in time.

"There are traitors everywhere," said Aaron.

Josh looked up at him. "That may be, but I don't think Fishman was one of them. His downfall was nothing more than naïveté and simple, human greed."

Aaron sipped his coffee, nonplussed. "I have even more interesting information," he said. "We discovered that Moshe is not Danielle's biological father. She was adopted."

Josh wasn't surprised. "When and how did her adoptive mother die?" he asked.

"Sophie died of breast cancer when Danielle was five."

Josh considered this for a moment, and then the question struck him. "Who are Danielle's real parents?"

"The adoption agency declared there were no records of her birth parents. She was dropped off at the agency only hours old, by a man who claimed to have found her abandoned in an alley."

Josh sat silently, thoughts racing through his head. The answers to many of his questions were getting clearer, and Josh knew that he was close to solving the rest.

"Josh, here's another surprise. Danielle and Alon have the same birthday."

"How would you know that?"

"Danielle was brought to the agency on May twenty eighth, 1977. Our records show that Alon was born on the same day—of the same year."

"Could they be twins?" Josh asked.

"That's a big leap. Obviously they weren't the only two children born in Israel that day. Still, it's something to consider."

"Who's Alon's father?"

"His name is Alexander Paul, a successful businessman

with excellent international connections. His family has lived in the area since before modern Israel existed. They claimed to have been here for more than a hundred years. Unfortunately, we do not have Mr. Paul's birth records. All we really know is from his bio, which states that he and his family are secular Jews, like much of our population."

"I've met Paul. He spends a lot of time around the IAA."

"He's a serious patron of the Jerusalem museum, but comes around to see us when he wants the VIP treatment. He likes to be in the know."

Josh's head was spinning with so much new information. Josh knew that it all tied together somehow, but the meaning eluded him.

"Are you going to question Paul?" he asked.

"Our people will see him later this morning."

"And what about the hostage exchange?"

"I'm going to find a way to stall the Guardians until tomorrow afternoon," Aaron told him. "If your tip about the basilica is accurate, we won't have to deal with a hostage exchange. If we do go through with it, though, we have a plan that will take you out of harm's way."

"What do you mean?"

"You're not the one who is going to deliver the fake scroll."

Josh put up a hand to stop the conversation. "I don't want anyone taking my place. I can't in good conscience allow anyone to put his or her life in danger. That's happened enough already. The Guardians want me to deliver the scroll and, if any person is to bring them the scroll, that person will be me."

Aaron watched Josh carefully with an expression that Josh couldn't completely interpret. "We'll discuss this further if it becomes necessary. I'm hoping *no one* will have to deliver the scroll."

"Let's go to the basilica, then."

"Not yet. Let my people run their investigation first."

Josh felt his blood pressure rising. "No more waiting, Aaron. I can't keep doing nothing while the Guardians have Danielle."

"You aren't doing nothing. You're coming with me to the IAA. In the meantime, I'll send an advance crew to the basilica. If there's something to find, believe me, they'll find it."

Josh knew there was logic in what Aaron was saying. Why, then, did it make him so uneasy?

Chapter 62

AT THE GUARDIANS' HEADQUARTERS IN NAZARETH, THE Master waited for the arrival of Father Andre, eager to engage his captive. He needed these moments of entertainment to keep himself sharp.

"Hello, Father," the Master said as Andre entered his office, escorted by two formidable guards. "I hope you're in the mood for a little debate."

Father Andre's brow crinkled and his mouth set in something approximating a sneer. He may have been frightened out of his mind, but he still had some fire in him. "What kind of debate?"

"How about religion?" said the Master, leaning forward in his chair. "I can't wait to hear how you defend your beliefs. Are you afraid? If you'd prefer to decline, I can always kill you instead."

"Now there's a choice," scoffed Andre. "You're going to kill me anyway, aren't you?"

The Master shrugged in mockery. "Let's make it interesting, shall we? I will give you a chance to save your life. All you have to do is win our debate."

"What happens then?"

"I'll spare your life and release you, of course. If you lose, I'll make sure you get the last rites. But if you turn me down..."

Father Andre interrupted, not needing to hear more.

"Do I have the freedom to speak my mind without any censorship from you?"

The Master straightened his back, delighted that the priest was taking the bait. "You can say whatever you want and I, as a religious man, will keep my promise."

"You have a twisted definition of religion," Andre accused.

The Master shrugged. "Let's not quibble over such things when we can have a more spirited discussion instead."

Andre laughed joylessly. "I don't want to debate you."

"Why...because you're afraid you'll lose?"

"No, because you're a madman."

"Clearly," said the Master, "you don't understand my point of view. How easily you must sleep at night, tucked in beneath your moral platitudes. You call me a madman, a crazed fanatic, and that is all you see because the truth is too complex for your feel-good religious outlook. I am a man of genius and generosity."

Andre scowled. "I never would call you generous."

"I've done more good for the world than you ever have."

Andre laughed.

The Master stammered with rage. "Don't mock me or I will kill you right now."

The blood drained from Andre's face. "If you're not a madman, then why do you do the things you do?"

"I do God's work," the Master said. "Everything I do is for the betterment of mankind."

Andre's mouth dropped and the Master chuckled.

"I see that you don't understand me. Yes, I manipulate a group of men whose brains aren't their greatest asset. They serve a purpose and they have a role." The Master moved from his chair and circled Andre. "I am committed to the truth—a truth that has been distorted by the lies of those who wrote the Bible and used it for their own purposes."

Andre twitched with anger as the Master continued calmly. "My work is to destroy not only the evil in the world, but also its major cause, the false god of the Old Testament—the Demiurge—who created our planet after falling from the grace of the true Creator God."

"The God of the Old Testament false?" said Andre cynically. "I doubt that very much."

But the Master was unimpressed. "You have been brainwashed by the Catholic Church," he said, waving away his opponent's ignorance with a flick of his hand.

"So you do evil in the name of the true God?" Andre asked, disbelieving.

"I do not do evil. I do what is necessary to glorify God and defeat the forces that control mankind." From inside his mask, the Master felt his eyes tearing. He rarely had the opportunity to discuss his mission with a man as learned as Andre and it returned him to the full force of his convictions. "I take righteous action," he bellowed, "what do you do? It is I who will be rewarded by the Creator God and his son, Jesus Christ. It is I who suffer for the sake of the truth."

"What is the truth?" Andre asked, intrigued by the very horror of what he was hearing.

The Master took a step toward the priest. "Father, you are a true man of faith. It's funny, isn't it, how one can be both learned and ignorant at the same time? Still, you are not to blame for your limited beliefs. As a fellow lover of mankind, I respect you enough to reveal to you the truth you seek: Jesus was not a man, but a purely spiritual being that came to earth to save the world. He never died on the cross, because Christ was not born of flesh and blood. He was an entirely spiritual being."

"I've read about that theory in some of the Gnostic literature," Andre said. "But how does that justify hatred and violence?"

"We incorporate some Gnostic teachings, but we are not Gnostics. Tell me, Father Andre, do you think the New Testament tells all of Paul's stories?"

"Absolutely."

The Master shook his head sadly. "You're so misguided. Not all of Paul's letters were included."

"What makes you an authority?" Father Andre asked sharply. "You and your group are a disgrace."

"Silence!" shouted the Master, his patience wearing thin. "I am trying to help you, and yet you insist on remaining ignorant. We are the only true Christians. It would do you well to know the real history of your beloved, heretical Church. For hundreds of years we survived by pretending to be devout Catholics. We practiced our own beliefs in secret in order to escape the sentence meted out to others who opposed the sham religion of the ruling class. Groups like the Cathars were not so fortunate; their members burned in agony at the stake…all in the name of your God of compassion. But the time came when we could no longer condone the immorality of the Popes. At first we had looked the other way. Most of the Popes of the Middle Ages, however, were more interested in politics and power than in spiritual matters, and so we broke away, went underground, and continued the tradition that had sustained us for more than a thousand years."

"If you're so pious," challenged Father Andre, "then why do you kill and hate?"

The Master sighed. Such remedial lessons could be so tiring. "We kill only non-believers. I had assumed you were capable of making that deduction yourself."

"But according to your beliefs, non-believers make up more than 99.99 percent of the world!"

"When our Lord returns," explained the Master, "he will rule over all mankind and there will be no non-believers."

Andre laughed. "And how do you intend to convert the Hindus, Buddhists, Muslims, Jews, and real Christians who don't believer the things you do?"

The Master stared through his mask at the reputed holy man. "They will convert or die," he sneered.

Father Andre threw up his arms. "Then you're destined for failure. Man must come freely of his own volition. As an archaeologist and I have searched for the historical Jesus. As I've studied the histories of other cultures, however, I have come to realize that all men are my brothers. "

The Master had no stomach for this kind of thinking. "You would think differently, Father, if you knew what happened at the Council of Jerusalem in A.D. 49."

"Enlighten me," Andre conceded, as if he had a choice.

"When Paul met with James, Jesus' brother, and with Peter, his favorite disciple, he agreed to continue that his converts would follow the Jewish dietary laws. Instead, he began the process of pulling away from Judaism, the religion that James and Peter still practiced. Jesus, you see, was not the founder of Christianity. It was the Blessed Paul, our first Master."

Andre's eyes opened wide. "Saint Paul was your first Master? That's impossible."

"In A.D. 70, before the first Gospel was written and after Paul was martyred, we were entrusted with a document that Barnabas, Paul's companion, had kept. It detailed Paul's work and contained secrets of what actually transpired at the Jerusalem Council of 49. We've kept this work secret over the centuries."

Andre sneered again. It was getting annoying. "I seriously doubt that such a document exists."

"Oh, it does," the Master assured him. "It is hidden in a secure place."

"Prove it," Andre challenged, and the Master laughed uproariously.

"I have no reason to prove myself to you," he said. "That is, unless you are considering conversion."

Andre refused to acknowledge the insinuation. "Saint Paul would never have been part of your sect," he said defiantly.

"There you have me," said the Master. "Paul is our honorary leader, the spiritual father of our lineage. Although he appeared to have been a Jew, Paul was truly a Gnostic Christian. His secret teachings were revealed to us by Marcion, our first official Master."

Andre took a moment to absorb this. "Marcion was thrown out of the church as a heretic in the second century."

"He was a true student of Paul," the Master corrected. "Marcion was excommunicated because he knew the true nature of our Lord, and of the original twelve disciples."

But Andre wouldn't let it go. "Marcion wasn't born until twenty years after Paul's death."

"True," said the Master, not interested in quibbling over details. "But he took possession of all of Paul's original writings, most of which are so secret that they have never been seen. Marcion alone saw the truth of Paul's life and message. For two hundred years the Marcionites thrived as an early Christian sect, but after the council of Nicea in 325 C.E., where the truth of real Christianity was distorted, they were declared heretics by the new Catholic Church. Marcion had his own sacred scriptures, though, which we have passed down through the ages. These are the sacred documents of the Guardians, which prophesize the return of Jesus and his new mission on earth."

Father Andre hesitated, his eyes growing dark. "Why are you telling me this?" he asked.

"Because it can do me no harm. I do respect you, Father, but I have no choice but to kill you."

The Master relished the fear he saw in the priest's face.

Did Father Andre truly believe that the Master would have given him a chance to win his freedom?

"You always have a choice," Andre said, his voice shaking. "Just know that if you opt to kill me, I will be united with my Lord in Heaven. You, on the other hand, will be condemned with the Devil in Hell."

The Master was giddy with delight. "Why Father," he taunted, "is that hatred I hear in your voice?"

But Andre merely looked at him with a sad smile. "No, my brother," he said, "it is pity for your lost soul."

With this the Master's blood turned sour in his veins. The discussion had ceased to be amusing. He gestured and the priest was seized by one of the Master's faithful servants.

Moments after Andre had been dragged from the room, the Master heard an anguished wail, and then another, which was abruptly cut off. The men knew that they were not to kill Father Andre. Anything short of that, however, the Master left to their discretion.

Chapter 63

JOSH SETTLED INTO AARON'S OFFICE, NOT CERTAIN what they were going to do there. His thoughts kept traveling to the basilica, wondering what Aaron's men would find in their investigation.

"I have your laptop, by the way," Aaron said casually as he sat. "You can take it back with you later."

The news surprised Josh. "Where did you find it?"

Aaron offered him a sidelong glance. "We didn't exactly find it."

"*You* stole it?"

"Of course. It was necessary. Do you really think our security men are as stupid as Boaz acted? I examined your files—as I said, this was a necessary precaution—and saw that you had photographed the Scroll. I considered deleting it, but then decided that you've earned our trust."

Josh wasn't sure he could say the same about Aaron. "You did what you had to do," he said darkly.

"Don't be angry. Besides, now that we've cleared this hurdle, we can truly consider you a part of our team."

"I'm not on anyone's team," Josh said curtly. "Let's get that much clear. We're after the same thing, though. If I can help, I will."

The phone rang and Aaron picked it up. It was the IAA front desk. "The call you've been waiting for is on line three."

Aaron thanked the operator, punched the speakerphone, and said, "Shalom."

"Have you made your decision?" The voice was garbled, as though processed.

"What decision is that?"

"Don't play coy with me or I'll hang up and you'll never see the hostages alive."

"I'm not playing coy," Aaron said quickly. "We will exchange the scroll for the hostages tomorrow at sunset."

"Our offer was for today and today only. If you choose not to accept it, the deaths of the hostages will be on your hands."

"We are willing to exchange the scroll for the hostages. We just need more time."

"There is no need for more time! You have the scroll and we have the hostages. There is nothing to prepare."

"I need more time with some of the authorities," Aaron said, stalling for time. "This isn't as easy as it sounds."

"Deciding to save lives seems quite easy to me. As a gesture of good faith, though, I'll make you a counter proposal. We will exchange one hostage tomorrow. If we determine the scroll is authentic, the others will be returned to you on Wednesday."

Josh's intuition nudged him. "What are the names of the hostages you're holding?" he asked.

"You know their names," said the voice on the other end of the line.

"There will be no exchange," Josh said, knowing that it was a risky proposition, "unless you give us the hostages' names."

There was a moment of silence. "The hostages are Danielle Ben Daniel, Father Andre Billet, and Jonathan Levi."

The kidnapper had just made a glaring mistake, and it

took all of Josh's will power to avoid shouting it out. The quick eye contact he made with Aaron told him that the agent felt the same way.

"We may accept your proposal," Aaron said, "but first I need to consult with some of my colleagues."

"You have sixty minutes," said the voice, and Aaron broke the connection.

"The Guardians aren't aware that we know Jonathan is dead," Josh said.

"Remember," cautioned Aaron, "we're only speculating that the ashes we found were Jonathan's, based on the discovery of his car. The man didn't say anything about Alon. Maybe the ashes were his."

Aaron was right. Was the kidnapper acknowledging that he'd already killed Alon?

One of Aaron's men stepped quickly into the room. "The call came from a cell phone. We checked with the phone company and the number belongs to Jonathan. The call was made from a location two miles outside of Nazareth."

"Thank you," Aaron said, dismissing the man.

Josh tried to factor this new bit of information into what he already knew. "What does that mean?"

"It means we're drawing closer to them."

In exactly one hour the phone rang again. Aaron and Josh eyed each other across the desk. With a nod, Aaron picked it up, activating the speaker.

"What is your answer?" demanded the voice.

"I have another question."

"No more questions! Answer now or the hostages die immediately!"

Aaron glanced at Josh and then looked down at the phone. "We agree to do the exchange tomorrow at sunset."

"Then follow these instructions exactly. Cohan is to

handle the exchange and deliver us the scroll. When we have it in our hands we will direct you to the hostage. Have Cohan at the ruins of the Roman Theater in Sepphoris at 7:30. And remember, no tricks or all hostages die. Do not bring any of your men. You can accompany Cohan, but he must be alone when he hands us the scroll. We will have men stationed around the area to make sure you follow our directions. Have I made myself clear?"

"Perfectly clear," said Aaron, playing along.

When the call ended, he didn't even stop to talk to Josh. Aaron picked up the phone immediately and dialed his security offices in Nazareth to update them.

"Our men have the entire area covered," he said when he was finished. "In the next few minutes we'll have one of our surveillance helicopters checking out the area around the Roman ruins. I still think it's a long shot that the hostage exchange will occur, but if it does, it will be on our terms."

Chapter 64

THE DARKENED THEATER WAS EMPTY AND STILL, SILENT except for the hushed tones of two figures robed in black.

"You have learned your lessons well, my son." The Master's voice was heavy with emotion now that they were finally alone. "You have become everything that I hoped you would be, and one day you will succeed me as the next Master of our line. We are destined to save this world, but to do so we must carry out our mission in utmost secrecy. The burden will be heavy at times and you may feel alone in all the world, with no one who knows your true identity. But you will be bolstered, as I have been, by the knowledge that your own son will someday carry on where you and I leave off. When he is of age, you will instruct him in the sacred teachings as I have instructed you."

"Master, I will keep my vows and never tell anyone our secret. You've taught me well. When the time comes, I will make you proud. Have we finished the preparations for tomorrow?"

"We have. Very few things are as satisfying as a masterful deception. Tomorrow night, after the exchange, I have planned an enormous celebration. Tonight we start early, as you create your heir."

"I'm pleased with your selection," said the younger man, his excitement growing. "But will she succumb?"

"She will be ready for you, my son," said the Master. "The drugs will ensure it."

Chapter 65

IT WAS NEARLY IMPOSSIBLE TO RELAX, BUT JOSH NEEDED to access the wisdom gained only through meditation. This might be his last opportunity for a very long time—maybe his last time ever. Josh forced himself to focus and began:

Ribbono shel Olam.
Ribbono shel Olam.
Ribbono shel Olam.

He saw swatches of bright red, green, blue, and purple and willed himself to go deeper, down to a place he had never been. He'd crossed some barrier, aided no doubt by the words gifted to him. This was where his past life memories lived. This was not a dream, a vision, or delusion.

This was real.

Josh saw the major life events of five people he knew instinctively as his ancestors. He saw Rabbi Hillel in 6 C.E. teaching a young Yehoshua ben Yosef to love one's neighbor as one's self. He experienced the courageous death of Rabbi Akiba in 135 C.E. He watched Judah ben-Bava, known as Judah the Prince, editing a part of the Mishnah in 193 C.E. He heard the voice of Rashi discussing the Talmud and the Torah in 1085 C.E. He observed Rabbi Isaac Luria discussing the mysteries of the Kabbalah in 1569 C.E.

Josh was connected to all of these great men. Their blood ran in his veins. But why was he seeing this now?

He emerged from his meditation, returning to the consciousness of the "real" world. Instead of insight, Josh had gained only more questions. As a scholar and a seeker of wisdom, he had studied all of these men to some degree. But he doubted that historical fact would aid him in the conflict ahead.

What he had connected to most during the meditation was essence of these ancestors—what some might call their vibration or spiritual signature. He sensed that it was this energy that could help him when he finally faced his adversaries. Josh decided to pray. Although prayer had never been a meaningful part of his life, he now instinctively understood its value, as he never had before.

He chose a psalm he knew by heart:

Our days are like grass,
We shoot up like flowers that fade
And die as the chill wind passes
Over them, yet Your love for those
Who revere You is everlasting.
God, Your righteousness
Extends to all generations.
May this generation finally know peace
And May all people be united as one.

His spirit nourished, Josh pondered the danger he faced. He didn't believe that Aaron would come up with a viable alternative to the hostage exchange. Nor did he believe that Aaron's men would find the Guardians' lair in Nazareth quickly enough.

With sudden certainty, he realized that only one person could undermine the Guardians and save Danielle. That one man was the descendant of Rabbi Hillel, Rabbi Akiba, Judah the Prince, Rashi, and Rabbi Isaac Luria.

Josh rose. The time had come for action.

Chapter 66

A SINGLE SPOTLIGHT PIERCED THE DARKNESS, ILLUMI-NATING the altar and suffusing the surrounding space with an otherworldly glow. The Master could sense the anticipation in the room. He, too, was feeling the stir of excitement brought on by the impending ritual. This moment happened only once in a generation. If all went well, his grandchild was about to be called into creation.

The Master walked slowly to the stage and gazed out at his Chosen.

"On this great night we celebrate the continuation of our lineage. Soon you will bear witness to the holiest of rites. I ask you to control your animal instincts and transmute the libidinous fire. Many of you have already shown me that you are weak in this way, but I implore you to learn from your recent challenge and turn your energies to the higher spirit of our cause. You have served me well, and now you will be rewarded. You will experience the continued rebirth of our sect. Let us all pray that our Lord will bless us with an heir."

The Chosen Twelve stood and prayed in unison.

The doctors had told the Master that the time was right. His instincts told him the same. Those imbeciles at the IAA thought they had gained the upper hand, but little did they know that their postponements served a higher purpose. The Master prayed silently, thanking God for the unexpected boon of perfect timing. They would have no interference tonight.

A second man appeared, dressed in a white robe and serpent's mask. There was a stir in the auditorium; never before had the Guardians seen another donning the sacred mask of their Master. The tension in the room increased, and the Master began to worry that the audience was too pitched, too capable of being overcome by their carnal yearnings. Several of them had been punished already for accosting Danielle outside the shower room. Tonight they must not cross the line. The Master would not allow anything to defile this moment.

The masked man waited at the altar for the appearance of his mate. Moments later, the beautiful woman appeared, flanked by two Guardians who held her up and led her to the altar. When they removed her white robe, the Chosen erupted in a collective gasp. Not even a few ugly bruises could diminish her radiance.

When he had discovered the woman's true identity a few days before, the Master paused to ponder his intentions. For the briefest instant, his human impulses had warred with his sense of mission. But then he realized how perfect—how pure—this opportunity was. Eternity itself seemed to be conspiring in their success.

When she was positioned in front of the altar, the Guardians who had led Danielle stood back from her naked form. As they did, however, she collapsed to the floor. Something was terribly wrong.

The Master moved swiftly to the spot where she lay and tried to revive her. "You fools!" he raged. "I told you to sedate her, not to render her unconscious. Unless she plays her part there can be no ritual! You will pay for this with your lives."

Chapter 67

J OSH PACKED HIS BAG WITH TWO SEMI-AUTOMATIC pistols that he'd purchased that day. He hoped he wouldn't have cause to use them, but he was prepared to do so if he had to.

As he was heading out the door, when the phone rang.

"I've got great news," said Aaron. "We found the Guardians' hideout."

Josh wasn't surprised, although he wished he could have been. He didn't need to ask Aaron how he'd done it.

In the past hour, he'd felt as though he was thinking with new clarity. With that clarity came the ability to see patterns that had eluded him before. He'd been expecting this call.

"That is great news," he said. "I assume that means there's no hostage exchange tomorrow evening?"

"I never felt comfortable with the idea of the exchange. Now we can forget it. I've come up with a new plan. While the Guardians are at Sepphoris waiting for the exchange, we'll attack their headquarters and capture their leader."

Josh was silent. He wasn't interested in Aaron's scheme; he had his own plan—though it, too, was one in which Aaron would play a significant part.

"Josh, are you still there?"

"I was just admiring how clever you are," Josh lied. "So how does your latest plan work?"

"I'll pick you up tomorrow at three o'clock and we'll drive to Nazareth," said Aaron. "We have to be there no later than 6:30."

"What if I met you in front of the Basilica of the Annunciation at 6:00?" Josh countered.

"I want you to go with me. Along the way, we can discuss some important details."

Josh tried to keep any inflection out of his voice. "That isn't going to work for me. I'm driving to some spiritual spots on the road to Nazareth and would rather be alone."

"But..."

"Aaron," he interrupted, "did you know that Nazareth means guardian in Hebrew and Arabic?"

"Of course I did." Aaron sighed and said grudgingly, "Okay, I'll meet you in front of the basilica at 6:00 tomorrow evening."

"Make sure you're well armed. I don't have any weapons. I'm counting on you to protect me."

Josh hung up and looked at his watch. It was 5:30. He had thirty minutes to get to his destination. He grabbed his bags and headed for the Old City.

It took Josh less than fifteen minutes to walk the mile to the Jaffa gate. He headed to the Christian Quarter and found the Sword of God souvenir shop that was the entrance to the Guardians' old hideout.

"I'm with Israeli security," Josh told the woman behind the register. "I need to inspect the rooms below."

"The priests aren't there," she said. "The only people who've been here today were policemen."

"I'm going down there anyway. What is the latest you can close the store?"

The woman looked at the clock on the wall. "Twenty minutes."

"I'll see you before then."

Josh took out his flashlight and headed downstairs. He moved quickly through the headquarters to the door that led to the tunnels under the Old City.

The passage was cold and dark. Josh walked a long distance down the main tunnel. He entered one of the smaller passageways, which led to the large stone slab that had blocked his way the last time he'd been there. He hadn't understood then what was on the other side. Now he needed to pay homage and respect. It was one of the last things he had to do to prepare himself.

When Josh reached the ancient rock, he put on a skullcap, fell to his knees and recited Kaddish, the traditional Jewish prayer said on behalf of the dead. Josh read it now for someone who hadn't had it said for him in nearly two thousand years. As he spoke, Josh was overcome with emotion at the significance of the act; but there was a deeper effect, as well—a pervasive sense of peace and faith that seemed to fill him with every word. "May God remember his servant Yehoshua ben Yosef," Josh concluded, kissing the stone. "May good deeds and charity be performed in his name."

Chapter 68

JOSH DROVE HIS RENTED RANGE ROVER TOWARD KFAR Nahum, also known as Capernaum, the City of St. Peter, on the northern banks of the Sea of Galilee. He hadn't gone more than ten miles when he noticed a white Mercedes following him. Josh had also seen a similar vehicle just before he left Jerusalem. He turned off the road and let the car go by.

After a few minutes, he resumed his journey, only to find that the car was soon tailing him again. Josh knew that it belonged to either the Guardians or Aaron's people. He wasn't worried. He had his two semi-automatic handguns loaded. If he was in danger, he could fire off twelve shots in less than three seconds.

Josh's thoughts turned to Danielle. They hadn't had much time together, he felt bound to her in a way that he couldn't explain, as if their connection transcended the limits of time and space. He longed to talk to her, to hold her, to meld their bodies together. He wanted to tell her everything she meant to him, how she'd changed his life permanently. He only hoped he would get the chance.

Josh drove up the coastal plain from Tel Aviv to Haifa. This was the path traveled by army after army throughout the centuries as they marched north from Egypt or south from the Euphrates to do battle. Despite its long and bloody history, however, Josh favored this road over the more direct, but considerably more dangerous route through the West Bank.

By the time he arrived at Haifa, the white car had disappeared.

Josh decided to spend the night in Haifa. He checked into the Dan Carmel Hotel in the central section of the city, when the check-in clerk forgot to ask for his passport, Josh used the name of John Coughlin, his old nemesis back at the University of Pennsylvania. It was more a gesture of precaution than anything else, as he knew all too well that if the Guardians wanted to find him, they would. But the name had come to him as he was walking through the entryway of the hotel, and Josh hadn't bothered second-guessing the impulse. It was funny, he thought, that after everything he'd been through lately he suddenly felt a kind of affection for the man. Josh realized that he was relieved to have let go of his pride and resentment. There were more important things in life than bruised egos. He thought again of Danielle, and of the danger they both were in. Josh was glad that he had decided to make this pilgrimage of sorts, and hoped that it would give him the strength he needed.

Haifa was situated on a hill overlooking a bay, and for this reason some people referred to it as the San Francisco of the Mediterranean. The hotel had impressive views of the city and the deep blue bay below. But Josh had other sights in mind. He peered out his hotel window, looking for the white Mercedes or any suspicious characters. After studying the neighborhood for several minutes, he concluded that, at least for the time being, he was safe. He went to bed for what could very well be the last night of his life.

The next morning, Josh woke up at 6:00 a.m. and went running. Then he checked out of his hotel and began the short drive to the Bahai Shrine which opened at nine.

As he pulled out of the hotel, he noticed that the white Mercedes was following him once again. It had to be Israeli security. The Guardians would have come after him last night.

Josh knew that he had to prepare himself spiritually for what lay ahead. He parked his car and beheld the shrine's beautiful gold dome and magnificent gardens, then went inside, where the remains of the religion's founder, Bahá'u'lláh, were buried. Josh said another prayer, this time taking in the energy of tolerance and unity that made up the foundation of the faith. Before yesterday, he hadn't prayed since his parents' plane went down, but now he found a deep comfort in the act.

Israel was home to more than 20,000 antiquity sites of all sizes and periods, each of which was protected by the Antiquities law and enforced by the IAA. But Josh had no time to waste. His agenda was specific, yet it wasn't the result of careful calculations or strategy. The Guardians weren't easily predictable or bound by any apparent moral code, which meant that his mind was of little use as he prepared himself for the confrontation that would determine his fate. Instead Josh let his intuition guide him, trusting that it would lead him toward the highest good.

As he left the shrine, Josh looked at his watch. In a little more than eight hours he would meet Aaron. He drove eighteen miles to Megiddo, the location named in the book of Revelation as the site of final battle between the forces of good and evil. At Megiddo, he went to the Tell of Armageddon, one of the largest and most impressive archaeological sites in Israel.

At each site Josh meditated and prayed, opening himself to whatever wisdom or energy may come. He surrendered himself to the path that lay before him and, as his fear fell away, Josh felt his resolve expanding to contain a new awareness. Reconciling himself to the true scope of his challenge, he released what was left of a lifetime of doubt.

Josh wished he had time to explore the ruins more fully, to adjust to his new perspective, but his time was running out. He had to get to Capernaum. The drive took longer than he had expected, though, and when he arrived on the northern shore of the Sea of Galilee it was just before 1:30. Josh went directly to the magnificent, Romanesque ruin that, according to some archaeologists, was built over an older synagogue where Jesus had preached and prayed.

The ancient walls still stood against a deep blue sky. Josh imagined what it would have been like two thousand years before. Had Jesus really prayed here? Josh felt something, but it was impossible to know if it was a real connection to the divine or the product of his yearning. He fell to his knees and recited the holiest of Jewish prayers, the Shema.

Hear, O Israel: Adonai is our God, Adonai is One.

When he finished, he noticed that the sky had darkened overhead, where the roof of the synagogue had once been. Josh heard the roaring sound of thunder, and the air was suddenly alive with electricity. With a crack of lightning, rain began to pour. Soaked to the bone, Josh ran to his rented Range Rover.

When he got to the parking lot he spotted the white car again, and this time, the men inside as well. Israeli security. Josh smiled at them, but kept running toward his own vehicle. He looked at his watch; he had less than four hours left, just enough time to pay his respects at the tomb of Moses Maimonides—or, by his Hebrew name, Rambam.

Josh arrived at Maimonides' whitewashed tomb, which sat high on a hill above the Sea of Galilee. He felt a special kinship to this man who had traversed the realms of science and spirit with expert wisdom, becoming not only a physician and philosopher, but also the greatest Jewish religious authority of the Middle Ages. Josh considered his own, seemingly schizophrenic position. Could he ever find such an elegant balance between the two worldviews? He prayed now for a unified vision in the confrontation to come.

When he opened his eyes, Josh saw that he had less than two and half hours to make the drive to Nazareth and meet Aaron. He focused now on only one thing—his mission.

Chapter 69

NAZARETH WAS A DIFFICULT CITY TO NAVIGATE. THE bypass road that wound around its perimeter was dotted with confusing signs, all pointing in different directions to the same location. Josh seemed to be going in circles, but finally he arrived at a parking lot a few blocks from the Basilica of the Annunciation. He had ninety minutes before he was to meet Aaron.

Josh changed in the car, slipping into a bulletproof vest, then grabbed his two guns and hid them under the legs of his pants. He decided to explore the area around the church. He noticed that the white Mercedes was parked in the same lot, but this time there was no one in it. His intuition spiked again, and he looked around to see where they might have gone. At the other end of the lot was a three-story office building that looked as if it had been built in the 1950s. Out front, a small sign read "Deus Enterprises." Josh spent about ten minutes walking around the building, watching from different spots to see if anything was going on. He didn't notice anyone going into or out of the place and was about to head to the basilica when two huge men in dark business suits approached from the rear and entered through the back door of the building. Their gait seemed strangely familiar. Were they Guardians? Josh took one last look around the premises and knew he would return.

He walked a short distance down Casa Nova Street to

the entrance of the Basilica of the Annunciation, which stood in the heart of the older part of town. Josh checked out the area, but nothing seemed suspicious. He didn't see any obvious Israeli security, but guessed that they were there, somewhere. At least, he hoped they were.

Unlike the other holy sites he had visited, Josh felt no emotional connection to the basilica itself. This struck him as odd, but when he checked in with his intuition he was left only with the sense that something wasn't quite right about the site itself. *This isn't where it happened*, he thought.

As he came around again to the front of the church, Josh noticed that the place seemed unnervingly still, like in the moments before an earthquake. Josh checked his watch. It was time to meet Aaron.

Josh stood outside the basilica for several minutes before Aaron arrived, flanked by the two large men dressed in black that he had seen earlier, going into the offices of Deus Enterprises. Their presence here, now, told Josh everything he needed to know. Up until that moment he had still hoped he was wrong about Aaron. It was a disappointment, but it didn't matter. Aaron could take him where he needed to go.

"So, gentleman," Josh said casually, "what's tonight's plan?"

Aaron pointed to the three-story office building. "That's the Guardians' hideout," he said. "But my men have reported that all of their members are in and around the Roman ruins in Sepphoris, waiting to make the hostage exchange. Their leader hasn't been spotted. We think he's in this building. We'll take him while he's not protected."

Josh nodded. He didn't want to say too much, for fear that his voice would betray him.

Aaron patted his shoulder holster. "Are you armed?"

Josh attempted to be surprised by the question. "No. Should I be?"

"No. It's better if you aren't. People who aren't accustomed to shooting guns tend to get themselves hurt in situations like these."

They walked up to the front door of the building and stepped inside. Aaron moved silently across the sterile lobby and opened a steel door. Inside, there was an elevator. Aaron went to a panel on the wall and typed in an eight-digit code. The elevator opened.

"You've learned an awful lot about this building," Josh said with what he hoped would pass for admiration.

Aaron pushed the button and the elevator began to descend. He looked at Josh with an expression of superiority and more than a little contempt. "Israeli intelligence is the best in the world."

"And you do your country proud, Aaron."

Aaron seemed baffled by the comment, but had no time to press the point. The elevator door opened to reveal a man in black robes and a serpent mask. Josh knew instantly that this was the Master.

"Mr. Cohan," the Master said scornfully, "to what do we owe the pleasure?"

Josh knew he had to play things cool. The next several minutes would determine everything. "I've been looking forward to meeting you," Josh said evenly.

"And I you." The Master looked at Aaron. "Is he armed?"

"I think guns scare him."

"Search him anyway."

The goons frisked Josh and found the two 9 millimeters strapped on either leg. Then they tore open his shirt and removed the bulletproof vest.

The Master regarded Aaron disapprovingly. "You are not paid to make amateur mistakes, For your sake, I hope that this one will be the last."

"I know this guy!" protested Aaron, masking his humiliation with bravado. "I knew he wouldn't be able to shoot a gun even if he had one."

"You're too much of an idiot." The Master backhanded Aaron across the cheek, drawing blood with his jewel-encrusted ring.

Josh fought to remain calm. He'd anticipated the worst and it was coming true. He watched Aaron wipe at his cracked lip. "What do you get for this, Aaron?" he asked. "What do you get for betraying me?"

Aaron chuckled as he looked at the blood on the back of his hand. "You're a nice guy, Josh, even if you are way too nosy. But money talks, my friend."

"It didn't work so well for Fishman," Josh said pointedly.

A sudden panic flashed across Aaron's face as the meaning of Josh's words sank in. He tried to cover it up, forcing a laugh that was too loud, too late.

"Silence," the Master said holding up his hand. He gestured to his right and one of the goons blew a hole in Aaron's head, spattering blood against the tasteful décor of the office's reception area.

Josh knew that the only way to live through this was to keep his emotions in check and his wits about him. He had known that the Master was ruthless, but seeing him kill with such utter nonchalance made Josh realize how completely out of his depth he really was.

"I was benevolent with Aaron and killed him quickly," said the Master, fixing his eyes on Josh. "You won't be so lucky."

One of the goons grabbed Josh from behind and he felt a sudden blow to the back of his head. In the next instant, everything went black.

Chapter 70

WHEN JOSH CAME TO, HE FOUND HIMSELF IN A DIM, candlelit room. It was only when he heard the sword being drawn from its scabbard that he realized he wasn't alone.

"Leave us," the Master ordered, his blade gleaming in the light of the flickering flame. His goons complied, leaving Josh alone with his enemy at last.

"Your archaeologist friends have caused us a good deal of trouble," the Master said. "They would have used the scroll to destroy our religion, but I have destroyed them instead."

Josh seethed at the lunacy of the fanatic's rationale. "They had barely begun the translation," he argued. "None of them knew what the scroll said."

The Master stepped toward him, lifting Josh's chin with the flat end of his sword. "But *you* know what the scroll says, don't you?"

Josh felt no need to lie. "It says things you couldn't begin to comprehend."

The Master laughed mockingly. "You do realize that it is a complete fabrication, don't you?"

"The words of the scroll are the words of Yehoshua ben Yosef known today as Jesus of Nazareth."

"Such passionate naïveté." The Master circled him slowly. "They are the words of a heretic in a sad attempt to invalidate the only true religion." The Master flipped a switch on the wall and a spotlight suddenly flooded the room. "This is what happens to heretics, Mr. Cohan."

Josh recoiled. Behind the altar, hanging upside-down on a cross was Father Andre, crucified like Saint Peter. Danielle, wrapped in a white robe, lay motionless on the floor with her eyes closed. Josh saw no blood, though, and he prayed that she was only unconscious. Then a slithering and hissing sound came from a serpentarium atop the altar. To his horror, Josh saw that it was an Israeli Saw-Scaled Viper, one of the most dangerous snakes in the world.

"You're a demon," Josh said with utter revulsion.

"Not true," corrected the Master. "In fact, I'm quite the opposite. Too bad you won't be around when the rest of the world finds out. You know, I actually had some reservations about Father Andre. His tenacity was admirable. When he turned out to be too empathetic to non-believers, though, he sealed his fate."

Josh forced himself to look at the crucified priest. He needed to draw on the outrage he felt at this atrocity. He needed to channel his anger, his love for Danielle, and his newfound faith into something he could use to take the Master down.

The Master brandished his sword once again, blinding him with the bright light that reflected off of its blade. Instinctively, Josh covered his eyes.

The Master laughed uproariously. "Too bright for you, Josh? I apologize. I certainly don't want to block your vision. By the way, that viper is for you. A special treat for a special man. The bite itself won't be so bad, but once he sinks his fangs into your flesh, your hours of agony will begin."

As the Master spoke, Josh thought he saw Danielle go tense. She was alive, but was she conscious? Knowing he was leaving himself open to attack, Josh closed his eyes. He

needed help. He needed to see the scroll. Josh knew that
there was something there for him, if only he could capture it.

Ribbono shel Olam.

Josh let his thoughts fade. The Master disappeared from
his sight, as did Father Andre and even Danielle.

Ribbono shel Olam.

The scroll emerged in his mind's eye. Josh expected to
see something new, but instead he was drawn to the last passage he had translated.

*Beware for these forces may have the face of righteousness.
This face is only a disguise. It is a mask even unto the demon
himself.*

The recognition struck Josh with a tremendous force.
He now knew something about the savage murderer in front
of him—a secret even unto *the demon himself.* He finally had
an edge. Ironically, the information had been given to him by
Aaron, the Master's late accomplice.

"Are you praying, Josh?" the Master taunted.

Josh opened his eyes and looked squarely at the masked
man. "I know all of your secrets," he said.

The Master chuckled. "You don't know any of my
secrets."

Josh took a step closer. "I know about the Council of
Jerusalem."

This drew The Master's attention. "That's impossible."

"It's not impossible at all. You could even say that I was
there."

"You know nothing."

Josh moved closer still, his certainty growing as the
Master's uneasiness gave way to alarm. "I know more about
you than you do," he said. "You say you hate the Jews."

"More than anything in the world. They are worse than
the pigs they refuse to eat."

"And yet you are Jewish yourself," Josh said, delivering his blow.

The Master drew himself erect. "Preposterous!" he hissed, raising his sword. "I've heard enough of your lies."

"You really don't know, do you?" Josh said, drawing out the revelation. "Your father never told you, but of course he wouldn't. Your birthday is September 30, 1943, is it not? You were born in Dachau. Your real parents were killed by the Nazis...because they were Jews."

The Master stopped only a few feet from Josh, sword still aloft. "Pure fabrication."

Josh stood his ground. "The commandant of the camp was a member of the Guardians. He knew that your adopted father was sterile, and that he desperately needed a male heir. He arranged to smuggle an infant to Israel."

"You missed your calling," the Master scoffed. "You definitely should have been a novelist."

Josh leaned toward the demon, not backing down. "A Jewish agency helped place the child with what they thought was a family of wealthy Jews. But the Pauls weren't Jewish, were they, Alexander?"

The Master staggered sideways and Josh took advantage of the moment to rip the mask from his face. The seething eyes of Alexander Paul stared back at him.

Paul let out an ungodly roar and began waving the sword maniacally through the air. Josh lunged at the man's feet, toppling them both as the sword clattered to the floor. Josh slammed a fist into Paul's face and then held the dazed man down with the full weight of his body.

"I know all about your religious group," Josh said, looking down into the face of pure evil. "When your followers fled their Jerusalem hideout, they left behind a Bible. I realized that you were Marcionites the moment I saw that it contained only the writings of Luke and Paul. But the real

Marcionites disappeared in the fourth century, didn't they? Your sect was nothing more than a perversion, a bunch of pathetic hangers-on."

Paul kicked his legs ferociously to dislodge Josh, who was thrown to the side. Josh knew Paul would go after the sword and would waste no time using it. He had to get there first. He scrambled to his knees, but when he looked in the direction where the sword had fallen, he found nothing.

Paul sprang to his feet and pivoted toward him, but he was unarmed. Their eyes locked in an instant of bewilderment before Josh once again saw the gleaming blade slice upward behind his adversary.

Responding to the look on Josh's face, Paul turned. But it was too late, and the arc of the sword found its mark— cleanly severing the Master's head.

As the lifeless body collapsed with a sickening thud, Danielle dropped the weapon. Josh's heart opened more fully than he ever thought possible and he rushed toward her.

But at that precise moment, the door flew open and both Josh and Danielle turned toward the sound. One of Paul's men charged into the room. He saw the body of his fallen leader and raised his gun. Josh ran to tackle him, but the thug fired at Danielle, hitting her squarely in the chest. Seconds later, though, the man himself crumbled, hit by another shot that came from the doorway. An Israeli security team stormed into the room, lowering their weapons when they saw that only Josh was left standing.

Josh rushed to Danielle's side. He could hardly feel her pulse and her eyes fixed in a distant gaze.

Don't take her, he prayed, *please don't take her. I need her much more than You do.*

Josh put his hands on the place where the bullet had entered her body and prayed even more fervently. He couldn't lose her. Time seemed to suspend itself as Josh held his hands in place. At last, he opened his eyes and looked at the woman he loved. Her eyes were closed now, but the bleeding had slowed.

Security had already called for medical assistance. Josh remained by Danielle's side, holding her limp hand in his own, until the paramedics arrived. As they radioed their dispatcher for a helicopter, Josh scanned the now crowded room, recognizing one of the security men from the white Mercedes. He had assumed that the car was part of Aaron's detail, but clearly, that hadn't been the case. A moment later, Giuseppe and Goner hurried through the door. They watched as the paramedics put Danielle on a stretcher.

"I'm sorry, Josh," Giuseppe said.

The paramedics began to move Danielle toward the door.

"I'm going with her," Josh said, moving toward the exit.

"We have a second helicopter that will follow the medical chopper," Giuseppe told him. "Why don't you come with us? We have a lot to discuss."

Josh shook his head. "I won't leave her."

Goner conferred with the paramedics and returned moments later. "She's in critical condition but stable," he said. "I can't explain it, but it seems that the bleeding had actually stopped before the paramedics even worked on her. She seems to be out of danger for the time being."

"I'm going with her anyway," said Josh impatiently.

"The medical staff has no extra room in their helicopter. They'd appreciate it if we met them at the hospital."

Josh reluctantly agreed as Danielle was led away. He looked down at the blood—Danielle's blood—on his hands.

Chapter 71

Josh, Giuseppe, and Goner rode in an Israeli Security helicopter toward the Hadassah Hospital in Jerusalem. Danielle's chopper was only a few minutes ahead of them. Josh searched the sky for it, but saw nothing.

"How did you find us?" Josh shouted over the din of the helicopter's rotors, trying not to let his worry consume him.

"We had men on you, we had men on Aaron, and we had our own men on the case," Giuseppe said. "We knew that one or all of them would turn something up."

Josh turned back to face the other men. "My instincts told me that Aaron was bad. I wasn't certain until yesterday, though."

"He's been under investigation for more than a year," Giuseppe told him. "We knew that he was double-dealing and taking bribes, and brought him into the situation with the Guardians because we had reason to believe he would eventually lead us to them."

"If he hadn't been killed tonight," Goner said, "he would have spent some serious time in jail."

Giuseppe's cell phone rang. He listened for a few moments and then snapped it shut. "That was one of our agents with more details from the scene. Before we found you, we were involved in a firefight in another part of the hideout. Eight of the Guardians were killed and three were critically wounded."

"Any reports on our men?" Goner said.

"Two wounded but not seriously." Giuseppe turned to Josh. "We caught the group by surprise. They were changing into their robes and only two of them had time to fire."

"Why were so many of them killed, then?" Josh asked.

"They were going for their weapons. We shot them before they could pull the triggers. One of them ran—the man who shot Danielle. But as you know, we killed him, too..."

"Wait a minute," Josh interrupted, "you got eleven of the Chosen Twelve, and Danielle killed their leader, Alexander Paul. But there's still one Guardian unaccounted for. That means that he either escaped or was never there to begin with."

Goner shook his head. "It was impossible for anyone to escape. We had the building surrounded."

Josh thought for a moment, and then it struck him. "Was Alon one of the dead?"

Giuseppe looked down at his cell phone as though he expected it to give him the answer. "We're still confirming it, but I don't think he was there."

Josh nodded. "Of course. Paul was smart enough to keep his son elsewhere in case something went wrong. I guess he didn't feel he was entirely invincible."

"If Alon isn't among the dead or captured, we'll begin a manhunt for him immediately." Giuseppe stared out the window at the earth passing beneath them. "Now we know who gave the Guardians all their information."

"Yes," Josh said. "Jonathan, Aaron, Alon, and Moshe."

"Moshe?" Goner and Giuseppe were shocked.

"Moshe unwittingly gave information to Alon, Jonathan, and Aaron. He wasn't part of the Guardians' plan, but he helped them to almost pull it off."

"It's amazing—half of your archaeological team was directly or indirectly working to destroy the scroll, and yet they didn't succeed."

Josh closed his eyes for a few seconds. "Most of the time, bad guys lose."

"We never did find Jonathan," Goner said.

"Yes you did," Josh told him. "You found his ashes."

Giuseppe nodded thoughtfully. "Tell me how you discovered the information about the Master's background."

"Ironically, I had assistance from Aaron. I followed the paper trail from some of the documents he brought me to a Jewish agency that was in charge of adoptions in Palestine back in 1943. They kept meticulous records. Only one of their babies came from Dachau.

"The Nazis treated most Jewish infants like all other Jews—they killed them. This one, however, was supposedly smuggled out of the concentration camp with the parents' wish that he be raised in Palestine. The only way a Jewish baby could leave was with permission of the commandant. The Guardians and the Nazis shared similar views. My guess is that the commandant was connected to the Guardians in some way."

"But why would the commandant want to give a Jewish baby to Alexander Paul's father?"

"He knew that Paul's father spied for the Nazis in Palestine and wanted to adopt a child. The commandant was probably delighted by the irony of the opportunity. Think about it, he placed a Jewish child in a supposedly Jewish home knowing that it would be raised to hate his own people. There are plenty of precedents for this, of course. Some of the worst anti-Semites in history were former Jews— including the Guardians' founder—or Jews who didn't know that they were Jews like the Master."

"Once I discovered that the Pauls had adopted the baby, it was easy to trace the family's history. They became Jewish converts just after the Balfour Declaration of 1917. They sensed the winds of change, and felt it was better for them both politically, and for their mission, to use the subterfuge of being Jewish."

"You should work for the Mossad," Goner said, but Josh didn't respond.

Giuseppe's cell phone rang again. "Alon is missing," he told them after hanging up. "He's not among the dead or wounded."

Josh had already assumed as much. "Consider Alon to be extremely dangerous. It's likely that he already knows what happened at the hideout. There are other Guardians besides the Chosen Twelve. Alon must be stopped before they have a chance to regroup."

As the helicopter began its descent toward the hospital's rooftop emergency pad, Josh could see Danielle being unloaded by a team of doctors in white coats.

Stay with me, Danielle, he thought, speaking to her silently in his mind. *Please stay with me.*

Giuseppe put a hand on Josh's shoulder. "Josh, you should be pleased with what you've accomplished today."

"Pleased? I don't think so. If I hadn't found the scroll in the first place, Michael, Father Andre, and the Reverend Barnaby would still be alive. They were good people."

"They're with God now," Giuseppe said. "And in some way, they helped you to destroy the Guardians."

Josh's face grew grim. "Not all of the Guardians were destroyed, Giuseppe. I guarantee you they'll be back."

Chapter 72

GIUSEPPE MADE HIS WAY BACK TO HEADQUARTERS FOR documentation while Josh and Goner hurried into the emergency ward of the Hadassah Hospital. Goner approached a nurse, showing her his identification card, and she addressed them in a whisper.

"She's in critical condition," the nurse told them. "Normally no one would be allowed to see her."

Goner started to say something and the nurse held up a hand. "But this is obviously a matter of national security. She's in room number nine. I'll have one of the other nurses escort you there."

Josh prayed quietly as they walked down the hall. He tried to reach out with his heart to feel Danielle's presence, to get some idea of how she was holding up in this struggle. All he got was the faintest sense: she was still alive, but only barely.

When they entered the room, Josh saw doctors surrounding an unconscious Danielle, working frantically.

"What's happening?" Josh said, pushing himself into their midst.

"Who are you?" one doctor said gruffly. "Somebody call security!"

Goner flashed his badge again and the doctor nodded, clearly irritated at the interruption.

"I need to be near her," Josh told him.

But the doctor pulled him away from Danielle's bed. "You can't come in here now. We're trying to save this woman's life."

"Tell me what's going on."

The man looked back toward the rest of the medical team and saw that they had things under control. He then turned again to Josh. He seemed reluctant to give up any information, but finally relented. "She's lost a lot of blood and her vital signs are extremely low. There was more internal bleeding than our paramedics realized. We're having difficulties stopping it."

Josh moved toward the bed. "I can help."

The doctor grabbed Josh by the shoulder and spun him around. "Look, you shouldn't even be in here. We're doing everything we can. You should wait in the lobby until we have something to report."

Josh shrugged himself free. "I said I can help."

Josh moved two doctors aside and took Danielle's hand. Another doctor reached over to stop him, but Goner stepped in to stop him. "Let the man do what he needs to do."

"This woman is in dire condition," the second doctor said, a vein throbbing in his temple. "He's preventing us from helping her."

But Goner wouldn't back down. "He may be her only chance."

Josh tried to block out all of the conversation and every distraction. He closed his eyes and, slipping deep into his unconscious mind, began to visualize the inside of Danielle's body. He'd stopped some of the bleeding back at the hideaway, but not nearly enough. He saw blood leaking from her chest and intestines.

Josh knew that this would be his only opportunity to save Danielle. He sank deeper into meditation, opening himself to the healing energy of the universal One. In his mind, he cast a white light on Danielle's wounds, bathing the torn flesh and internal organs with its healing brilliance. His hands grew hot as he held them over his lover, and only when the light began to dim on its own did he pull them back enough to examine her again. Her internal tears had mended.

"This is not possible," one doctor said as Josh rose from his meditative state. "Her pulse and blood pressure are returning to normal."

"Is she going to be all right now?" Goner asked.

"I...I believe so." The doctor wore an expression of utter disbelief.

"I wasn't asking you," Goner said. He locked eyes with Josh. "I was asking him."

Josh glanced appreciatively at Goner and then back to Danielle. "She's going to be fine."

Goner hesitated then whispered, "Josh, may I have a word with you in the lobby?"

When Josh finally tore his attention from Danielle, he saw that Goner's expression was serious.

"Only for a moment," he said. "When she opens her eyes I want to be the first person she sees."

Chapter 73

G ONER AND JOSH SAT IN THE QUIET, DESERTED LOBBY
of the Hadassah Hospital. In the early morning hours, with
no one scurrying around, the place seemed eerie and fore-
boding.

"That was quite a trick you pulled off in there," Goner
said.

Josh didn't know what to say.

"The doctors are going to have a few questions," Goner
continued.

"They'll have to go elsewhere for answers," Josh confessed. "I think I know where this comes from, but I'd be
lying if I told you I could explain it."

"Does it have something to do with the scroll?"

Josh stared at his hands, wishing that he could offer a
simple explanation. "Something, yes. And a lot to do with
something bigger. I'm just beginning to understand it now."

Goner stood and clapped Josh on the arm. "Well, we're
going to have to come up with something official for the file.
I'd better talk to those doctors and make sure that word of
this doesn't get out. After that I'm going to go home to try
to get some sleep. You should do the same."

"My place is in Danielle's room. For all kinds of reasons."

"Do you want me to stay with you?"

"It's not necessary," Josh told him. "I can handle it."

Goner reached out a hand and Josh extended his to shake. When he did, he noticed that Goner was giving him a gun.

"You may still need this."

Josh took put the gun in his pocket and thanked him.

When Goner left, Josh returned to the ICU. The room had cleared out considerably, and only one of the original nurses remained. She was checking the various monitors and reporting her readings to a doctor who Josh had not seen before. He immediately recognized the blue eyes behind the doctor's surgical mask.

"Nurse, give me a hand," the doctor said as Josh entered. "Let's take the patient up to her room." He turned and noticed Josh. "Who are you?"

"I'm with her."

The doctor shook his head. "Not tonight."

Josh took a step in the doctor's direction. He'd break the man's neck right here if necessary.

"He's okay," The nurse intervened. "I think he's her fiancé. He's been cleared by Israeli Security."

The doctor grumbled, but relented.

You have no choice and you know it, you bastard, Josh thought.

They wheeled Danielle's bed into a large private room that smelled of cleaning fluids and meds.

"After you're finished getting her comfortable," the doctor said to the nurse, "please leave us alone."

She nodded, completed her work, and left the two men alone with Danielle. Josh hoped that she would remain unconscious long enough to miss what was about to happen. She'd been through enough already.

As soon as the door was closed, the doctor dropped all pretenses and stared at Josh with obvious disdain. "Stop playing games, Cohan. You know who I am."

"Yes," Josh replied, his voice somehow steady, "I've been expecting you, Alon."

"Because of you, my father is dead."

"Your father brought his death onto himself."

But Alon dismissed this last statement. "You realize, of course, that he's only dead in his physical form. His spirit is as powerful as ever."

Josh didn't doubt that it was true. "Let's deal with this one plane of existence at a time."

Alon tore off his surgical mask. "You are so smug. But that self-righteousness will be your downfall."

"Your father failed, Alon. The Guardians have failed. Acknowledge that and you might avoid eternal damnation."

Alon laughed loudly and viciously. "Who knew you were so funny, Josh? Let me tell you what's really going to happen. First, I'm going to snuff out your little life. Then I'm going to take Danielle—my sister—away from here and honor my father's memory. When she is stronger, we will produce an heir; and when she is done serving her function as a vessel, I'll send her off to meet you, okay?"

Alon slashed at Josh with a long surgical knife. The movement was so quick that Josh only barely got out of the way. Alon came at him again and Josh ducked under the move and drove a fist toward Alon's temple. Alon clearly didn't expect this and the blow knocked him to his knees, the knife clattering to the ground.

This gave Josh the chance to pull the gun that Goner had given him. He wasn't sure he could use it, but Alon had no reason to know that.

"This is done, Alon."

But the man's face grew feral as he released an inhuman scream and then rose from his crouch to charge. Josh had no choice but to fire. For the briefest moment, Alon stared at him with pure evil in his eyes and then collapsed.

Josh kneeled over the fallen man. He was still breathing.

"You don't know what you're up against," the Master's son rasped, blood spurting from the wound in the side of his throat. "You're one man against an army more powerful than you can imagine."

But Josh wasn't listening to what Alon was saying. He reached out his hands and held them over the dying man. He prayed that he could set his own bitterness aside, that the healing light could cleanse the hatred from them both. But it was too late. Alon drew a final, sputtering breath and was gone.

Chapter 74

THE ISRAELI POLICE WERE THE FIRST TO ARRIVE. Minutes later, Goner and Giuseppe were on the scene, joined by Moshe, who went directly to his daughter's bedside. He kissed her forehead and took her hand, then looked over at Josh. "I heard what you did here tonight."

Josh watched Danielle's face, so peaceful, so perfect. He simply smiled.

Moshe smiled back, tears welling in his eyes. "I owe you an apology, Josh. I said before that you were no match for my daughter—I was wrong."

Josh felt his heart soften. The past few hours had been a whirlwind.

Giuseppe signaled Josh over to a quiet corner in the room. "I don't know how Alon got through our security," he said.

"I'm guessing that he didn't. I think he got here before your people were in place. At that time there would have only been a metal detector. Alon came in unarmed, so he just walked right through. You knew him; he was brilliant, manipulative, and resourceful, just like his father."

"I'll handle the police," Giuseppe said, "but they'll want to meet later for a full briefing."

The door opened again and a uniformed officer strode through the door, followed by three hospital workers with a gurney. They lifted Alon's body and wheeled it from the room, one of the orderlies staying behind to mop up the blood that had pooled on the scuffed linoleum.

Josh still couldn't believe he'd used the gun. He had no choice, of course, but he felt a kind of sickening grief no less. Had there been another way? Was there some part of him that had wanted to do it? Josh replayed the scene in his mind—the firing of the shot, his own hesitation as he extended his hands over the wound. Why hadn't the healing energy flowed? When the time came, had some part of him refused to help? Or had the bullet just done too much damage? Josh had no answers, and so he shook the questions from his mind.

He grabbed Moshe's hand and gently pulled him away from Danielle's side "I know that Danielle was adopted," he whispered.

Moshe's face turned pale, "Please don't tell her...she doesn't know."

"I won't. That's between the two of you. But when she gets better you should tell her." Josh took a breath, "There is something else, though..."

But Moshe's attention was back with Danielle. "Hmmm?" he said, looking over his shoulder as if to make sure that she was still there."

Josh realized that nothing good would come from telling him who his daughter really was. Instead, he patted Moshe on the shoulder and said, simply, "Nothing."

He turned back to Giuseppe and Goner. "I need to talk to you," he said.

"Do you want to go get a cup of coffee?"

"No," Josh told him, "I need to stay here with Danielle."

Giuseppe nodded and directed Josh toward the foot of the bed.

"The Guardians are stronger than I thought," Josh said. "I figured if we killed the Master and destroyed the Chosen

Twelve, we'd be free of them. But I realize now that I was wrong. Two thousand years is long enough to build a powerful organization, especially with fanatical hatred fueling the fire."

"You're right," Giuseppe said. "Our intelligence reports estimate that they have at least 3,000 members in more than twenty countries. The Master's henchmen were likely nothing more than muscle, but some of their members are men of influence and power. Most are in America and Western Europe, not in Israel. They look at Israel like Catholics look at Rome. We haven't paid them the attention they deserve because, since 1948, they've been keeping a low profile and hadn't caused us any problems. That changed when you discovered the scroll."

"The scroll," Josh said, rubbing his temple, "I know. It has so much to offer, but it's come at a considerable price, hasn't it?"

"All of this would have bubbled up to the surface eventually," Goner reassured him. "The scroll just proved to be the catalyst."

"You're right about the price, though," said Giuseppe. "That's why we've decided not to release it for publication."

The news stunned Josh. "Why?"

"It's not the right time. The government has weighed the situation carefully, but the climate here is already too politically charged. The scroll is just too controversial…"

Josh was incredulous. "The scroll could be a major tourist attraction for the Israel museum. Even if it wasn't authenticated, it could be presented as the possible words of Jesus. Look at all of the people who visit the Shroud of Turin even though dating tests have proved it to be a fraud."

"We may release it eventually. But you've said it yourself; it's too explosive. And there are too many things we still don't know about it. We know the scroll is authentic, but is it really the work of Jesus Christ? Joseph was a common name 2,000 years ago, and any number of them could have had a son named Joshua. There could have been hundreds of people named Yehoshua ben Yosef living and writing at that time."

Josh leaned in closer. "The scroll was written by Jesus of Nazareth. I know it. Look at the text. Some of the stories are similar to the New Testament, and those that aren't have the same spirit."

"I don't disagree with you," Giuseppe said, "but there are parts of it that could draw negative attention. Our country is sensitive to world opinion. We have no choice but to be guarded in this situation."

Josh wasn't ready to give up. "The scroll is pure; it's the original source. The world is entitled to hear his message. We need it now more than ever. And besides, Jesus was betrayed 2,000 years ago. He deserves to finally be heard."

Giuseppe had a guilty look. "Josh," he said, changing the subject, "even though the government has decided not to release the scroll, I wanted to ask you a few questions about it."

"What do you want to know?"

"I haven't read the Scroll," Giuseppe whispered, "but there is a great deal of speculation about it among the agencies involved. We suspect that you're the only person who's translated the whole thing."

"I've translated most of it," Josh told him.

"Then how do you think different groups will react to what it says?"

Josh considered the question for a moment. He wanted to think that people would be able to look beyond their own dogma and see the scroll's message of unity, but he knew enough to know it wasn't likely. "You can never be sure of any reaction," he said. "It depends on people's beliefs."

"What kind of a response do you expect?"

"If the scroll is authenticated as the work of Jesus, it would certainly make theologians revaluate their position. There are similarities in the scroll to the image of Jesus that progressive Christian scholars have already formed. However, it would be upsetting to fundamentalists and traditionalists because it doesn't validate Jesus' divinity or their literal interpretation of the New Testament. The scroll's message would reverberate throughout Christianity and spark numerous debates among religious scholars, clergy, and religious people."

"How do you think our people would react?" asked Giuseppe?

"If they're secular..."

"The majority of Israelis are."

"They'll find it both ironic and satisfying."

"Satisfying?"

"Jesus shows great concern and love for his people—the Jews."

"That's surprising, after so many of us have been killed in his name." Goner said, his eyes widening.

"That's the ironic part," Josh said. "Jesus never killed anyone. People who had their own agendas rewrote parts of the New Testament for their own purposes. Today we call it spin. There are always people and governments that look for a scapegoat when they can't handle their own problems. Look at the Guardians."

"What about religious Jews?"

"I don't think they would care one way or another. Some of them may be surprised that Jesus was one of them and loved the teachings of the Torah, but I doubt the scroll would have any effect on them."

Giuseppe looked off into the distance. Josh could only guess what went on in his head. Someday, this discussion would be more than simple speculation. Someday the world at large would see the scroll. It was too important to remain a secret.

Danielle was still sleeping, and Moshe came to the edge of the bed to join them.

"I'm going to find a way to convince you all that the author is Jesus," Josh said.

Moshe put a hand on his shoulder and squeezed. "Do that if you can, Josh. Plenty of us would love to believe it. I'm not sure that it would change our decision about publishing the scroll, though."

Josh's brow furrowed. "We'll see." He paused for a moment to appraise the men around him. "How much do any of you know about St. Paul?"

Giuseppe and Goner just shrugged, but Moshe said that he had read a fair amount about him.

"Did you know," Josh asked him, "that in 49 C.E., James, Jesus' brother, and Peter, Jesus' favorite disciple, met with Paul? Of course James and Peter knew Jesus personally; Paul did not. It was twenty years after Jesus' death. James and Peter were in charge of the Jerusalem sect that followed the teachings of Jesus, even though they still followed Judaism. History claimed that the meeting with Paul ended in a compromise and that Paul had agreed to waive circumcision but uphold the dietary laws when preaching and converting the Gentiles.

"But history is written by the winners. The followers of Jesus in Jerusalem hated Paul, and they had good reason. He never followed up on his agreement with them; instead he decided to go with his own vision, one that wasn't the same as the Jerusalem disciples. Christianity was born that year. It began right after the Council of Jerusalem."

"Why are you telling us this now?" Moshe said.

"I've just been thinking about it since I...had my run-

in with Alon. He said something about how determined the
Guardians were and it brought me back to Paul."

Josh noticed that Danielle had begun to stir. "Gentlemen, can you please leave us alone?"

Chapter 75

DANIELLE'S FACE WAS PALE AND HER VOICE WEAK, BUT when her eyes fluttered open they were as bright as ever. "I dreamt you were here," she said, and Josh could barely believe how happy he was to have fulfilled her wish.

"I guess that makes me the man of your dreams," he said, with a goofy grin. Danielle laughed, but her wounds were tender and the movement made her ache all over. There were tubes and sensors everywhere Josh didn't want to hurt her, but he needed desperately to hold her. He sat down beside her on the bed and wrapped his arms around Danielle as gently as he could, kissing her lightly on the cheek. When he pulled back his face was wet, though Danielle didn't seem to be crying.

He kissed the bridge of her nose and then, ever so softly, her lips. "I always believed we would have this moment."

Danielle touched his lips tenderly. "I made myself believe the same thing. There were days..." she shut her eyes and it didn't take much imagination for Josh to know what she was thinking. "...But I kept believing."

"No one can hurt you now. The Master and the Chosen Twelve are dead."

"It was Alexander Paul," Danielle said, as if remembering after a long time.

"Yes."

"He always seemed like such a nice man."

Josh's mood darkened. "They say the Devil wears many disguises."

Danielle's eyes grew distant and she appeared lost in thought. "Did I...was I the one who killed him?"

Josh thought about the guilt he felt over killing Alon and wondered if he should try to spare Danielle any similar conflict.

"With a sword," Danielle said. "That was real, wasn't it?"

Josh squeezed her hand, kissed it, and held it to his cheek. "That was real. You were remarkable, actually."

"How'd I wind up here?"

"One of Paul's henchmen shot you. But he's dead now. An Israeli security man killed him."

"Is everyone else okay?" she asked, suddenly panicked. "Is my father safe?"

"Your father is fine, but some of the others weren't so lucky. Paul did a lot of terrible things."

Danielle took a deep breath and tried to sit up, but the effort was too much for her and she sank back into the bed.

"We'll talk about this later when you have your strength back. Right now, you only need to know two things. The first is that you're going to recover completely."

A look of relief passed over her face. "What's the second?" she asked.

"That I plan for us to grow very old together."

She broke into a mischievous smile. "Is that a promise?"

"That is definitely a promise."

As he held Danielle close, Josh could feel the syncopated beating of their hearts coming slowly into unison. He knew that their story together was only beginning, and that it was likely to take several unexpected turns; but he would do everything he could to keep his promise.

Chapter 76

DANIELLE HAD FALLEN BACK INTO A DEEP SLUMBER, BUT Josh still sat in the chair beside her bed. For the first time in weeks, he didn't have a clear objective. The Guardians were far from vanquished, and he knew instinctively that his path would meet up with theirs again; but for the moment, this was the only place he wanted to be.

Knowing that Danielle would likely be out for hours in her condition, Josh shut his eyes and began to meditate. There was, of course, one thing left to do—translate the final passages of the scroll. Calling the images up from where he stored them in his mind, Josh began to read. Now that the imminent threat had passed, he found that the translation fell into place nearly instantly.

> *The existence of evil in the world can be attributed to mankind alone. As long as he wages war, man is a savage, for war is a savage act and is a blockade to enlightenment. The day will come when there will be justice in this unjust world. When all people realize their potential, the impossible will happen.*
>
> *Darkness and evil will be defeated and light shall rule the world. The light will shine on all the generations of men and women that ever lived and led lives of love and righteousness. They will know their destiny and meet God.*

Isaiah says that there will be a suffering servant, but I see a suffering people. I have frightening visions of my people being persecuted to the brink of destruction. The suffering servants are my people. My worst fear is that I will be indirectly involved in their calamity, though the greatest of these tragedies is hundreds of thousands of days away.

After the great destruction, I see gentile sects that are yet to be born, battling each other and bringing devastation on the world. They will fight to the death, slaughtering many in the several names of their shared God. When humans face their darkest hour, the hour of annihilation, when the people can no longer breathe, a light shall appear. The light shall bathe the adversaries in love and understanding and tolerance will prevail.

The Messiah will eventually come, but he will not come in the way that people expect. Has the prophecy been fulfilled? Is there peace on earth? Does brotherhood and sisterhood reign supreme? It hasn't happened yet. Fear not, for that day will dawn. There will be much pain and suffering, and much blood will flow from now until that hour, but the good in men will overcome the evil.

When man is at the precipice of disaster, when the end of days appears to be at hand, it is then that one of my blood shall appear. He is the harbinger of hope for humanity. He will be blessed with faculties the world has never seen. Yet all that he is, your future generations can become. He will show the way. Only then will my work be finished.

I have sealed this scroll with my own blood as a testament to my words.

Whoever finds this Scroll must help to deliver

its message. In two thousand years, on the day when the moon covers the sun for the longest time and the world is in darkness, a colossal battle will begin. Never has there been such fire, and most will not survive it. The disaster must be averted before the spark catches, lest it scorch the earth and scatter the souls of all mankind.

Josh began to rise from his meditative trance, but for the first time, he felt his path to consciousness blocked. There was something more he needed to see—something related to the message in the scroll's final passages.

As though another power had taken temporary control, Josh felt himself dipping deeper into his superconscious. There he saw a set of numbers, the same numbers he had decoded from the beginning of the scroll:

155778

The numbers faded and Josh regained his ordinary consciousness. As always, he felt a bit gauzy when he first emerged from meditation. The numbers, however, stayed fixed in his memory. *155778.* He'd pondered their meaning before. Now, though, he understood that they were directly related to Jesus' final message in the scroll—the prediction of a conflict 2,000 years after his death that would destroy most of the world. Could the numbers be a date? If so, they made no sense.

Except in the Jewish calendar—the calendar Jesus would have used.

155778.

Josh reflected again on the scroll's prophecy that the final battle will occur on the earth's darkest day. But was it a riddle? If so, what could it mean? Taken literally, Jesus could have been talking about an eclipse. Josh knew from his studies that the longest lunar eclipse of this century would occur on July 27, 2018.

The corresponding date in the Jewish calendar was Av 15, 5778. *155778.*

That was the message that Josh needed to hear. On that day, unless humanity's free-fall toward destruction was somehow broken, the greatest catastrophe in human history would take place.

It was a little more than a decade away.

Whoever finds this Scroll must help to deliver its message.

Josh's carefree time without a mission had lasted less than an hour. He had no idea what his first step would be, but he knew what he had to do.

Danielle stirred in bed, shifted slightly, and settled again.

I promised you a future, he thought. *It may not be a peaceful one, but it will be ours.*

Chapter 77

Josh packed his belongings into his rented Jeep and headed back to the desert. Danielle had made significant progress in the past few days—enough that he could let her have some much-needed time to reconnect with her father while he was away. There was something Josh needed to do, something he had realized as soon as he had read the final passages of the scroll. He had three stops to make in only two days' time.

Deep within the bowels of the Old City, Josh returned to the tunnel he had visited before. Alone, he trudged through the dark passage toward his destination some three hundred yards down, not far from the secret entrance to the Church of the Holy Sepulcher. He stopped outside the ancient tomb where he had said Kaddish for the most famous martyr in history and leaned into the ancient stone with full force; but the slab held fast. Josh heaved with all his weight and will, and still the stone wouldn't budge.

Frustrated and out of breath, he sat down on the cold ground to think, his back against the giant rock. From that vantage point, he again noticed the small opening between the slab and the ground. Josh pulled a small shovel out of his backpack and began to dig around the narrow space. In his mind's eye he envisioned the stone itself. It seemed to radiate an energy of grief that washed over Josh and wrung his heart. Instinctively, he began to dig deeper, pouring with sweat, Josh dug with all the determination he could muster. The hard ground began to give and within minutes he had dug a small entry.

Josh turned toward the newly created space. His heart was pounding and his adrenaline flowing. He knew he needed to go in, but he wasn't at all sure what he would find.

It was pitch dark inside. Josh stepped into the blackness and simply allowed himself to sense the presence of the space. He could tell that it was small and dank. As he stood in the darkness Josh felt the resonance of long past events. He knew that this was the place.

But when he flipped on his flashlight and shone it around the chamber, he found that it was empty. What had he expected to find—ghosts? Human remains? Josh had known that there would be nothing of the kind, and yet he felt a pang of disappointment.

Josh moved his light around the chamber, searching around the sacred burial block for any kind of sign. Incredibly, that was just what he found. The beam moved across a plain but ancient plank of wood lying on the floor. When he turned it over, Josh saw that it had been carved in Aramaic and read: *King of the Jews*.

Beside it were two rusted nails. Crusted with blood.

Josh drove up the winding road to the summit of the Judean hills, 2550 feet above sea level. From this perspective, he could see most of Jerusalem spread before him. It was a remarkable city, but one that had seen far too much bloodshed and sorrow. Sadly, he knew that it would only see more of both in the decade to come. It had been foretold, and he would be a part of it—hopefully, part of its resolution.

Josh turned and looked at the Judean desert below. He felt the presence of those who had been there over the last

3,000 years. It was here that David and Solomon had dwelled, the prophets walked, and Jesus meditated and prayed for forty days and nights.

He closed his eyes and invited these spirits inside of him. *One, one, one...*he thought.

Perhaps they had been there all along. Josh let the voices swell in his ears, knowing that he would need them now, more than he ever had before. Smiling, he turned his face to the sky, felt the gentle breeze on his cheeks, and listened for the sound of wings.

The sun was lifting itself over the Jordanian mountains when Josh reached his final destination. It was the brightest sunrise he had ever seen.

Josh parked the Jeep on the side of the road and hiked out toward the cave where he had discovered the scroll and where Jesus of Nazareth had left it 2,000 years before. He had the whole day ahead of him, and when he reached the cave he would spend most of it in meditation and prayer. Now, though, in the perfection of the present moment, Josh felt the texture of the solid earth beneath his feet—the crunch of small rocks and the uneven grades of the parched land. His mission had only just begun.

Author's Note

THE SECRET SCROLL IS A MIX OF FICTION, HISTORICAL speculation based on thousands of hours of research, and fact.

The scroll itself is historical speculation. It's my creation, built from a synthesis of viewpoints and opinions of the historic Jesus held by a number of the world's leading Biblical scholars.

With the exception of the Guardians' hideouts, all sites mentioned in the book are real places. Many of these are among the holiest sites in the world.

The portrayals of historical figures such as Pontius Pilate, Marcion, Constantine, et al. are, to the best of my knowledge and research, accurate.

The portrayal of St. Paul is historical speculation, again based on extensive research.

The historical events described in the book are factual with the exception of the Council of Jerusalem, which is also historical speculation.

The Guardians are based on an early Christian religious sect that existed for two hundred years. This novel makes the assumption that the group still exists, which is, to the best of my knowledge, fictional. Some of the ideas and methods the group expounds are similar to those of some sects and fanatical groups today. These sects bear different names, but the hatred and intolerance they preach are the same.

331

The Israel Antiquities Authority is one of the world's leading organizations in Biblical archaeological discoveries and advancement. All of the IAA characters portrayed in the novel are fictional and are not based on any real people.

The University of Pennsylvania Museum of Archaeology and Anthropology in Philadelphia is one of the finest educational museums in the United States. All characters associated with the Museum are fictional and are not based on any real persons.

Research on *The Secret Scroll* took me more than two years. It involved more than seventy-five books, dozens of interviews, and a wide variety of other reference materials. A more extensive description of the research involved in this book can be found at www.TheSecretScroll.com.

Reading Group Guide

1. Early in *The Secret Scroll* we learn about Josh Cohan's first archeological find. How did that experience impact his actions after finding the scroll?

2. The concept of trust plays a large role in the plot. Who does Josh trust? Is he correct in his judgment? How has misplaced trust changed a situation in your life?

3. The Israeli Antiquities Authority (IAA) is comprised of experts from a variety of religious and national backgrounds. Do you think this diversity helped or hindered their review of the scroll?

4. Josh hid the scroll in a few different places before turning it over to the IAA. Do you think he was right to hide it? What would you have done?

5. Josh asks his friend Avner to hide the scroll for a while. Avner's involvement leads to his death. Is Josh responsible for Avner's death? Is the scroll's preservation worth his friend's sacrifice?

6. *The Secret Scroll* supposes the existence of a secret gospel written by Jesus of Nazareth. Do you think it is possible that such a text exists? Would its existence change the way you think about religion?

7. The Vatican has confirmed that there are many unreleased gospels in its library in Rome. Do you think such texts should be available to the public? Should archeological findings such as the one in *The Secret Scroll* always be made public? Are there situations in which discoveries should be kept secret? Why or why not?

8. What role does adoption play in the plot? How do you think this twist adds to or detracts from the story?

9. The identity of the Master is revealed only at the very end of the novel. Did you guess his identity earlier? How does this affect the way you read the book?

10. What do you feel is the main message of the novel? Do you agree with the message?

11. A line of the secret scroll translates: "The existence of evil in the world can be attributed to mankind alone" (p.324). Discuss.

Acknowledgments

Writing *The Secret Scroll* was the experience of my life-time. The writing process was both joyous and painful, but mostly exhilarating, as my story and characters came to life, and things happened that I'll never be able to explain.

A writer's journey is a solitary one, but I was fortunate that I had people I could talk to who helped me take the bare bones of the first draft to the final draft. The following are many of the people who were inspirational in my four-year writing adventure that led to *The Secret Scroll*. My sister Ilene Rose had the patience to let me read to her what I had written each day while I worked on the first draft. She became my first reader and one of my two muses. Jeff Gelb, a dear friend, a brilliant mind and a talented writer, was always there for me, and his inspiration and advice helped me immensely. Jeff was my second muse. Every day while I was writing the first draft I listened to tapes of *Stephen King on Writing*, which helped and inspired me throughout the writing process.

Mike Garrett and Leonard Tourney were also enormously helpful first readers. Publishing legend, Lou Aronica, liked the book enough to become my editor and friend, and Courtney Arnold, a talented and bright woman assisted me with final draft. I also want to acknowledge friends and booksellers who helped with their inspiration and positive comments. Thanks again to all the above people.

Jason, my oldest son, was always there to give support. Jason and his lovely wife Maris have just blessed me with my first grandchild, Maya.

Special thanks to my wife Lori, the love of my life, who stood by me, encouraged me and read most of the drafts and gave me important feedback. Both Lori and my son Max had to put up with me for four years as I disappeared into my office seventy hours a week and was obsessed with writing *The Secret Scroll* 24/7. I love you.

During the publication of *The Secret Scroll* I worked with some exceptional people: Margot Atwell, Erin Smith, Meryl Moss, Skye Herzog, Todd Stevens, MJ Rose, Steve O'Keefe, Robert Aulicino, Thomas Krafft, Don Goldberg, Cevin Bryerman, Joe Murray, and Jenn Risko. Thank you.

To you my readers, I appreciate you choosing to read *The Secret Scroll*. Thank you.

About the Author

Ronald Cutler was a radio personality in the 1960s, radio station owner in the 1970s, and the creator, producer, and writer of many successful national radio shows and services from 1979 to 1997. These shows were heard by millions of listeners and won many awards. In 1987, Frank Murphy, then Program director of the CBS Radio Networks, called Ronald "the Steven Spielberg of radio" in an issue of *Broadcasting* magazine. In spite of his love of radio, Ron always aspired to write a novel. He began reading and researching for *The Secret Scroll* in January 2004, and started writing soon after that. Ronald currently lives in California with his wife.